IN THE SHADOW OF A KILLER

ROBERT SANDILANDS

Ordering Information:

Prime Seven Media
518 Landmann St.
Tomah City, WI 54660

Printed in the United States of America

Table of Contents

CHAPTER 1

*I*n trembling hands, the alcohol spilled over her fingers. The glass slipped and crashed to the floor at her feet. Stepping back from it, she pleaded into his cold grey eyes. "Please, Declan, I'm telling you the truth. I couldn't do anything about it. He snatched the package and ran."

Declan slapped her across the face and grinned as she fell back against the bar and slid down to a crouching position at his feet. He landed a kick to her thigh and revelled in the sound of her cry as he reached down and grabbed a handful of her dyed red hair and pulled her up. He grinned as she screamed, and he threw another slap to the side of her head. "You're a lying little tart. You got the cash; the guy almost died. Swore he gave it to you."

He knew he could do what he wanted with this woman or, for that matter, any of the six he had working for him. They wanted money, drugs, and booze that he could supply, and he relished the control he had over them. He laid out the punishment to demonstrate to the others that they should not attempt to mess with him. Wilma had been given a simple job: hand out a package to a patron and collect the money from him. The patron, according to her, snatched the package and did a runner. He had sent two of his goons after this patron. They caught him and brought him back. In the back office, they beat him so badly that they had to resuscitate him a few times. But through it all, the guy swore he had given her the cash. Declan turned to the goons standing close by in audience. "Take this into the back office, gag her, and tie her up. I'll deal with her later."

He slipped behind the bar, turned on the lights, and checked that all the glasses had been washed and stacked in the right places. When satisfied all was ready for the customers, he signalled to the doorman to open up. Declan was proud of his achievements with his club. He had worked hard to get it to where it was now, through three years of struggling and fighting against the opposition. In the end, they came to an agreement to share the clientele and not to undercut one another's prices, and always to consult each other when a good deal was on offer. But Declan wasn't 100 per cent happy; he had agreed only to this to save his club from being burnt down. It had come at a price in human life; he had lost three of his best team—shot down at the back entrance when taking empty bottles out the back door to the bin.

Declan's routine was to keep an eye on the entrance to see who was coming in. Any strangers would be carefully watched. This didn't happen too often, as the doorman would turn them away unless they had a regular member to vouch for them. He retired to his office at the back of the lounge, where he had a monitor and could watch the door. This was his nightly routine. But this time was different—he had a whore to deal with first. Had he ignored the whore, he would have seen the big man enter. The doorman listened for the buzzer that would let him know that Declan disapproved.

The buzzer never sounded, so Barton ambled up to the bar and ordered. Knowing what clubs like this were like when strangers entered, he had held back and tailed in behind some of the regulars. Barton remembered Wilma's words and the tone of her voice on her mobile. She had said she was frightened for her life. She had explained to him what had happened and finished by begging him for help. He picked up his drink and sat at a table at the back, where the lighting was subdued. He studied the girls as they worked the tables. To the naive patrons, these girls were waitresses. The owner had them dressed in costumes. Barton knew better. He had been briefed by Wilma and knew they were peddling drugs and their bodies as well. A few of these girls were attractive, with good bodies, and he could see why the owner had hired them. He fancied them himself. He couldn't find Wilma amongst them. This was where it got tricky. He would have to ask for her, and if she was in trouble, he could be joining her.

In his experience in clubs like this, one never caught the girls' eyes but had to be patient and hope they approached. He emptied his glass and placed it on the middle of the table as a signal that he wanted attention, but still no girl came over. Could this be because he was a stranger in the club? Or maybe he had been spotted and the girls had been warned to be cautious.

Her long, straight black hair swayed over her brown shoulders as she rose from the table she was attending and strolled past the bar, maybe on her way to the toilet. Barton held up his empty glass, and she smiled and indicated with a long finger where she was heading. He had guessed right. A few minutes later, she stepped out a door and looked at him and diverted herself to his table. She smiled, picked up his glass, took it to the bar, got it refilled, and returned. "Would you like a drink?" Barton asked before she had a chance to turn and walk away.

Again, the smile. "Maybe later." She winked and pranced back to the table she had left.

His eyes followed the black girl as she walked hand in hand with an oldster out a door at the far corner of the bar lounge. In the few moments the door was open, Barton noticed a long corridor leading to a stairway. He wondered whether this was where Wilma was—up those stairs with a client. But he decided against that thought, remembering that he was amongst the first to enter the club and she wouldn't have had time to solicit a punter. He carried his empty glass to the bar this time and got it filled by a nervy bald man with thick-lensed glasses that made his brown eyes look like beads.

"Never saw you in here before," the bartender commented as he counted the change Barton had handed him. Barton picked up his drink, nodded, and turned to walk back to his seat. Just then the black girl came through the door, followed by the oldster. They parted company, and she smiled and approached Barton.

"I wouldn't mind that drink now," she said, and she hooked her arm around his and steered him back to the bar. The beady-eyed bartender already had her drink placed on the bar, and she reached out for it. Barton headed back to his table and towed her along with her arm still hooked around his. "What's your name?" she asked as they got seated.

Barton took a long swallow from his glass. "Does it matter if you know my name?"

She grinned. "No, but I have to call you something if we're to have a chat."

"Was that old man your first john tonight?"

She nodded and sipped at her drink.

"Well, you can call me number two."

She gave a soft laugh. "Would you like the same service as number one?"

A faint light flickered, catching the corner of his eye. He turned and saw that another door a few feet away from the one the girl had used was slightly open. A figure stood looking through the gap. Barton couldn't make out the features for the light behind but guessed they were those of a man. Inch by inch, the blade of light became broader. He had guessed right. It was a man who quickly stepped out and closed the door. "Is that the boss?" Barton asked, nodding his head at the man walking towards the bar.

She grinned and nodded. "Yes, he owns this place."

"Have you worked here awhile?"

She shrugged. "Long enough."

"Maybe you can introduce me to him."

"You'll have to give me your name," she replied with a giggle. "I can't very well say, 'Boss, this is Mister Two.'"

"You seemed quite nervous when he walked in. Is he that bad?"

"No, he's not the worst I've worked for. He's okay as long as we do our job properly."

"And if you don't do your job properly, what then?" he asked, lifting his glass, holding it close to his lips, and looking over the rim into her brown eyes.

She shook her head vigorously. "I don't know. I've always done my best to do my job."

Barton took a sip from his glass. "Do you know of any of your mates who failed to do their job properly?"

She jumped up and stared down at him, lifted her drink, and said, "You ask too many questions, Mister Two. Not good for you in a place like this." She then turned and strutted away to another table.

A jittery little character, he conceived, and he watched as she weaved her way around the seated patrons to attend to another client. Her boss must have noticed her stomping away from him. Barton watched as he approached her, though she was already with another customer. He drew her to the side, and a conversation took place. Barton drew the conclusion by the man's demeanour that it wasn't very friendly. They parted, she went back to the customer, and her boss spoke to a couple of goons who were stationed close to the bar. Barton lowered his head but could sense their eyes were on him. The two goons approached.

"The boss wants a word," one of them said.

Barton lifted his glass and drained the last of the beer. "What about?" he asked, and he slammed the glass on the table with a thump that got the attention of a few of the patrons.

"Just get on your feet and you can ask him in his office," the bald- headed one snarled, and his mate stepped forward and tried to grab Barton's arm. The goon was too slow, and Barton swiped his hand away, causing him to stumble against Bald Head.

They regained their balance and dived at him, and the pair soon had him pinned to the floor, but not before Barton had landed a few kicks at them and a punch that met with Bald Head's nose. Kicking, punching, and swearing, they wrestled Barton into the back office, with the rest of the patrons silently spectating. The two goons had to get help to hold him down so they could secure him with cable ties and press duct tape across his mouth. He was finally tossed down next to Wilma on the floor.

She looked comatose. He managed to nudge her with his shoulder. She moaned and eventually responded after two more attempts. Her eyes lit up when she saw him, and she tried to form words behind the gag, shaking her head vigorously. Barton took it as an apology.

The early-morning sun shining through the dirty office window woke him. He hadn't intended to fall asleep and had fought to stay awake for the past few hours. That was one of his downfalls; beer always had the effect of a sedative when he drank it too fast. He found himself lying on his side, facing away from Wilma. He tried to move his legs and nudge her to see whether she was still awake, but he felt nothing. He wriggled his body about and finally got himself back into a sitting position. She wasn't there. *They must have come in and taken her.* How could he have not heard them? Surely she must have made some kind of noise when they grabbed her—a warning, of some sort. Or was there more in his drink than just beer? The place was silent. *Where has everybody gone? What happened to the music that was blaring when*

they dragged me in here? Surely he couldn't have been asleep that long. He had no way of knowing what time it was; he could remember one of the goons ripping the watch from his wrist to secure the ties.

CHAPTER 2

*D*eclan Craig prided himself as being a safe driver, always keeping to the speed limit, keeping an eye on the surrounding traffic, and regularly glancing in his mirrors. He had been driving for fifteen years and had never been involved in an accident that was his fault; he'd never even received a parking ticket. Not many drivers could say that. If he ever needed to go at speed, he would get one of his goons to do the driving. This morning Badger was in the driving seat; he was a big man with a deep, rasping voice, and when he laughed, his whole body quivered. Something Declan said started him off. Wilma wasn't laughing; she was the butt of Declan's humour. She had been bundled into the back seat of Declan's silver Range Rover. The reason the two men in the front were having a joke was because she had wet herself. Spraying deodorant into her pants hadn't worked; they could still smell her. "Put the foot down," Declan told Badger, "before that whore gases us to death." The cold winter breeze stung at his features through the open windows, but it was better than breathing in her urine. "I'll have to get this thing valeted when we're finished with her." Badger had to engage four-wheel drive up the steep, muddy incline on the narrow track. They were bounced about, and at one point Declan thought he would bash his head off the roof; had it not been for the seatbelt, he probably would have. Even with the duct tape around her mouth, they could hear Wilma's screams. "Shut the fuck up!" Declan shouted back at her.

The deserted red brick building appeared as if by magic. One had to be looking for it amongst the shrubs and trees to spot it. It was still well concealed at this time of the year, when the foliage had blown off. According to the developer's report from when Declan purchased the place, it was once used as a family-owned cotton mill. At the time, he thought it conspicuous, but he had since learned that mills like this were dotted all over Lancashire. It had earned its purchase in the past for him and would do so in the future, without his having to spend much money on it.

Badger pulled up as close to the steel-shuttered door as was possible so that he wouldn't have to carry the whore far. Declan got the door open and held it to let them in. Wilma, slung over the big man's shoulder, was shocked to see signs that people had recently been living in this place. Matrasses lay on the floor all the way along the walls on both sides.

She was being carried all the way to the end of the building between the mattresses and could see three doors at the bottom. One on the right was marked "toilets". On the left, a sign said "kitchen". She was barged through the one in the middle and found herself in a well-equipped office. A large desk with three computer monitors and keyboards on top of it took up most of the space. She felt herself being dumped onto a leather chair, and she landed so hard she was sure it must have caused her to get whiplash.

Badger's big hand grabbed her arms and sat her up so she was facing Declan, who was seated behind the desk. "Wilma"—he smiled and leaned forward—"I have a few questions to ask you, and I want an honest answer. You know what will happen if you vary from the truth." She stared into his cold grey eyes. A lock of blond hair fell over his forehead, and he flicked it back with sideward jerk of his head. He then nodded to Badger, who leaned over and ripped the duct tape from her mouth.

She yelped at the sudden pain and felt her eyes water. "Honest, Declan, I've told you the truth," she whimpered.

"That's not what I'm talking about."

She shook her head in confusion. "What *are* you talking about?"

"That big guy we dumped beside you in the back office—who is he?"

She shook her head. "I don't know; I've never seen him before."

"I hope for your sake you're telling the truth." He lifted her mobile off the desk and held it up, "I'm going call a few numbers on this that you have saved. My guys are with him just now; they have his mobile. If it rings, you're dead and so's he." Declan began going through the stored numbers.

Barton's mother called his mobile at the same moment Declan hit the third number. Mrs. Barton's call got through first. The goons grinned at each other, knowing the pleasure they were about to get from beating up the big guy currently locked in the back office. They didn't bother to check whether it was Wilma's number and didn't bother to answer before they disconnected.

The back office had been used as a storage room and was partially filled with discarded furniture. An old piano had been upended, and parts of the wooden panelling were missing. Barton noticed that a sharp corner of the angle-iron frame was exposed and hobbled over to it using his feet and buttocks. It took him a painful ten minutes to get to it and more exertion to get onto his feet.

Rubbing the cable tie on the sharp corner was tricky, and he often pinched the skin on his wrists. He could soon feel blood running onto his fingers. As he was almost at the point of giving up, the tie fell off, landing at his feet. A gentle tug got the tape away from his mouth, but no matter how carefully he pulled at it, it stung as it pulled the bristles from his designer stubble. The ties on his ankles posed no problem; he had them off in a matter of seconds.

While he stood nursing the torn skin on his wrists, he noticed a short length of scaffolding pipe on top of a chair, and he soon grabbed hold of it. It was about three feet long, just the right size for a club. With the weapon behind his back, he returned to the position he had been dumped in and faked unconsciousness.

The silence continued for what felt like an hour, and he was beginning to think that he had been left in here to die of thirst and starvation when the lock on the door rattled. All three of them charged in; the distance they had to cover before reaching him was about ten feet. There was no time for Barton to get up, but plenty of time to swing the pipe at the head of the first one who tried to grab him.

The goon stumbled sideways with the blow, knocking his mates off balance, and Barton was up and swiping at them. He felt the pipe hit its target on another, but the third managed to get hold of him. Barton had the advantage of momentum and soon had this one on the floor; he managed to keep control of the pipe and thrust it spearlike at full force into the goon's mouth.

Still wielding the length of pipe, Barton rushed out the door,expecting to be challenged by more goons. He was surprised when he reached the outer door and had encountered nobody. He turned to see whether the three he had fought with were giving chase, but no movement came from there. He was about dive out and run for his car when he noticed his mobile on the bar. Luckily it was at the near end, and he soon scooped it up and made his escape.

It wasn't until Barton got back into his flat that he remembered to check his mobile. He saw his parents' home number on the screen. *This can't be good*, he thought. They seldom called unless it was serious. He hit the reply button, and his mother answered in her usual panic mode, saying she thought his father was being paranoid.

"He thinks a man with white hair is following him. He claims that every time he looks back, he sees this person behind him."

"Does he say anything about what this man looks like?" Barton asked.

"Not much," she replied in a shaky voice, "just that he has pure white hair, is tall and thin, and wears dark glasses."

"Is Dad at home just now?"

"No, that's the reason I called you earlier. He wouldn't let me; says he can handle it."

"Where is he?"

"He's in town somewhere. Says he knows a guy who can get him cheap tobacco, but I think maybe he's trying to nab this guy to see what his game is."

"Okay, Mum. I'll be over soon."

His father was at home when Barton arrived knocking at their door. Tom answered. "This is a surprise; what brings you here?"

"I was passing and thought I'd come in and see how you were."

"I see you've been in a fight. That's some black eye somebody's given you," Tom Barton remarked, sitting down on his regular chair whilst rolling a cigarette at the same time.

"I walked into a door."

Tom grinned. "Yes, okay. You've said that so many times in the past, it's starting to sound a like a greeting."

His mother walked in carrying a tray holding cups of tea. She placed the tray on the small table between them and said, "The reason he's here is because I phoned him about that man you said was following you. Personally, I think you're getting paranoid in your old age."

Tom blew smoke out the side of his mouth. "Okay, if that's what you think, then maybe I am."

"What does this guy look like?" Barton asked, lifting his cup.

"As your mother says, I'm getting paranoid, so just forget it."

"I can't forget it. This guy sounds like someone I've met before."

"Another one of your thug friends?"

"If it's the same guy, he's not a friend and is dangerous. I think you both should go on holiday for a few months to be on the safe side."

Tom almost chocked on his smoke. "Where do you think we'll get the money to do that?"

"You don't need to go that far. Stay in this country. Go and stay with Mum's sister in Cornwall."

His mother lifted her cup and sat next to him on the sofa. "That won't work; your aunt Molly can't stand the sight of your father."

Tom jumped up, almost toppling the table. "Look," he cried, "I'm not running away from this creep! Who's to say he won't follow us to Cornwall?"

Barton cut in. "The question that's bothering me is, why is this guy following you?"

Tom shrugged. "Could be something connected to your or Corrie's activities." He sat back down again and resumed belching smoke from his cigarette.

"What has that got to do with you?" his wife asked, holding out her hands. "Surely whoever this man is can't blame you for what your sons have done?"

Barton caught his father's eye, and that look told the older man that his son knew why but wouldn't discuss it in front of his mother. That will have to come later. "When was the last time you saw this guy?" Barton asked.

Tom stubbed his smoke out on the ashtray on the table. "I'm not sure. I think it was the day before yesterday, but I have that feeling that he's there watching me and following when I go out."

Barton was familiar with that gut feeling and knew it wasn't something one ignored. But sometimes he had discovered that it was the result of an overactive imagination brought on by the kind of life he had lived. That was his personal excuse for it. He got up and nodded at the older man. "See me to the door, Dad."

Tom was invited to take a few steps farther than the door and found himself sitting in his son's car. He reluctantly answered the questions his oldest son fired at him and finished by saying he could handle it. "You take nothing to do with it; you must have enough to worry about looking after yourself," he concluded, and he stepped out of the car.

CHAPTER 3

eclan showed Wilma around the interior of the building. They first visited the shower room, and then the kitchen, which to her surprise was well equipped with all the modern facilities. He opened the door to a small room that had been recently added, built with plasterboard walls and wooden frame. "This," he informed her, "is your private quarters. You'll find a change of clothes and everything you need."

Wilma, still with her hands secured behind her back, gave him a puzzled look. "What's all this in aid of?"

"I've decided to give you a second chance, but that all depends on how you perform."

"Perform what?"

He laughed and nodded to Badger, who reached around her with a knife and cut the cable ties. "I have some gentlemen guests coming to stay here for a few days. You know what I mean when I say 'perform'. On top of that, you will cook for them and do anything they wish of you."

She knew what would happen if she refused, but she also knew the danger she was being forced into. No matter the outcome, death was inevitable. She would be here on her own with strangers. She had no way of knowing who they might be, but she could guess, with Declan involved, that they had to be crooks—most likely on the run.

"I've got someone outside watching this place. If you try to escape, he has orders to shoot you. These guests will be arriving tomorrow morning, so you have all night to make up these beds." He waved his hands at the mattresses. "You'll find the bedding in that cupboard next to your room."

Wilma stood staring at their backs as they left, locking the door behind them. She was never a great lover of mobile phones and had always looked at them as an invasion of privacy, but now she would give all she ever owned to have one just for a few minutes. But on further thought, she realised she had no way to tell Barton her whereabouts. She had no idea where she was; they had blindfolded her on the way here and more than likely had come the long way round. She began to wonder about this guy Declan spoke about who had orders to shoot if she tried to get away from this place. Was he bluffing, and where would this guy be? They had removed her blindfold after they had entered this place; she had no way of knowing whether there were other buildings close by. She still ached from the latter part of the journey; they must have travelled on a dirt track or an old farm road. That could mean this place was well out in the country. Even if she did manage to escape, where would she go? She remembered watching a programme on the television about how a lot of walkers got lost in Dartmoor, to be found dead weeks later. The cupboards in the kitchen had been well stocked with food, and the fridge and freezer were packed. This, she decided, had been planned or maybe was an ongoing racket Declan ran. If the latter was the case, then who was her predecessor, and what had happened to that person? Her biggest fear struck her. *Probably murdered by one of Declan'sguests.*

"Do you want to go out on that rough road again?" Badger asked.

Declan shook his head. "No, take the proper entrance; that was to confuse that bitch, make her think she was miles from anywhere. That way she'll not try to do a runner."

"What time is that truck supposed to arrive in the morning?" Badger asked as he turned the Range Rover onto the main road.

"Not sure; the driver is going to give me a call when he's getting close to the old mill."

"That means we'll have to be ready to leave at any time?"

They sat in thoughtful silence until Badger drove into Declan's driveway. "I'll see you at the club later," Declan said as he got out of the vehicle. "Take this with you. Get it fuelled up. I'll drive myself in with the Bentley." With that he bounded up the steps into his house.

Sitting in the lounge, July placed her glass of orange juice on a side table and jumped up to greet Declan. She was one of his most treasured possessions. Yes, she worked as a hostess in his club, but she was not like the other girls. She was his live-in lover and partner. In his eyes, she was the most beautiful woman he had ever loved. She was also his top informant, and bloody good at the work. She had eyes and ears all over the place, and she could tell at a glance when a new face came into the club whether that person was a copper, a rival gang member, or just a troublemaker. Over the years, Declan had developed total trust in her, the only person he could trust. He could never get used to the sensations he got when he gazed into her wide-set ebony eyes. He loved the touch of her soft, dark body and enjoyed running his fingers through her jet-black hair. After a session of hugs and hungry kisses, he asked, "What's your day been like?"

"Had a lovely day," she promptly replied. "Visited my parents, had a run-in with my younger sister—but that was to be expected. I never could understand what goes through that girl's mind."

They sat down on the huge white leather sofa, and he put his arm around her. He was about to get settled for a night with her to watch a movie she had recorded when his mobile sounded. "What!" he barked into it. "How the fuck did that happen? He was tied up, gagged, and I left three of you to watch him!" He jumped up, listened for a while to the excuses the caller supplied, and put the phone back into his pocket. He turned to July. "That guy you told me about—did you get his name?"

She shook her head. "He didn't give me it. I asked, but he never said. Why? What's happened?"

"We dragged him into the back office, as you know; had him secured with cable ties and gagged. I left three of those stupid clowns to keep an eye on him, and guess what? He got away! Beat the fuck out of the three of them with a metal tube!"

She stood up beside him and put her hand on his shoulder. "is this guy going to make any difference to your operation.? We don't really know who he is. I'm sure he's not a copper. I don't think he's a member of another gang. He might just be new in town and decided to try the clubs."

Declan walked away shaking his head. "I'm sure he came into the club for a reason. I'm wondering If that bitch Wilma had anything to do with him turning up."

"Now that you mention it, I did see her on her mobile while you were dealing with that patron who did a runner and didn't pay her for that bag of cocaine."

He grinned. "That's all I need to know. If she survives her time looking after those immigrants, I'll need to have a word with her."

Barton strongly suspected who this stalker was, but why was he tailing an old man like his father? Was someone paying him? That being the case, who would go to that expense and trouble unless he had a good reason? On the drive home to his flat, he decided the only way to find out was to nab this stalker, but in the meantime, he had told Wilma he would help; it was the least he could do for her to return the help she had given him in the past.

After a quick shower and a microwave meal, he headed back to that club. He decided the only way to find her was to chance nabbing one of the goons that dragged him into that back office. He parked his car a way off and decided to walk to the area of the club. He ambled along with other pedestrians on their shopping tasks. It was obvious the place was closed, although the tubular lights were still on, displaying the name: "THE WESTERNER'S CLUB". Barton wondered whether there could be people inside, such as cleaners or staff, preparing for the night's business. He certainly wasn't going to attempt to get inside, knowing full well what would happen to him. He called his home number, and luckily his father answered. "The only way we're going to nab this guy who's following you is for you to get into town and hope he decides to tail you. That way I'll know for sure who he is." He could imagine the row between his father and mother about the plan, but he could see no other way to find the man and at the same time keep an eye on the club and see whether any goons turn up.

Tom reluctantly agreed, and he told his wife, who wasn't too happy with the idea but acknowledged it could prove that her husband wasn't just getting paranoid.

Over an hour had dragged past, and there had been no sign of any of the goons. Barton had walked the length of the street regularly, stopping at a shop window to look back at the club entrance. At one of his stops, he felt a hand pat his shoulder.

"Don't turn around," his father said. "I'm going to continue along the street. You stay there. If this guy is stalking me, he should pass you."

Giving a slight nod, Barton realised his father would be already walking away. Through the corner of his eye, he watched the older man stroll along, pretending to do some window shopping at the same time he had eyes on the club. As his father got nearer a crowded area, he had to move along slowly to keep sight on him. As he approached the club, a silver Range Rover indicated to turn left along the side of the building. Barton stepped out to see where it was heading. At the same moment, he noticed the tall white-haired man step out of that turning. Although he was about twenty yards away, there was no mistaking it; this was the same guy he'd had contact with in the past. His father had turned and was heading back along the street on the opposite side, Barton turned towards a shop window and could see the old man's reflection as he passed.

Quite a few minutes passed before White Hair appeared and, like himself, pretended to be window-shopping. Barton crossed the street and followed. At the junction, his father crossed over at a pedestrian crossing, but by the time White Hair reached it, the lights had changed and he had to wait. Barton quickened his pace, caught up to him, and grabbed his elbow. "This is a surprise," Barton said. "Didn't expect to see you again so soon."

White Hair turned. "Who are you?" he said, with a slight hint of an accent.

"I'm a blast from your past." Barton smiled at him, but he couldn't study the man's expression for the dark glasses. "What are you doing here?"

"I don't know who you are, mate, so why don't you fuck off." The lights had now turned to green, and he pranced across. Barton decided not to pursue, and his father was gone—probably having darted up one of the narrow lanes and headed home. When he got back to the club, the Range Rover was waiting at the junction to get out onto the main street. He was tempted to rush to it and dive in, but the risk of the passenger's door being locked was a chance he decided not to take. He held back until he saw which direction the driver took, and he then rushed for his own car. It was a wild guess that the Range Rover wouldn't turn off before he caught up with it, and for a while he thought he had guessed wrong. At the large roundabout that led to the M6, he saw it behind a convoy of HGVs. He chased after it as it overtook the line of trucks, but no sooner had it joined the motorway than it turned off again. At the end of the slip road, he was stopped at traffic lights. The Range Rover was nowhere to be seen, and he had no idea which road it had taken. Making another wild guess, he took the street to the left. After a short way, however, he found that the street had been blocked off for some construction work. He made up his mind to go back to the club later.

CHAPTER 4

All the mattresses had been made up with fresh bedding. Wilma had made herself a snack, had a shower, and jumped into the bed. Sleep took a long time to come, and she was aroused by the sound of a truck pulling up outside. She jumped up, quickly dressed, and dived for the only window. The early morning was dull and overcast with black clouds. What she could see was the headlights of the vehicle as it reversed along the side of the building. She was shocked to see a shipping container being parked close to the door. The driver got out, though she couldn't see what he was doing. The unit then pulled away, leaving the trailer behind.

Wilma sat at the kitchen table and drank a glass of milk to see whether it could quash the need for a cocaine fix. It didn't work, and as time wore on, the craving got worse. The pains started, and her whole body was soon in agony. The shivering became out of control, and she could no longer hold the glass.

The kitchen door burst open, and in charged Declan and Badger. A packet of cocaine suddenly appeared in front of her. She grasped it and tore it open, and soon she started sniffing with a straw. A few seconds later, the world was again a wonderful place to live in.

"Don't overdo it with that." Declan pointed to the powder. "I need you to look after our guests."

Wilma got up, unsteady on her feet. "Give me a minute," she said with a wide grin, "until it settles down, and I'll be fine." She swept her red-dyed hair back from her face and watched them walk out of her room, leaving the door ajar. Declan, she noticed, stood at the main door, and Badger continued out towards the container. The heavy metal doors opened with a noisy crash, and the next thing she heard was voices cheering. Declan waved an arm, and a crowd of men rushed towards him. Wilma counted fifteen of them. As they strolled into the building, each one selected a mattress and dumped his bag on top of it. They spoke loudly in a language she couldn't understand, and she could see Declan didn't understand it either.

Declan led them to the open door of her room. A broad grin dawned on his face. She stepped back, forcing a smile. He shouldered his way through the men and waved for her to join them. "This lady will look after you all!" he shouted at them. Reluctantly she edged her way towards him; she could feel all eyes were on her. A cheer rose from them in words she had never heard before but could guess the meaning of. Declan explained the conditions and pointed to where the toilets and the kitchen were. One of them who seemed to understand translated. Another cheer broke out, and one of them stepped towards Wilma; he was the tallest of the group and had greedy brown eyes and a cropped black beard. He eyed her hungrily and reached out and touched her hair, withdrew his hand, and sniffed his fingers. He shouted to his companions, and they cheered and laughed.

In a low voice, Declan said, "You'll be all right as long as you do what they want willingly."

Even through the effect of the cocaine, Wilma felt nervous, and she could feel the drug wearing off swiftly. She decided it wasn't the purest she had ever had. "What do they eat?" she asked.

Declan shrugged. "Just serve up what you have. If they don't eat it, then they'll have to starve; but I don't think it's food they have on their minds." He laughed and walked away to join Badger standing at the main door.

Wilma retreated into the kitchen intending to lock the door but was shocked to see the lock had been removed. She hastily armed herself with a large knife from the utensil drawer and placed it on the worktop for easy reach. She had learned that the men liked thick black coffee, so she prepared some and carried it into them on a plastic tray in a large jug with paper cups for them all. Their dark brown features lit up, and broad smiles appeared all round; they in turn approached and helped themselves when she laid the tray on the floor.

Wilma quickly returned to the kitchen. An hour later, she served them large bowls of boiled rice, and curried chicken on plates. She discovered they were all laid out on the mattresses, sound asleep. She made extra noise lifting away the cups, and a few of them awoke. Soon the noise started again as they all got aroused and helped themselves to the food.

Wilma lay on the bed and listened to them in prayer, and soon after they came to her door and entered. To save her own life, she had no other choice but to accommodate them all, and this she did, sometimes three at a time. This went on all through the night until the morning sun shone through the dirty window and they all returned to prayer. Cold turkey was beginning to set in, and she kept herself busy washing dishes and making meals for them. The large knife was still on the worktop, and she decided that the first one to come in here and want to have his way with her again would get it.

She was all set to make an attack at the first one when a heavy diesel engine sounded and the noise of the truck picking up the trailer drowned out the sound of the foreigners getting their belongings together.

Long after things went silent, she went in to see that the place was in turmoil. The bedding was strewn all over the place, the mattresses had been upended, and a strong smell of urine stung her eyes. "Dirty bastards!" she shouted aloud, but no one was there to hear her. In desperate need of cocaine, she got to work cleaning the place up, but no matter how much she pushed herself, the pains and the shaking got stronger as the day wore on. She told herself that she was lucky to have survived the night.

As she loaded the last of the bedding into the washing machine, the main door opened and Badger strolled in. She expected to see Declan behind him, but that didn't happen. "What's happening?" she asked.

He approached her and handed her a package of cocaine. "Your wages." He laughed. "I could do with a cup of coffee." he walked towards the kitchen, and

Wilma followed, desperate to get the package open and sniff a line. As Badger waited for the kettle to boil, Wilma had already started, with the straw at her nostril. "You'd best use that sparingly," Badger said. "You won't get another lot until the next lot of immigrants arrive."

Wilma sat back in the chair and grinned broadly. "When will that be?"

Badger shrugged and got up to prepare his drink. "It could be today, next week … whoknows."

She resealed the package and put it in her jeans pocket. Her head was spinning, and her vision was well out of focus. A sudden stabbing in her chest forced her to buckle over and topple off the chair.

The next thing she saw was Declan's face so close she could smell his breath. "Is this you sleeping on the job?" he said, slapping her on the cheek.

She tried to get up, but strong hands held her down. "What happened?" she yelped.

"You sniffed too quick," the deep, guttural voice said from behind. "That was the real deal I sent you. You're not supposed to take as much as the shit you usually sniff. I told Badger to warn you; he must have forgot. That lot was supposed to last you for a few days."

"Let me up; I need to go to the toilet or I'll shit myself," she cried, fighting against the restraining hands. She heard them both laughing as she ran to the toilet; she didn't have time to close the door and just got her jeans and pants down in time.

Barton reasoned that because of his encounter with the tall, thin man with the white hair, he may have made the man more cautious, making it more difficult to nab him again. It was well into the small hours in the morning. He lay awake on top of his bed fully clothed and decided he would have to somehow nab this guy and find out what his orders were. Barton realised he had seen the man before, and it suddenly dawned on him where. But he couldn't understand why the man was tailing his father. What had old Tom done to attract the attention of some big criminal boss? It was obvious the white- haired guy was a pro. And he must be getting paid—but by whom?

After a shower and some food, he decided to recce the Westerner's Club and see whether the silver Range

Rover had been parked back there. Before he managed to get his car started, his mobile sounded. He noticed his parents' home number. *Trouble again*, he thought.

"Richard," his mother stated, "that man your father said was following him is standing across the street from our house. It's taking me all my strength and persuasion to stop your father going out to confront him."

"I'll be there in a few minutes," Barton assured her. "Just don't let dad go anywhere near him."

This being Barton's home turf of his younger days, he knew all the backstreets and alleys, and he parked his car a few streets away. The shortcut to his home, the one he took on his way home from school all those years ago, hadn't changed. This he was glad of, and he knew that if that man was across the street from his parents' house, he should be able to come up from behind. The narrow lane between the houses across from his parents' home was where Barton hoped this guy would be standing. He stopped at the back corner of the two buildings but couldn't see the man standing at the other side. He slowly edged his way along to the end and looked carefully in all directions. The only movement he saw was that of a young woman and a child walking towards him. He stood there for a minute and let the woman pass before he stepped out across to his parent's door, dreading the thought that this white-haired man could have barged in on them.

He examined the door. It didn't show any signs of being forced or kicked in. When he tried the handle, he found that the door was unlocked. He quietly entered, crept along the passage, and dived into the living room.

Tom had been listening and had heard the front door handle being turned and was prepared to jump on whoever entered his living room. Armed with a golf club, he let it fly, and it slammed into his son's shoulder.

Barton fell forward with the impact but managed to regain his balance by grabbing the back of the sofa.

His mother ran in from the kitchen. "Are you trying to kill our other son?" she put her arms around Barton and helped him onto the sofa. "Are you all right?" she asked.

"I'll be all right," he replied. "Luckily it was just the shaft that hit me and not the club end."

Tom was beside him, apologising. "I thought it was that guy."

"Don't worry about it, Dad; at least I know you will defend yourself if he ever tries to get in."

"Did you see him hanging about outside?" his mother asked.

Barton shook his head. "No, he was nowhere in sight. I came up through the lane across the street, hoping to catch him."

"What do you think he's playing at? Is it scare tactics or what?" Tom asked.

Barton had decided that this was a routine check, but he kept it to himself. He had heard about it from gang members he had associated with in the past. A shooter first gets to know his victim's routine; this is the part that takes up most of his time. Once he's sure what the victim will do next, he'll pick his spot. The puzzling part was why anyone would want to hire a hit on an old man whose worst crime was that he was forced to deliver a bag and failed to do so. "I don't know what this guy is up to. If his intentions were to harm you, he would have done before now."

He returned to his car the same way as he had arrived, in case this white-haired guy might still be hanging about, but he was nowhere to be seen. Maybe Barton approaching him on the street that day had, as he had previously decided, made him more cautious. Before he got his car started, he sat feeling guilty. He had pacified his parents but hoped he hadn't put them off their guard.

The Westerner's Club had on its lights above the door saying that it was open for business. Barton had parked a distance away from it, but not so far that he couldn't see the action at the door, which at this early stage in the evening wasn't much. *'Mr. Craig' that black girl called him—is he the owner of the silver Range Rover?* It was no matter; Barton had decided he had a score to pick with him for the way he had been dragged out of that lounge and banged up in that back room.

The silver Range Rover wasn't in the parking area behind the club. Barton had taken a stroll to the end of the street where he could see the vehicles that had been left there. What got his attention was a large metallic blue Bentley pulling in and stopping at the rear door. A casually dressed man got out of the driver's side, and Barton thought, *This must be a driver*—until the man turned. *Ah! Mr. Craig.* Had Barton been closer, he would have rushed at this man and given him a good doing over, but that was out of the question. *His time will come. More than likely, this area is covered with CCTV cameras.*

A group of noisy youths came through the front entrance. Barton was tempted to follow them in but resisted—and was glad that he did. The Range Rover drove past him and turned into the parking area. A tall, heavily built man got out, and he, too, entered through the rear door. Barton recognised him as one of the goons that jumped him in the lounge. Knowing that they would be in there all night doing their job, he headed back to where his parents lived and parked up in a lane where he knew he could observe the whole street without being spotted. If this white-haired guy turned up, he knew he wouldn't have time to rush him, but he would be able to do something if he attempted to enter the house. He made a quick phone call to his parents to warn them of his plan, telling them to lock the door. Time wore on, and with no sign of White Hair, he was about the call his parents to cancel the plan for the night when a knuckle knock came to his passenger's window. White Hair leaned down to the window and indicated for Barton to wind it down. This he did.

"You looking for me?" White Hair said with a heavy accent.

"What makes you think that?"

"If you are, I'm here. What do you want to do about it?"

"Well, as you're asking." Barton jumped out his side of the car and gazed at White Hair over the roof. "Why are you following my parents?"

CHAPTER 5

Declan had been extra vigilant since that big guy entered his club, and his eyes seldom strayed from the CCTV screen. He had the feeling he hadn't seen the last of that long-haired ape; those brown eyes gave the impression of someone on a mission who wouldn't easily give up. What puzzled Declan was the nature of his mission. Surely he did not intend to protect that junkie whore, yet a voice inside him said they were somehow connected. There had been a peculiar look in her eyes when his goons dumped the big guy next to her. A knock on his door disturbed his train of thought, and Badger stuck his head around it.

"I'm not a hundred per cent sure, Boss, but that big guy who smashed Pinkie and Robo with that scaffolding pipe—I saw him outside standing watching the club door."

Declan jumped up from behind his desk. "Get one of the boys and get out there and nab the bastard. Bring him here. I want to know what he's about."

"He's a tricky fucker, Boss. I think that to be sure we can nab him, I might need at least another one of the boys."

Declan nodded. "That's okay; just don't take any of the door staff."

When Badger turned to leave, July squeezed past him and, as she always did, left the damn door open. Declan grinned and waved his finger towards the door, and as always, she closed it with her foot. "You're looking quite concerned," she said, sitting herself down on the seat opposite the desk.

"I am," he confessed, and he sat back down. "That big thug we banged up in the back office got away and smashed a couple of our boys with that scaffolding pipe that got left in there. How the hell did that get there?"

July leaned forward on the chair. "That place is full of junk; that just happened to be part of it."

As she spoke, he wondered what it was that attracted him to her. She was a beautiful woman, and he loved the feel of her brown skin, the firmness of her breasts and bottom. He loved to comb his fingers through her long black hair whilst gazing into her ebony eyes. "I'll have to get that place cleaned out; the problem is I'd have to hire a skip, and there's no place to put it."

"Could put it in the car park."

"That would leave little room for the customers' cars, and we'd get all the bums around scavenging for what they could sell, and what they couldn't, they'd leave lying around."

She nodded, agreeing with him. "How's Wilma getting on in the old factory?"

"I'm sure she and that big thug are in some way connected. According to Badger, that thug is hanging around the door, watching it. I've sent him and a few of the boys to nab him and get him back here."

July stood up. "What do you intend to do with him?"

"Get a few answers from him."

"Then what?"

"Let the boys get their own back at him for bashing them with that pipe. He left one with a broken jaw and no teeth."

"I got the impression that won't be so simple; he looks like somebody who can handle himself." She walked out the door,leaving it open.

"Shut the fucking door!" Declan roared, but she was gone and out of hearing distance, into the din of the club life. *If it wasn't for the feeling I have for you*, he thought as he got up and slammed the door, *I'd have you working with that whore Wilma*. He never got to reseat himself, as the door flew open and Badger stuck his head in.

"Sorry, Boss; the bastard was gone by the time we got out there."

Declan slumped down on his chair and slammed the palm of his hand on the desk. "We've got to find out what the creep's game is. I think he's working for someone. Can't see him taking risks for a junkie whore."

"Who do you think he's working for?" Badger asked, and he took the seat July had sat on.

"That I intend to find out." He picked up the phone and punched in the numbers. He knew it was risky, but it was a chance he had to take. After a brief conversation, he replaced the receiver and gazed at the big man sitting opposite him. "He's not a copper."

Badger grunted. "Boss, I could have told you that; I don't think a copper would bash people with a scaffolding pipe. We searched him and found no identity on him."

"Well, somebody must be hiring him; he's too good to be just a punk looking after a whore."

"Maybe that's all he's doing, Boss. He could have feelings for her; stranger things happen."

Declan sniggered. "Well, he can't be living off her immoral earnings; she's not all that good at enticing the customers for a quickie. That's why I knew she was lying about that pack of drugs she delivered. She was always scrounging off the other girls for money to buy more drugs and fags. The temptation when she got that cash in her hand was too much."

A long silence followed. All that could be heard was the creaking of the chair Badger was sitting on. He jumped up and said, "When are you expecting another group of immigrants?"

"Soon; just waiting for a call. But we need to be careful that big guy doesn't follow us out there."

With his hand on the doorknob, Badger turned. "Now there's an idea. Why don't we set a trap for him. Tomorrow we could get the boys out there waiting for him to turn up when he follows us there."

"Do you think he'll follow us?"

"Well, if it's Wilma he wants, he will."

"And if it's not the whore he wants, what then?"

"Then we'll know he has been hired by someone."

Declan grinned. "That could be fun. You get that arranged … but not too early; give the big ape time to get here and see us leave."

Badger nodded, grinned back, and slipped out the door, closing it softly. The club was in full swing, the music deafening. Patrons were crowding the dance area, but only a few were dancing, if what they were doing could be termed dancing; they seemed to be just standing there bobbing their heads to the beat. Badger caught the attention of one of the doormen and waved him towards the bar. "Get a couple of the boys, the biggest and the hardest, to be here by nine tomorrow morning."

Pinkie could hardly hear what he had been told. He waved a hand at his ears and then pointed to the toilet door. Badger repeated the instructions after making sure they were alone. "Why? Is there a problem?" Pinkie asked.

"I hope not," Badger replied. "Just giving you a chance to get back at that guy who bashed you with that length of pipe." He told Pinkie what the plans were, and a broad grin dawned across Pinkie's face before they returned to the deafening thumping of the dance area.

Over the roof of Barton's car, White Hair held out his hands and said, "I wasn't aware I was following your parents." He brushed a hand through his hair.

"It's pure coincidence we happen to be at the same place at the same time."

"Then what are you doing here, at their home?" Barton asked, and at the same time he began walking around his car. By the time he got to the front bumper, the man had already started running and was well on his way to the end of the street. Barton cursed himself for not anticipating this and jumped back into his vehicle to give chase. It seemed White Hair had vanished into thin air. Barton drove along the streets, darting from one to the other, sometimes getting out to search the narrow lanes and back doors of the neighbouring houses. After an hour of fruitless searching, he gave up and returned to his parents.

"He might have had someone waiting for him with a car; that's the only way I can explain where he disappeared to," he told his father.

"That being the case," Tom said, "there must be some organisation backing him up."

Barton shook his head. "I wouldn't go as far as to suggest that."

"Well, how do you explain how he could disappear so quickly if, as you say, you were right behind him?"

"There're some dark corners up those lanes and behind the back gardens; he could be hiding somewhere. Might even have ducked into an empty house. Remember: I was trying to catch him, not trying to find him."

"So what do I tell your mother?"

"I'll stay here the night in case he's hiding and comes back."

Barton spent the night on the sofa, didn't get much sleep, and jumped at the slightest of sounds. When his mother touched his shoulder in the morning, he jumped up, almost knocking her off her feet.

She yelped and stepped back out of his reach. "That doesn't look too good. Are you always like this when someone wakes you?"

"Sorry, Mum; I've been up and down all night, sort of expecting that guy to turn up and try to get in."

"Well, you can relax; it never happened."

"What do you mean it never happened?" a familiar voice interrupted from behind. They turned to see Tom at the door, holding up a sheet of paper. "I found this on the dressing table." He handed it to his son.

"What is it?" his mother asked.

Barton read the scrawled writing. "'You live one more day, but the countdown has already started.'"

"What does it mean?" his mother asked.

Barton stood up and stared at them both. "It means this guy is good and has taken a contract out on you, Dad, and he won't stop until it's fulfilled."

His mother threw herself down on the sofa, her eyes staring and her lips quivering. "Call the police," she cried, and she slumped over with her head in her hands.

"If the police catch him, whoever has hired him will get someone else to fulfil the contract."

His mother jerked her head up and stared at her husband. "What have you done to deserve this?"

Tom shook his head, shrugged his shoulders, and fell back in his chair, trying to roll a cigarette. "I don't know." The paper and shag fell out of his shaking fingers. "Honest, I just don't remember doing anything to deserve this."

She turned to Barton. "Do you know what he has done? This is your kind of life. Is it something you have done to someone to make them want to take revenge out on your family and make you suffer?"

Barton shook his head. "Mum, you watch too many movies."

"She might not be too far wrong," Tom butted in.

"None of my associates know I have a family, so Dad, think back; you may have offended someone without realising it." Barton knew what his father had done and could tell his father knew as well. But he dared not admit it in front of his wife.

"Is there not such a thing as police protection?" his mother asked.

"You don't need protection; I told you both to go to visit Mum's sister in Cornwall for a week or two; I'll get this mess sorted out."

"When?" Tom barked at him.

"Now." He turned to his mum. "So get on that phone and get it arranged. I'll run you to the station."

The rush was on. An hour later Barton dropped them off at Piccadilly Station in Manchester. The rush was so intense that he failed to notice the black Citroën private hire that was on his tail.

Herman Goth, a.k.a. Judd, instructed his driver to pull up a short way from Barton's vehicle. They watched while the big guy lifted his parents' cases out of the boot.

Their goodbyes didn't last long before the old couple entered the station and Barton drove away.

Judd pulled the hood of his jacket up over his head and got out. He held back to let them buy their tickets but was not so far away that he couldn't hear them mentioning their destination. The day was going well. He smiled to himself. *Soon this job will be over.*

Barton, satisfied he had done all he could for his parents, decided to head for the Westerner's Club in search of that silver Range Rover. As he slowly drove past the entrance to the car park, the vehicle in question stopped to wait for a gap in the traffic. Barton slowed down even further and got a few blasts from the cars behind. He pulled into a bus stop lay-by and let the convoy pass. The Range Rover glided past, and he let a few vehicles continue behind it before following. When they reached the suburbs and the speed restrictions increased, the Range Rover kept to the inner-city limit. The danger lights began to flash in Barton's head; he could see the signs, when you want someone to follow you, make sure they don't lose you. Whoever the driver was, he was making sure that didn't happen. Barton was sure the driver didn't know his car, so he assumed the driving pattern was intended to serve as a process of elimination. Although there were quite a lot of oncoming vehicles and most of the drivers in front overtook the slow-moving Range Rover when the chance came, Barton knew he had to do the same to avoid being noticed.

Although Badger kept a vigil through his mirrors, Declan was constantly looking through the rear window for signs of a following vehicle. He had told Badger to slow down while he watched for a following car to do the same. This never happened. "If that guy is tailing us, he's a crafty bastard or he's not back there. Just carry on as normal; we need to see what that whore is up to."

The three men Badger had sent on ahead rushed over. "Is this guy following or what?" Pinkie asked.

"We're not sure," Badger replied, jumping out and slamming thedoor. "You lot get out of sight just in case."

Declan and Badger went inside, leaving the others to deal with the big guy if he turned up. Wilma was stretched out on top of her bed. Declan slapped her across the face but got little response. Again he slapped her, this time much harder. Her eyes half-opened and were rolling in all directions. Blood ran from her nose into her mouth. They both grabbed her under her arms and carried her into the shower room. They dumped her on the tray, where she buckled over and lay in the foetal position. They then turned on the water to the coldest setting and walked out. "Bloody useless whore," Declan commented. "I hope this guy turns up to see her in that condition."

"We're not sure it's her the guy is interested in," Badger said as they stepped out into the sunlight.

Pinkie and his mates came out of their hiding place behind some shrubs. "Looks like that guy's not coming."

"We'll hide inside for half an hour," Declan said, "I think he's a tricky bastard; he might be holding back or hiding somewhere in those bushes." The half hour turned out to be a full hour as they sat in the kitchen, drinking coffee and playing cards. Pinkie and his mates took it in turn to stand inside the door with it slightly open to watch for any signs of the big guy. Wilma staggered out drenched, a trail of water dripping behind her. They looked up from the game and burst out laughing.

"Fuck off, the lot of you!" she shouted, and she stormed into her room.

"She got an overdue wash," Declan said, and they started to laugh again. He got up off his seat. "I don't think that guy's coming. You three get back to the club; we'll stay here and get some info out ofthe whore. I've a feeling she knows more about that guy than she's telling us."

Wilma was in the process of changing into dry underwear when Declan and Badger burst in. "Have you used up all that stuff I gave you?" Declan demanded. Wilma nodded and continued fastening her bra. "If you want more," Declan said as he sat on her bed, "you'll have to earn it." She grinned and was about to remove her pants. "Not that way!" he snapped at her. "I want information about that big guy who got dumped beside you in the back office of the club."

"I don't know what I can tell you. That was the first I had seen him."

He stood up and smiled at her. "Okay, if that's how you're going to play it, you won't be getting any more sniff until you decide to cooperate." He dug into his pocket and tossed her mobile on the bed. "When you're ready to talk, call me." He gave Badger a nod, and they both walked out to the Range Rover. "The first thing she's going to do is phone that guy; she can't tell him where she is, but she can give him a description of this car." Declan went on as Badger started it up. "Then he will follow us, and I'll also be sure of his mobile number. We'll return when she starts to get cold turkey, then we tempt her with the goods, then she'll tell us what she knows about him."

"What do you plan to do with her when she gives you the info you want?" Badger asked after he got the vehicle in motion and back onto the main road.

"Hopefully she'll give him the details of this car. If he's as good as I think he is, he'll tail us. Then we can nab the two of them together; you and the boys can do what you like with them."

"So you've made up your mind that it is her this guy is after?" Badger asked when they pulled up at the first set of traffic lights.

"I've phoned around a few of the organisations, and it seems they know nothing about him."

Badger had his doubts but made no comment. He knew well enough that when a big guy like this one is doing the rounds, word soon gets out. As an afterthought, he recalled that the night he and the few others fought the guy into the back office, he thought the guy looked familiar. But he'd thought no more about it until the day when he spotted him observing the club entrance. "I've a feeling I've had some kind of connection with that guy before." He finally added, "Can't be a hundred per cent sure; it's just something about him that sets off alarm bells."

"Funny you should say that." Declan said, watching Badger try to remember where he had seen that big man. "I get that feeling too; it's been bugging me since that time he managed to escape from the back office."

"Do you think he's some kind of pro?" Badger asked as he pulled up the handbrake close to the back door of the club. They both got out the Range Rover, slamming the doors at the same time.

"If he's a pro as you say," Declan said, unlocking the door of the club, "who's hiring him, and why is he interested in a junkie whore?"

"We may find it all out when she's in need of a fix."

CHAPTER 6

When the big silver four-by-four pulled off the main road, Barton carried straight on and decided there was nothing he could do, but at least he knew where the turn-off was, and maybe that would be the place to start next time rather than the club. He pulled into a lay-by just as a truck was pulling out and phoned the mobile he had given his parents. He had spent some time with them teaching them how to operate it. His father answered, saying everything had gone to plan and he could see no sign of the white-haired man. Half a second after he ended the call with his father, his phone sounded, and Wilma's name came on the screen. "Hi, Wilma. Where are you?" That was the one question she couldn't answer, but she spent a lot of time explaining all that had happened to her. "How can I help you if I don't know where you are?" She had described the bumpy road they had taken her on, and when she ended the call, he decided to take the turning that the Range Rover had made.

Although it was classed as a B-class road, it was wide and smooth. He had turned off onto few rough, narrow roads only to discover they finished on a farmyard or a dead end. He called Wilma, asking her to describe the building she was in. All she could tell him that she thought it might have been a factory or a warehouse at some point. "The only thing I can do is follow that silver four-by- four and hope it leads me to you."

"Don't do that," she pleaded. "When they come here, they bring a gang with them."

"I'll work something out," he said before ending the call. Had she remembered to tell him that a truck had been driven there, things would have changed; and then he would have realised that it must have been a wide road. Instead he was searching for a rough track. He gave up and went back to the place where the four-by-four had turned off, on the off chance that they might come back. He parked in a lay-by not far from the turn-off, where he could just about see if a vehicle turned into it. A large beech tree blocked most of his view; luckily at this time of year there were no leaves.

As he wiped condensation from his windscreen, it struck him: why had she suddenly managed to phone him at that time and not before? It looked obvious that they had given her mobile back to her for this reason. He quickly returned her call and told her to hide her phone. "Just don't let them get hold of it and be able to check who you contacted." He could tell she wasn't very pleased at having to be without it again. A time check informed him he had sat there for half an hour, and the only vehicles that had turned into that road were a van and a few farm tractors. To pass the time, he decided to call his parents, and his father informed him that they had arrived and got settled into his sister-in-law's home and had seen no sign of the white-haired man.

Daylight was fading, and he decided to head for home. There was no point of hanging about any longer. He couldn't see the junction, and he was feeling hungry and in need of the toilet. As he got on his way, he noticed headlights travelling along that road and decided to investigate. He turned in and drove along, using his parking lights only. Up ahead, the headlights took an unexpected right turn. He pulled in and watched them disappear into what looked like a shrubby area. A moment later, all went dark. Barton decided they must have reached their destination. He parked his car as far off the road as possible, got out, and started to walk.

He soon came to a wide entrance. The road looked well used although the surrounding area was overgrown with bushes and trees. Keeping close to the side under the darkness of the trees, he made his way and soon came to the dark shadow of a structure. Here the concrete road widened into a courtyard. The vehicle he had been following was parked close to the front of what looked like a long warehouse or redundant factory. This place was close to the description Wilma had given him. As he crept closer, he discovered the vehicle wasn't the silver four-by-four; it was the same colour but a different make. Confused, he wondered whether he had made a mistake; he couldn't remember seeing this car parked at the club.

Before stepping out into the open, he did a recce around the building, looking for a window, but it seemed that they had all been bricked up, leaving only a small one facing the side farthest away from where the vehicle had been parked. To look inside it, he would have to cover open ground, and anyone looking out that window would surely spot him. He ducked past the car and listened at the double wooden doors. He was sure he heard voices from inside. He couldn't make out what was being said, but the speakers were definitely men. A moment later, he heard what he had hoped for; a female shouted, and he recognised the voice. It sounded as though she was begging or in pain. He resisted the urge to burst in and retreated into the shrubs. He just managed to get ducked down when the doors opened and the light from inside shone directly at him.

He didn't wait to see who was there or how many; all he could think of was to get back to his car and get it moved before they spotted it parked at the roadside. He raced through the long grass and shrubs, stumbling a few times, and managed to get to his car before the vehicle parked at the building got there first. Without lights, he drove a few hundred yards and then parked. He sat there waiting, looking through his rear-view mirror for the headlights coming out of the lane and turning off onto the road. It never happened. Instead, another set of lights entered the lane and headed for the building.

As he had done a few times in the past, he decided to leave July in charge of the club for the evening, promising to be back in a few hours. She wasn't too happy about the arrangement, complaining that Declan had left her short of staff. "How are we going to handle things if they get a bit rough?"

"It should be quiet tonight; Mondays are always quiet," he assured her.

"What's the score, Boss?" Badger asked as he drove out of the car park. "I've sent a few of the boys out to the factory to make sure that bitch was looking after the place, and at the same time to see if they could get that big guy to follow—and hopefully nab him. Pinkie phoned to say the guy hadn't followed but has the feeling he's sneaking about in the woods. He said one of the boys went out to the car for his fags and thought he saw something moving about in the shrubs."

Declan grinned and patted his jacket pocket. "I've brought some reassurance, should he show face."

"Thought you got rid of that after you shot that woman with it?" Badger said as he drove onto the main road.

Declan grinned. "She deserved all she got, bloody undercover cop."

"I wondered if that big guy is one of them," Badger said. "You checked that out; he could be from a different department, and they haven't informed the locals."

"I thought of that; that's why we need to nab him." When Badger turned off the main road, he slowed to a crawl and switched off the lights. They both scoured the wooded area, but by the time they reached the old factory, they hadn't spotted anything moving. "He had to have come here by car," Badger said as they both got out of the Range Rover.

"Where could he have parked it?" Declan said, walking through the door as Badger held it open. Pinkie and his two mates were sitting in the kitchen, playing cards. The room was clouded in cigarette smoke, and empty beer cans lay on the table. "What do you think you lot are doing?" Declan shouted at them. "I need you all to be on the ball in case that big creep is out there." He tipped the table over, scattering their game and drinks. "I want you all out there looking for him!"

Hearing the clamour, Wilma stormed in. "What's happening?" she shouted. Declan swung round and could see she was close to suffering from withdrawal. He grinned and grabbed her arm. "I've a few questions to ask you." He steered her back into her room while Pinkie and his mates picked up the table and chairs. He threw her onto the bed, and Badger rushed to the other side and held her down by the shoulders. "I want the name of that big guy we threw down beside you in the back office." Declan grasped her throat and squeezed.

"Honest, Declan, I've never seen him before," she managed to gasp out.

"You're a fucking liar." He squeezed more tightly, and she started to choke and gasp for air. He let her go, as did Badger. "Okay, if that's the way you want it, we'll hang on for another half hour, and when you're screaming for a sniff, I'll give you what you need when you tell me that guy's name." They left her lying on the bed,coughing and gasping.

Pinkie was on his own sitting at the table. He jumped up when Declan walked in. "The boys are out searching for that guy; I thought I'd stay here in case he charged in on you."

"Have you heard from them?" Declan asked as Badger went to the door, opened it slightly, and had a look out at the darkness.

"Be lucky to find your own nose in this darkness," he shouted back at them.

"That lot couldn't find their noses in broad daylight." Declan glared at Pinkie. "Get out there and help them."

"Okay, Declan." Pinkie jumped to his feet and stood a good six inches taller than Declan. He jabbed a thumb at the door. "In that terrain, you could be standing next to that guy even in daylight and not know it."

"I've brought a few torches," Declan said. "Badger will get them out the car for you. I need to be sure that guy's not sneaking about out there. Now get to it." When Badger returned, Declan was seated at the table with a mug of coffee in front of him.

"Any of that left?" he pointed to the mug.

Declan nodded. "Make yourself one. The bitch isn't screaming yet."

Badger had managed to get only a few sips from his mug when Wilma burst in and staggered towards them, falling on her knees in front of Declan.

"Please help me, Declan."

"What's that guy's name, and who does he work for?" he asked calmly, sipping at his drink.

"I don't know his name; honest. I've never seen him before," she sobbed.

He pulled a packet of cocaine from his pocket and slapped it on the table. "If you want it, give me what I want."

Wilma shot her hand out to grab for it but was too slow. Declan slammed his fist on her arm. She screamed and fell back onto the floor. He jumped up and landed a kick to her thigh. Another scream. "What's his name?" he shouted down at her. He got no reply and kicked her again, this time in the crotch. She let out a deafening howl. "What's his name?" he repeated. She lay on her side, doubled up, holding her groin.

"Barton," she managed to mumble out.

Declan turned to Badger. "Does that name mean anything to you?"

Badger shook his head. "Doesn't ring any bells."

"What is he to you?" Declan asked. "An ex-pimp or something?" He was set to land another kick.

"No, he's an old friend," she cried.

"Who does he work for?" Badger butted in.

Wilma shook her head. "I don't know," she replied. She braced herself for the other kick, but it didn't come, and she chanced to look around at them as they spoke silently at the other side of the table. They turned and walked out. The moment the door closed, she got up painfully and grasped the package from the table. A few minutes later, she had it spread out in two lines and was sniffing it through a straw. She lay back on the nearest chair and let the world float by as the pain slipped from her body. The world was now a beautiful place to be in, and she was enraptured by her surroundings.

Unfortunately, Declan didn't feel the same way about his surroundings; he shivered in the damp coldness as he watched his goons search the scrub with the lighted torches. After about ten minutes, he had had enough and got into the vehicle and started it up with the heater on full blast.

Badger joined him and was expecting a rebuke, but Declan just sat there staring out the windscreen. "I don't think that guy's here," Badger said eventually. "If he was, I think he's be long gone by now. Can't see anyone suffering this cold for a bitch like that."

Declan wiped the condensation from the window. "I can't take any chances. If he or anyone sees what's going on here, we're all in deep shit."

"We could all jump into the cars and drive to the end of this road, park up, and sneak back," Badger suggested. "If he's hiding in there somewhere, he'll be watching and think we've given up. He'll try to get in, and that's when we nab him."

Declan nodded. "Get them back in, and make sure the cabin lights in the cars are switched off. Don't want him to see us get out down there." This was an old trick he had learned from his past: never let the enemy see who's in the vehicle when the door gets opened; even with tinted windows, the light from the front window might give them away.

CHAPTER 7

Helping Wilma was no longer a priority on Barton's mind, although he would help her when he discovered what was going on in that old factory. *Must be something big for them to go to all this trouble.* The number of times the goons had walked past his hiding place and never thought to look up the tree made him grin. He could follow their every move—more so when they got torches. Now he watched as they all climbed into the vehicles and moved off. From his vantage point, he could watch them drive all the way to the end of the road with their headlights on. What alerted him was the suddenness when all the lights were doused at once. *An old trick*, he thought. He knew what would happen next. He wasted no time climbing down from the tree and made a wide route back to the main road and soon found where their cars were parked. A few minutes later, he had slashed all the tyres with his flick knife.

A short jog later and he was back at his own car and drove off.

He had instructed his parents to leave a light on to fool the white- haired man into thinking they were still in the house. He parked a few streets away and walked through the narrow lanes and walkways, searching for any sign of White Hair, but he turned up nothing. Using the key they had given him, he entered the house. He checked all the rooms for signs that the man had been in, and again the results were zero. He realised that White Hair was good; he had got in without being detected and left that note his father had found on the dressing table. He snatched his mobile from his pocket, and when his father answered his call, Barton said, "I think that guy has followed you."

"We haven't seen any sign of him," Tom replied.

"Have you been keeping an eye open for him?"

"No, but if I had seen him, I'd know him right away with that head of white hair; it stands out like a beacon."

"He could've been wearing a hat or a hood over his head."

A long moment of silence followed before the older man replied, "If that's the case, what can we do about it?"

"You need to stay indoors and stay away from the windows," Barton replied, and he cut off the connection before the barrage of objections began. He had visited his aunt in Cornwall only once, when he was on a school holiday. His parents and younger brother had taken the long train journey to Redruth and were met by his uncle and driven to a cottage near a village he couldn't remember the name of. They stayed only a few days, so he didn't see much of the countryside around that area. But from what he could visualise of that visit, it would be difficult to follow someone there without being spotted, as there was a lot of open, flat country with narrow roads. He hoped things hadn't change too much since then.

Time was wearing on, and he decided to stay the night at his parents' home, get up early—which was a task for him, having never been an early-morning person—and get back to that old factory before dawn to make sure the goons had got their vehicles going and had left. He had been informed by Wilma that she had been locked in and decided the small window was his best way to get inside.

He had no idea what had woken him, and when he checked the time, he was glad his sleep had been disturbed. He reckoned he had only an hour till daylight, and he had planned to get there before dawn, giving him time enough to recce the surroundings before climbing in that window. He had lain on their bed fully clothed. With no time for a shower or to eat, he rushed out to his car and raced onto the main road.

A relief came when the goons' cars were gone. He wondered how long they'd had to wait for a breakdown service to arrive. Not too keen on wading through the wet grass and bushes, he walked cautiously along the road. When he neared the building, a scarlet dawn silhouetted the factory. At this point, he entered the shrubs and circled around without losing sight of the edifice. When sure no goons had been left behind, he approached the window. Seeing nothing but darkness inside, he rapped on the small panes and got no response.

His last resort was to get Wilma on her mobile and hope that she was alone. Her phone rang about six times before she responded. "Where are you, Richard?" She asked in a slurred voice before he could get a word in. The alarm bell sounded in his head, and he guessed she was not alone in there. He hoped she had hidden her mobile in a place where they couldn't hear it; he also hoped they hadn't heard him at the window.

"Where are you?" she repeated in a slow, sleepy voice.

This told him they were listening, and he could tell she was dictating. Someone was with her; he was sure of that now. "Oh, you know, with some friends. Haven't found a decent flat yet." He hoped he had sounded convincing.

A long silence followed, and then she said, "We need to meet."

"I thought you were staying in that old mill; you said you were locked in?" A few moments passed.

"They let me out."

While he was engaged with her on the phone, he started picking at the old wooden widow frame with his knife. The years had taken their toll on the wood, which was held together with the many coats of paint. "Where would you like to meet?" The silence continued to the point where he thought she had cut him off, and then she came back, saying, "I've got my job back at the Westerner's. If you could come in about nine, I'll meet you."

The window was almost free, he had only about twelve inches to work at and it would slip out silently in his hands. But he had to keep her talking to create a distraction. "I'm not going back there after what happened the last time." He could almost hear the brains working on overdrive at the other end of the phone.

"Okay," she finally said. "I'll take a break and meet you outside at nine." Her voice lowered as if she were falling into a deep sleep.

He managed to catch the frame as it unexpectedly came free before he had completed stripping the cement seal. "Okay," he said, "I'll see you there." He placed the window on the ground against the wall and squeezed himself in on his side and silently crept along a dark passage. At the end he noticed a slit of light shining beneath a door. He crept towards it and put his ear to it. At first no sound came from within. A footstep at the other side of the door made him take a step to the side and press himself against the wall. The door swung open, sending a beam of light down the length of the building. A shadow appeared, and a figure stepped out.

Barton drew his knife and dived at the figure, dragging it to the floor. He held his blade to what he discovered was a slightly built man. Although this man was small, he was well muscled and put up a fight until Barton jagged his neck with the point of his knife. "Make another move and I'll slit your throat!"

Barton shouted. The man stopped struggling and lay still beneath Barton. "Who else is in there?" he asked.

"Just the girl," the man replied.

Still holding the blade against his neck, Barton dragged the man to his feet, turned him around, and pushed him back inside. Wilma lay naked on the bed, her brown eyes rolling around under half-open lids and her mouth wide open. Wilma's wrists were bound to the wooden headboard, and her legs were wide open. Barton saw red and launched himself at the man, punching him several times in the face until the man fell, and still he kept up the barrage of punches. Finally, when there was no more movement from him, Barton got up and went over to the bed and released her. He had promised to help her and was determined to do so. To be sure the man wouldn't regain consciousness, he landed another kick to his head and began dressing Wilma with the clothes that were lying around on the floor.

A search in the man's pockets revealed a set of old iron keys. He left Wilma sitting on the bed and ran to the doors. One of the keysopened them, but he had to fumble with them to find the right one. At a fast jog, he got to his car and drove it up to the doors. A few minutes later, he had Wilma in the back seat and was driving home.

He had to carry her up two flights of stairs to his flat; she hadn't improved any on the journey. He lay her on his bed to give her more time to recover. After a quick microwave meal, he checked on her and found she had rolled over. *That's a start*, he decided, and he gave her arm a shake. That got a moan from her, and her eyelids fluttered. His next attempt was a cold, wet cloth on her forehead; this made her jump.

"No! No!" she screamed, and she threw her arms about and sat up, looked at her surroundings, and caught sight of him. "What's going on? Where am I?"

"You're in my flat," Barton replied, and put his arm around her.

"How did I get here?"

"I brought you here; how else do you think you got here? That moron they left you with must have given you a rough time."

She pulled herself away from him. "What the fuck do you think you're doing?"

"You asked me to help you, remember?"

"That was when I thought they were going to kill me, not now. Declan gave me the job of looking after the old mill and his guests. I'm all right now—well … I was until you messed it up for me."

"You could have let me know that on the phone."

"I thought you might have guessed instead of playing the big hero."

"When I found you, you were lying on that bed naked with your hands tied to the headboard; your legs were wide open. I automatically thought that guy had drugged and raped you."

"Well, maybe he had; what difference does it make? I'm used to it."

"How did he manage to get you to take the drugs?"

"Oh, for fuck's sake, are you blind or something? I've been on drugs for years. Thanks to you I no longer have a supplier."

Judd's mobile sounded as he got settled in a seat in the next carriage to his target and a woman. He pushed his hood back and held it to his ear. "When are you going to get that job finished?" the voice at the other end asked.

Thankfully the carriage had emptied at the last stop and no one was within hearing distance. "I'm working on that now." He could visualise the dapper little man sitting in the front room of his mansion on his white leather chair with a glass of brandy in his hand. Judd had been in that room on several occasions. Unknown to the little man, he had been in every room in the house. That was another of his talents; he was a successful burglar and had never been caught in all the years he had been at it. He had once entered the little man's bedroom while he was having sex with a young boy, and they never detected his presence.

"It's been almost a year now; surely you must have had an opportunity to get it done in that time?"

"I'm trying to make it look like an accident, as you instructed in the contract. That takes time to set up; plus I've got that big oaf of a son snooping about."

"Right," the little man replied, "I'll get in contact with the son and give him a job that takes him away for a spell." It was on the point of Judd's tongue to ask why he wanted this old man hit, but he thought better of it. One of the unwritten rules was never to ask that question.

"You do that, and I'll have the job done in a few days."

"Where are you now?" The little man asked.

Judd never answered and cut the call off. That was another of his golden rules—never to reveal his location. To resist the temptation to simply shoot this old man, he had left some of his firearms hidden in the cellar of his home. One of his thoughts was to steal a car, do a hit, and run, but that would need to be executed when the oldster was on his own; the last thing he needed was witnesses. He also thought of using the mugging technique, and that also had to be done without witnesses. Suicide—making it look that way was tricky. The old man's relatives would swear he had no reason to take his own life. The final one was his choice—no mess, no fuss, and witnesses wouldn't know what had happened, so they couldn't say anything to help the police in their enquiries.

He wasn't exactly sure where he was when the train pulled into the station and he noticed Tom Barton and the woman—his wife, Judd presumed—get off carrying two small cases. He quickly got up, made sure his hood was well over his head, stepped out of the carriage, and was soon close behind them. He stood at the station gate as they hailed a taxi, and as soon as they were inside it and on their way, he did likewise. He handed the driver a few notes and told him to follow the cab in front.

"No problems, mate," the driver said. "I heard it on the radio where they were heading; this is the same company, so there's no need to panic if we get held up."

When the couple's cab stopped at a cottage gate well out in the countryside, Judd told his driver to take him to the nearest hotel or B&B. The driver grinned widely when Judd handed him more twenty- pound notes. "Give me a number where I can call you when I need you, and if anyone asks, you never saw me, never had me as a passenger." He got a thumbs up from the driver as he pulled away from the small hotel with ye olde English exterior.

Furniture polish hit his nostrils the moment he opened the door, A grey-haired heavyset woman in her middle age grinned as he approached the reception desk.

"Can I help you, sir?" she asked.

"I would like a room for a few days." He gave her his warmest smile.

"Certainly sir. Do you have any means of identity?"

Judd handed her his false passport and watched her examine it carefully,

"We have to hold on to it until you leave, sir— the rules, you understand." She tucked it under her desk. "Do you have any idea how long you might be staying?"

Slowly shaking his head, Judd replied, "Depends on the job. Put me down for a week, to be on the safe side."

He signed the register, and she turned it round and glanced at the name. She smiled again. "That will be a hundred twenty pound, Mr. Burrows." He paid her in cash, which seemed to surprise her. She handed him a key and instructed him where to find the room.

The king-size bed didn't spare him much space. A big antique wardrobe at the far side restricted his movements even more. But there was enough room for what he needed. He sat on the only wooden chair and eased the container out of his inside jacket pocket and placed it on the bedside cabinet. He opened the lid, and there was his chosen weapon. He had filled the syringe before he left his house and had put a rubber nipple on the point for safety. The container was his own design; he'd made it look like a wallet so that it didn't protrude from his jacket. It had been a nervous time loading the syringe with the venom of the black mamba; even the slightest drop on the skin could be fatal. Two thousand pounds these little vials had cost him, but they had paid for themselves over and over again. Most of his victims had been diagnosed as having had a heart attack. The last thing an autopsy in this area was going to conclude was that a death had been caused by the venom of a snake from hot tropical regions.

There wasn't a definite plan on his mind as to how or where to administer the injection. One thought was to get the victim in a crowded area and bump into him and then get lost in the rush. Another one was the mugger's assault, but his favourite was simply to come up from behind and stab the syringe into the back of his neck. For that he would need an escape route and would have to be well disguised.

Never had there been a time when it was difficult to tail Tom Barton; the bright blue flat cap he always wore stood out like a crow in a budgerigar cage. If that old man had had the sense to discard it, the job would have been more difficult. Living in that cottage at the side of a main road with nothing but fields surrounding it, it was going to be a challenge for him to watch without being spotted himself. His hope was that because they were far from home, they might relax and assume he hadn't been followed. Just how long they had planned to stay there was another problem. He got up off the chair and gazed out the small window that looked out at the front of the building.

Three field lengths away, a tractor worked. He gazed at it for a while before a bunch of cyclists suddenly went past on the road below. The idea struck. He had done quite a lot of cycling in his past to keep fit, so he shouldn't look too much like a novice. He skipped down the narrow stairway to the reception. The mature lady had been replaced with a younger girl; Judd thought she was a teenager, but she wore a lot of make-up. It seemed a strange life when he thought about it; young girls slap it on to make themselves look older, and older women wear it to make themselves look younger.

"Can I help you sir?" the girl asked with a lovely smile.

"I was wondering where I could buy a cycle and the clothing that goes with it?" He returned her smile and stepped closer to the desk.

She diverted her eyes to the laptop that was next to her on the desk. "I'll Google it for you," she said, and her fingers swiftly began tapping at the keyboard. A moment later, she said, "There's a shop in Redruth." She grinned. "They sell that type of thing, along with other ironmongery, I'd advise you to phone them first and see if they have what you want." She quoted the number and also wrote it down on the back of their business card. He thanked her and got on his mobile to the number she had given. They had everything he would need. His next call was to his friendly taxi driver, with whom he arranged to be picked up the following morning.

The menu was nothing fancy—basic English food. This Judd didn't mind, and he ordered. To get to the restaurant, he had to pass though the bar, and he noted quite a few patrons, some standing and others sitting at the table. The place was tiny, and it looked crowded, but there were only about a dozen people in there. He wondered whether the people who lived in that cottage where the old couple were staying frequented this place. If his luck held out, there was a chance they would pay this place a visit.

The young girl who had been in the reception earlier was now doubling as a waitress and was playing with her mobile at the kitchen door. Judd was staring at her, wondering whether it would be wise to make a few enquiries about the people who lived in the cottage. A voice from the kitchen shouted, "Lisa, come and get the gentleman's food!" Lisa reluctantly put her phone away, and a few moments later she was at his table, carrying a tray that held his meal.

He waited until she had it placed out and asked, "Do you know the people who live in that cottage along the road?"

"Around here, everybody knows everybody," she replied. "That's the district nurse, Mrs. Townsend."

"Do they come here for a drink or a meal?"

"Her husband is a regular; she comes now and again."

"Do you think they might visit this evening?"

"I heard they have friends living with them, so I'm not sure what their plans will be."

CHAPTER 8

"*I* want that bastard found today," Declan shouted at the three goons. "He ruined the plans I had made; now he's killed Donnie and pissed off with that whore. Fuck knows what she's told him about this operation."

"Where do we find this guy, Boss?" Pinkie asked.

"Let's hope she has her phone with her." He pulled out his mobile from his jacket and thumbed in her number. A trembling female voice answered. "That you, Wilma?" he shouted.

"I'm sorry, Declan; he grabbed me. I couldn't fight back."

"Who grabbed you? Where are you?"

"Barton. I don't know where I am."

"You're a lying bitch!" he roared, "If you want more of that good stuff I've got, you'd better start telling me who this guy Barton is and where you are."

"I can't; he's standing here next to me, listening."

"Ask him what the fuck he wants."

"I'll tell you what I want." The gruff voice came on unexpectedly. "You to leave this woman alone and to explain why your thugs jumped me that night in your club!"

"Who the fuck do you think you are?" Declan barked back.

"I could be your worst nightmare if you harm this woman."

"What's your interest in that junkie whore?"

"She's a good friend, and I intend to help her; she says you were going to kill her."

"That was just a heat-of-the-moment idle threat, and instead I gave her another job."

"What, looking after foreign immigrants and possibly getting herself raped and maybe killed?"

"That won't happen," Declan sighed. "I've got guys looking after her; she'll not come to any harm."

"That's an old song; I've heard it so many times."

Declan gave another deep sigh. "Look … just bring her back to that old mill, and we'll sort this out man to man."

"You keep singing those old songs; you're breaking my heart."

"I'll break more than your fucking heart when I get my hands on you."

"Now we're talking business."

"I'll tell you what to do," Declan snarled, gripping his mobile so tightly his fingers began to cramp. "Dump her somewhere in town. You can get lost, and she can phone me and tell me where she is."

"What's your interest in her? As you say, she's a junkie whore."

"Never you mind what my interest in her is. Just you dump her, and we'll forget that you slashed our tyres, killed one of my boys, and beat another with a steel tube." Declan cursed when he realised the call had been disconnected.

Pinkie and his three mates had moved out of hearing distance and stood at the door.

Declan stormed towards them, kicking a few mattresses on the way. "I want the bastards found. Get every one of your friends out there looking for them. You know what she looks like; he'll be with her. The one who finds them, I'll make sure he gets a good payday." Pinkie and his mates jumped into their car while Declan got into the Range Rover beside Badger. "You were keeping yourself out the way there. Why?" he asked as Badger followed the other vehicle onto the main road.

"Keeping an eye on the cars," he replied after a moment's thought. "You know what happened the last time we were here."

"Don't remind me; I'll tear that bastard apart when I get my hands on him."

Expecting July to be in his house when he got dropped off, Declan went to the foot of the stairs and called her but got no response. "Where the bloody hell is she now?" he cursed as he searched from room to room. He sat down on his chair in the lounge and called her mobile. The voice that responded was familiar but not the one he was expecting.

"You … what are you doing with that mobile?"

"I've got your girlfriend," Barton said. "I picked her up in town, and she came quite willingly. I thought we could do a deal."

"What kind of deal are you talking about?" Declan roared as he jumped up off his seat.

"Wilma is developing cold turkey; she needs some of your good cocaine. If you want your girlfriend back, you'd better supply her with some."

"Tell her the only way she's going to get it is if she comes back to do the job I gave her. As for my girlfriend, you can have her."

"Oh, I've had her a few times, and she's good."

"Put her on the bloody phone."

July seemed relaxed and said, "Hi, honey, what's the trouble?"

"Where are you?"

"I dropped my phone, and this kind gentleman returned it to me."

"Get back here now!" Declan shouted, and he threw his phone on the sofa. "Another one who thinks I'm stupid. She needs a lesson on how to be honest with me. If the whore Wilma doesn't come back, she'll take her place at the factory." After pacing from his living room to his kitchen numerous times, he picked up his mobile and called Badger. "I think that bastard's got July. Get as many of your friends as you can muster and search for them."

"Give us an idea where they are?" Badger replied.

"I've no idea. I think they're in town somewhere. He picked her up while she was shopping, I think."

"Boss, they could be anywhere. Could take days."

"Just get in there; you might get lucky." He switched off his mobile, tossed it on the sofa, and began pacing, his mind in turmoil. He had another load of immigrants due to arrive in two days and had nobody to entertain them. At the last moment, he decided to go and help with the search. He didn't like parking the limo in town but couldn't stand being on his own; he always had to have someone close by.

"That bitch July. Who knows that what made her decide to go out, knowing he could turn up at any time."

He had become friendly with the taxi drivers in his localarea through Badger, who had been one of them in the past, and this was his advantage; he knew Badger would have informed them all to keep a lookout for that big guy and the girls. With the taxi idea on his mind, he called for one rather than risk getting his pride-and-joy limo damaged. On the taxi ride, he called Badger again and arranged a meeting but had to wait for a while for him to arrive. He was standing at a shop window, pretending to be interested, when he noticed a familiar figure reflected on the glass. He froze, frightened to move should the figure notice. There was no way he could forget that big guy, with his long black hair tied back tightly into a ponytail, his tanned features, and developed physical demeanour of someone full of self-confidence. This scared Declan; he had never confronted anybody like this before. He felt like a schoolchild who had been moved to a new school. Luckily, the big guy had moved on down the street when the Range Rover pulled up at the kerbside next to him. He jumped in beside Badger. "I've just seen that big guy walk past a few minutes ago. Get some bodies here quick and nab him."

Badger's eye flashed from side to side, and he looked in the mirrors. "I can't see him; are you sure?"

"Of-course I'm bloody sure, do you think I'm cracking up or something?" They drove down the street slowly,their eyes addressing every man they passed. When the shopping area came to an end and joined a busy main road, they hadn't seen any sign of the big guy.

"Maybe he's in one of those shops," Badger said.

"Pull up over there," Declan said, pointing to a bus stop lay-by. "We can see all the shops from there. If he's in one, we'll get the boys on him. Where are they?" he asked, gazing up and down the street. "They should be here by now."

Badger got Pinkie on his mobile and was told they should be with him in a few minutes. Declan kept looking at the shop doors. A few people came and left, but there was no sign of the guy he was looking for. "We're sitting here like clowns, and for all we know the big bastard could be miles away by now."

Glancing at Declan, his face showing concern, Badger said, "This guy had the two women. Where are they if you didn't see them with him?"

"I was wondering about that. He might have them locked up somewhere. He said the whore Wilma was on the verge of cold turkey; that'll make it harder for him to keep her quiet and might distract his attention from July. Take another drive up the street; by that time the boys will be here, and they can do a walking search."

At the end of the shopping area in a parking slot, Pinkie and a few guys were standing about talking and looking around themselves like a bunch of lost sheep. Declan rushed up to them, and they instantly surrounded him. "Split up into two groups, one group on this side and the rest the other. Search inside all the shops. For those of you who haven't seen this guy, he's big, black hair tied back in a ponytail, and about a month's growth on his face."

Declan led one group, and Badger the other. An hour later, they met up at the last shop and had nothing to report. Declan decided to risk calling July's mobile again, and she answered on the first ring. "Where are you?" he demanded.

"We're at home," she replied.

"What do you mean, 'We're at home'?" he shouted.

"He forced me to drive us here."

"Who forced you?" he yelled.

"The guy your boys gave a beating to in the club."

Declan slapped his forehead in confusion. "That can't be right; I just saw that guy walking down the high street about an hour ago; we're here searching for him."

CHAPTER 9

arton had sat with her and could see the gradual change come over her. He knew Wilma's body was starting to crave drugs; she'd got to the point where she was constantly using. "I'm going to a chemist. I know a guy who might help me get something for you." He stood up, and she curled herself up on his sofa, shivering. "All self- inflicted," he mumbled, but he couldn't help feeling sorry for her. He knew there were two chemists on the high street, both at the other end from where he had parked his car. His reasoning for this was that he knew of a little guy who could get drugs and did some dealing, but he wasn't sure whether this guy might have been picked up by the police. His last resort would be the other guy in the chemist's.

As he ambled down the pavement, a woman was walking in front of him. He recognized the sway of her hips—or was it the waving long black hair? He wondered where he had seen her before. When she stopped to look in a shop window and he saw her face reflected, it struck him. She was the girl he had spoken to in the Westerner's Club. He stopped, letting her take her time window-shopping. She unexpectedly turned, and they came face to face. He approached her. "I've got a gun in my pocket," he whispered harshly, loud enough for only her to hear. "Where's your car?" If he was expecting her to get into a state of panic, he was so wrong; she grinned and walked on willingly.

"At the end of the street," she replied.

"Okay, let's get it." He was expecting her to walk in front; instead she hooked her arm around his and smiled up at him. He, in turn, couldn't help but smile back; it was contagious—a real pleasurable genuine expression. This black girl was beautiful, with shoulder-length straight black hair, warm ebony eyes, and a set of movie-star teeth. Barton couldn't control the fluttering in his whole being.

"Even if you had a gun, I know you wouldn't use it on me," she said as they walked side by side to where she had parked her car.

He couldn't believe he was having this conversation as she drove out onto the main street. It felt more like he was on a date with her; they were chatting about silly nonsensical subjects like teenagers using their best chat-up lines.

"Where do you want to go?" she slipped in unexpectedly in a humorous manner.

"To your boss's house?"

"Why?" Now she was serious; the smile vanished, and she gazed through the sides of her eyes at him.

"You know Wilma? Well, she's in need of some narcotics—the kind your boss has been supplying her."

The smile returned. "I don't think he keeps them at his house … Where is she?

"She's in my car about half a mile up the road. We can pick her up on the way." When they pulled into the lay-by, Wilma was slouched over at the side of his car, trying to bring up the contents of her gut.

"I hope she's not going to be sick in my car," July complained.

"I'm okay now," Wilma assured her.

Between them they got her into the back seat of July's car. Barton slipped in beside Wilma to keep her sitting upright; that way if she were going to be sick, he could push her head out the open window. He carried Wilma into the large house behind July and was shocked when she pulled out the keys from her jacket pocket and led them into a huge lounge. It was obvious she had spent a lot of time here; maybe she was her boss's lover or partner. "You seem to know your way about this house," Barton said.

July smiled and nodded. "Declan and I have been together for a few years now."

They eased Wilma onto the sofa, and Barton sat next to her. "All very cosy," Barton commented. "A big house and an expensive set of wheels … You're doing well for yourself."

Settling down next to them, July replied, "Like a bird in a gilded cage."

Nodding towards Wilma, Barton said, "I bet she would like to change places with you." He could smell her perfume; this made him gaze into her ebony eyes and lean closer to her. She reacted the same. Their shoulders touched. Barton felt her hand resting on his knee, and he moved closer and placed his hand over hers. Slowly he lifted his hand and put his arm around her shoulder and drew her in closer. She met his kiss eagerly, and then her mobile sounded and they jumped apart.

"Saved by the bell," she said with a smile as she stood up and answered the phone. She held up a hand to indicate for Barton to be silent.

"The bastard's in my house; he has her and the whore with him!" Declan shouted to Pinkie. "Get the guys together and get over there pronto."

The charge began, and they all got into their cars and raced for Declan's house but arrived too late; Barton, July, and Wilma were long gone.

"No trace of a struggle," Badger said as he searched the lounge and kitchen.

"I bet that bitch July went willingly," Declan said, slapping his palm on the arm of the sofa. "She's going to regret this; they all are."

"I wouldn't be too hard on July," Badger said. "She'll be playing it cool to save herself. I've been there; it's the best way to play it."

Declan sighed and slumped down on the sofa. "To think that guy has been in my house with that whore Wilma. We need to find them, and soon."

"That might be a lot easier than you think," Badger cut in. "Remember: he wants drugs for the woman. We could set a trap for them when they come to collect." Declan's calling Wilma a whore left a bitter feeling in Badger. He had developed a strange relationship with her, although not a sexual one—more like a sister-brother connection. Every time he heard Declan address her as such, it sent a chilling feeling through him. In reality, though, he could see that was what she was—just an addicted whore. Maybe he just didn't want to see her that way. "Get July on the phone and arrange something," he suggested.

Declan's mobile sounded as he was about the make the call to July. He cursed and put it to his ear. "Mr. Crow, what can I do for you?" For a long two minutes, he listened. "I don't think I need another bouncer; I have already got half a dozen, and that's been enough," Declan complained. When the call ended, he stared at Badger. "I have to take on another bouncer."

"Did he give you any information who it is?" Badger asked with a shrug.

Declan shook his head. "No, but according to Crow, he's one of the best—been trained in the army in special forces, did a lot of work for him before, comes highly recommended."

"Doesn't sound like the run-of-the-mill bouncer; maybe we could use him in the factory instead of one of the girls."

"Or along with one of the girls," Declan corrected.

"If he's so good, we could send him out after the guy who's got your girlfriend and Wilma, that way we could get on with business as usual."

Declan mulled over that for a while and finally shook his head. "it sounds good, but I want to get my hands on that guy personally. I need to know what he's up to. There's got to be more to him than just trying to help a junkie whore." He lifted his mobile and made another attempt to call July. This time he was successful, and she answered after a few rings. "Is that guy there?"

July handed the phone to Barton. He listened for a moment.

"I'll get you what you want," He heard Declan say.

"All I want is some of your dope for Wilma," Barton said. "Nothing else."

"Don't give me any of your crap!" Declan shouted. "You have to be wanting more; men like you don't go to all this trouble to help a drug addict whore."

"That's all I'm doing!" Barton shouted back. "If you don't get the stuff, I'll get it somewhere else, and you'll never see her or your girlfriend again."

"Okay, okay," Declan replied, struggling to calm himself down. "Where can we meet?" He nodded to Badger and stuck up a thumb.

"We don't meet. You'll meet Wilma and give her what she needs. If you harm her in any way, you'll never see your girlfriend again."

The signal went dead, and Declan lobbed his phone onto the sofa. "That's one crafty bastard!" he shouted, pointing at his phone.

"So what's happening?" Badger asked.

"He's just sending the whore to collect the drugs. If we harm her, I won't see July again. I don't care about not seeing the July bitch again; I want him."

"Wherever we have to meet Wilma, he'll not be too far away; he'll be watching our every move."

Declan nodded. "We'll have to get a good team in the area to find out where he's hiding."

"If he's as crafty as you think, he'll choose a busy area with lots of people going about. That way Wilma could snatch the dope and get herself lost in the crowd."

Declan grinned. He remembered seeing her in a desperate need of her fix. "That whore won't be fit to get herself lost in the crowd; I doubt she'll be able to walk to where she has to pick up the drugs."

"I wish you'd give her the respect of calling her by name," Badger said under his breath. He then said in his normal speaking voice, "If she's as bad as you think, we could give her a bag of French chalk; she won't know the difference at a glance."

Declan sniggered. "I was intending to do that, then follow her, if our chaps can't locate that guy." His mobile sounded again. He jumped and grabbed it. July's name came up. "Wilma will be in the Fox Bar Pub at one o'clock." Her voice sounded hollow, and the line went dead before Declan could say a word. He smiled over at Badger and passed on the information. A glance at the time on the wall clock and he jumped onto his feet. "Let's get there early and set something up. I know Gabby, the guy who runs that place; he'll help us." His next call was to Pinkie to get everybody to get to that pub and meet him outside.

Gabby didn't have much respect for the laws on indoor smoking, and the small bar room was an eye-stinging breath-catching fug. Declan squeezed his way to the bar and had to wedge himself in between bodies to catch the attention of the little bald fat man serving pints.

His eyes lit up when Gabby saw Declan, and the moment he finished pouring beer into a pint glass and handing it over to a customer, he stepped over, grinned, and said, "It's a long time since I had you in here; what can I get you?"

Declan held up a hand. "Nothing, Gabby. How is trade these days?"

"The same as usual—good days and bad."

"I need a favour," Declan said, leaning over the bar. "I've got one of my girls coming in here at one o clock; I need to nab her and haul her into your back room to ask her a few questions. I want to leave a couple of the boys in here to do that."

"As long as there's no trouble."

Declan held up his hand. "You won't even notice; just leave your back room unlocked."

Gabby nodded and returned to serving his customers. Badger stepped closer. "All set, Boss?"

Declan nodded, and they both squeezed their way out into the fresh air. "Get two of the boys to stand in there, but be sure they're not ones that she would recognise. Tell them to let her settle for a minute or two, then quietly take her into the back room. Phone me when this is done, and we can go in and work on her."

Badger delayed a moment and gave his boss a sideward glance. "I'm not too happy with this; it all looks too simple. That guy Barton, he doesn't strike me as someone who's going to fall for that trick."

"What are you suggesting?"

"We get more than a couple of the boys in, in case this guy's hiding in there amongst the rest of the punters. With all that fag smoke you can hardly see five feet in front of you."

Declan reluctantly agreed; he had wanted people outside to search the area for this guy, who, in his opinion, was planning to make a move the moment he saw Declan's team take the girl outside. "Okay, get another two in there. But only two of them must approach the whore; the other two can watch their backs without making it look obvious."

CHAPTER 10

A nervy young man led Judd through the front shop and into another room where all the cycling gear was displayed. "Is it a road bike or a mountain one you would like, sir?" he enquired.

Judd grinned. "Do you hire them out? I'm only here for a week."

The young man shook his head. "Not normally; lost a lot that way. I do have some second-hand bikes out in the storeroom. What we normally do is sell you one of those, and when you're finished with it, bring it back and we'll buy it back from you. We won't give you what you paid for it; we would deduct what it would have cost to hire it."

It had been a long time since he had cycled, and he was struggling after only a mile. Up ahead was a slight incline. He rumbled through the gears to the lowest, but before he got near the top his legs were screaming with pain. He was about to jump off and rest when the cottage came into sight; this gave him incentive to keep going. There was no sign of life as he passed the cottage, and he wondered whether they had gone out. He could see no car parked at the side, where a narrow driveway passed the building and led to an old wooden garage that had seen better days. He carried on past and stopped a short distance up the road where he could see whether there was any movement near the building. After a while, his sweaty clothes began to get cold, and he shivered and decided to head back the way he had come.

It wasn't much of a movement on the front window curtain, just a flicker as he slowly freewheeled past. A quick glance in another direction and he would have missed it. He was confident they wouldn't recognise him with the cycling helmet and a face windshield. He didn't look any different from the bunch of cyclists he had noticed passing the previous day.

Another of young Lisa's jobs was to tidy the guest's rooms before they returned in the evening.

She was an inquisitive young woman and liked to nose though the guests' belongings. The man Burrows didn't have much to look through, just his clothes that were placed on the chair where he had left them when he had come back to change into cycling clothing. Her first search was of the breast pocket of his jacket; she pulled out what felt like a wallet and opened it, expecting to find some information and cash.

She was shocked to see a hypodermic syringe that had been placed in this specially designed wallet. *Maybe the man's a diabetic or an addict*, she thought. Suddenly she heard the sound of someone climbing the creaky stairs. In a panic, she fumbled to replace the strange wallet, and it slipped out of her hand. It lay open on the floor at her feet; the syringe had slipped out and rolled under the bed. She kicked the wallet under as well and pretended to be busy dusting, expecting her boss to come in.

Whoever it was didn't enter the room, and she heard the person walk past. After a few moments, she decided it could be another guest. She reached under and pulled out the wallet and then reached for the syringe. She hardly noticed the faint pinprick on her finger, and soon she had it all back together. The only thing that was missing was the small red rubber nipple. She knew she would be lucky to find it under the bed and didn't bother to search for it.

Almost at the end of his energy store, Judd approached the hotel. An ambulance was parked in front of it with blue lights flashing. Preferring to ignore it and all the action going on, he wheeled his cycle around the back of the building and propped it up against the wall. As he approached the front, the medics were carrying someone out on a stretcher. The grey-haired woman was asking what could be wrong. The medic, with a clipboard in his hand, said, "It's too soon to say; we have to take her to hospital and do some tests. Could you give me her name and address so we can contact her family?"

"I've already phoned her mother," the woman informed him. "She'll be at the hospital when you arrive. Her name is Lisa Alexandria, and she's worked here for about six months now."

Judd edged his way in and headed up to his room, desperate to get into the shower. After he had dried himself and got dressed, he dug the custom wallet out of his pocket. He knew at a glance it had been tampered with by the way it had been placed in his pocket. When he opened it, the first thing that caught his eye was that the red rubber nipple was missing. Now he knew why the ambulance had been there. whoever had been in his room must have searched in his pocket and tampered with the syringe. He searched the floor but couldn't find the nipple.

Not wanting to attract attention, the last thing he needed to do was make enquiries into who this person was who had entered his room. It was obvious this person must have searched his pockets, found what looked like a normal wallet, opened it up the wrong way, and caused the syringe to fall out. The person must have pricked a finger when he or she tried to pick it up and replace it. The question that was now puzzling him was, Would there be enough venom in the needle to kill a person? The best way to discover what had happened to the person who had been lifted away in the ambulance was to go down to the lounge and earwig; Judd knew it must be the topic of conversation.

"It certainly wasn't something she ate here," the heavily built woman with the grey hair was saying to a customer. Judd walked past them and sat at the nearest table. "One minute she was standing at the desk in Reception, playing with her phone; the next she was lying on the floor." The woman ranted on before she turned her attention to Judd with a smile.

"Can I get you something, Mr. Barrows?"

He ordered his drink and said, "Has someone had an accident? I noticed the ambulance earlier."

She shook her head. "Nothing too serious, just one of the staff took a bit of a turn." She walked away to the bar to get his drink.

"Must have been quite a turn," he said when she placed his drink in front of him.

She grinned. "Young girls, you know what they're like. She's probably gone and got herself pregnant."

Judd suspected differently. He had a good idea what had made the young girl pass out, and he hoped there wasn't enough venom on that needle to kill her. If that happened to be the case, then his plans would have to be changed. He couldn't have two people dying with the same symptoms in the same area; that would create an enquiry, and they would surely discover what had killed them and eventually be led to him. The investigation would soon conclude that the last job the girl did was in his room. To leave the hotel so soon after he said he could be here for a week might draw attention as well. The only young girl he had seen was the one who had told him about the cycle shop and served him his meal. He hugged his drink, deciding to delay and see whether she was the one the grey-haired lady had been talking about.

He finally drank the last of his drink and got up, deciding that if she was the girl who was carried out, he must play it cool and act ignorant.

The grey-haired woman came over to him. "Can I help you with something else?"

Judd shook his head. "No, I was just wanting to thank the young lady who provided me with the information about the cycling shop."

"I'm sorry, sir, but she's not here; she was the one who was taken to hospital."

"Is she going to be all right?"

"I've not heard anything yet; her parents are with her just now. I'm expecting them to call me and let me know."

He stood up, excused himself, and went back to his room to work out his next move. If that girl survived and started talking, it could mean trouble for him. If she died, it could be equally troubling. After long, hard thinking, he decided to check out of the hotel in the morning and head back and wait for the old couple to return to their home, and he would then wait for an opportunity to administer the venom. That way, with two people dying the same way hundreds of miles apart, the connection might never be made. He wished he had been there to see the girl's reaction to be certain that it was the venom that caused her to collapse. It was possible the dose she got wasn't enough to cause the reactions he had witnessed on previous victims. Had it been enough, surely the medics would have had her on a breathing system. He hadn't noticed that when he passed. As the woman said she collapsed, that sounded normal; the girl would have lost control of her legs.

Judd had booked an early breakfast, after which he called his friendly taxi driver and then signed out. With the driver's help, they managed to get the cycle into the boot of the vehicle and dropped it off at the shop. He had an hour and a half to wait for his train. While waiting, he phoned Crow and explained what the delay was. His description was basic, leaving out the part with the girl, which would have meant divulging his method. The little man came back saying he had got in contact with the old man's son and had pointed him in the direction of a job.

With his report finished, he strolled into a paper shop in the station. That was when he noticed the bright blue flat cap. The Bartons had decided to go home early,and together they had carried their luggage onto the platform only a matter of ten feet away from Judd. Had he been on his own, he would have had a good laugh at his luck, but he restrained himself, not wanting to attract attention.

"You know what will happen to you if you step inside that bar!" Barton shouted at her. "He'll have a squad of goons ready to jump on you."

"Why did you arrange for me to meet Declan there?" Wilma sobbed, still curled up on the sofa, her body shaking like a dry leaf in the breeze.

"As a distraction. I want him and all his gang there. I want to do a job in that old factory."

"What kind of job?" July asked.

"It's best you don't know," Barton replied, zipping up his leather jacket.

"What are we supposed to be doing while you're doing this job?" July asked.

"You're both coming with me; I'm not going to let you both out of my sight. I can't trust her not to phone this Declan guy the moment my back's turned."

"How can she do that? You've got both our mobiles," July complained.

"In her state, she would find a way of getting in touch with him." He grabbed one of Wilma's arms and lifted her up from the sofa. "Get hold of her other arm, and we'll get her into your car."

"Where's this place?" July asked, standing at the side the car and looking around while Barton got Wilma out of the back seat and onto her feet.

"You've never been here?" Barton asked, as he half-carried, half-walked Wilma towards the building.

July followed behind them. "What's this place used for?"

Barton stopped and looked into her ebony eyes. "You'll have to ask Wilma; she's been staying here."

Wilma lifted her head and gazed at July through half-closed eyes. "Foreigners sleep on mattresses on the floor." Her head dropped. "I had to cater for them." It all came out slurred. They had to listen carefully, finding it hard to believe what they had just heard.

"What's this got to do with Declan?" July asked as they reached the door.

"He owns this place," Barton replied.

"Are you saying that Declan is involved in people smuggling?"

"It looks like it," Barton replied as he worked on the lock with a device he had extracted from his pocket. "I suspected something like this; I wanted to fuck his operation up for the way he used Wilma."

When he got the door open and they walked in, July gasped in shock. "Is this where he hides them?"

Barton nodded. "It must be. He and his thugs have been scouring about this place, looking for me."

"How did you get to know about this place?" July asked as Barton placed Wilma on the bed in her makeshift room.

"I followed them here. I promised to help Wilma, and I decided they must have her hidden somewhere."

"What do you intend to do with this place?"

"First, see if he stashes his drugs here."

"And second?"

"Destroy the place."

"How are you going to do that?"

"Burn it down."

"Do that and Declan will get every thug in the area out looking for you."

"That'll cost him; thugs don't come cheap."

"That won't bother him. He can't stand to lose, no matter what it costs."

"Even if it costs him his own life?" Barton asked as he began searching in the kitchen.

"So do you intend to kill him?"

"If I have to."

"That might be difficult; he's always got his goons around him," July said, following him around the kitchen. She let out a yelp as he ripped the units off the wall and threw them onto the floor, and she had to jump out of the way when he toppled the fridge-freezer over on its side and emptied all the contents out. "I think you're wasting your time searching for drugs here."

He stopped and gazed at her. "Why? Do you know where he keeps them?"

She shook her head. "That's one thing he'll never divulge; I think that's where all his money is."

He walked out of the kitchen and started pilling the mattresses on top of each other in the middle of the floor.

She stood at the kitchen door, watching. "Are you going to start by burning that lot?" she pointed to the pile.

"Not yet," he said as he threw the last one on top. "First you have to drive into his club and tell him that if I don't get those drugs within a given time, I will. If he attempts to follow you, the same thing. You pick up the drugs and get back here; I'll work out the timing. He'll not want to lose this little earner." Barton followed her out to her car, watched her climb in, and said, "You'd better get back here in an hour exactly. I want enough drugs to keep her going for at least a month."

He watched her drive away, the tyres on her car kicking up gravel and dust as she sped off. The only thing left untouched in the kitchen was the gas cooker; he had a good idea that there would be no working gas lines to this place; it would have been cut off when the company closed the place down. *So there must be cylinders stashed somewhere.* After checking Wilma was still sleeping, he began searching outside. It didn't take him long to find one. He turned off the supply, cut the line, and then rolled it into the building.

July loved her blue BMW. She drove it with care and spent many hours washing and polishing it. Considering the situation she was in now, she knew she was going to lose it. She could tell by the tone of Declan's voice that she was nearing the end of this luxurious life. If she turned up at the club, it would mark the beginning of the end for her. He would toss her into prostitution and ply her with drugs till she couldn't live without them. Listening to the other girls that worked his club, she knew it was only a matter of time until he got fed up. Wilma, she decided, must have been one of his lovers. She remembered her lying on that bed in pain, her body trembling out of control. No way was that going to happen to her. She pulled up at the front door of Declan's mansion, rushed inside, piled all her clothes and belongings into a few cases, stuffed them into the boot, and drove off heading north on the M6. Her intentions were to get as far away as possible, find a place to live, and then abandon the car. This, she knew, would hurt. She knew she would have to drive it a great distance before torching it. If she kept it and she was sorely tempted, Declan would get a few of his police friends to trace it and find her. For this she would need help, and the only person she felt she could trust was Barton. The big question was, Would he help after what she was in the process of doing—abandoning him and Wilma.

Thanks to Declan, she had a good sum of cash in her bank account, and she decided to pull into Gretna Services to fuel up and get some food and visit the toilet. The break gave her time to think where she was going. *Needs to be a large town or city—easier to get lost that way.* She cursed Barton for taking her mobile; she didn't need it to find a hotel or B&B for a few nights until she found a flat, but she would have felt better if she could have called and booked in advance.

CHAPTER 11

*J*ean and Tom Barton got out of the taxi at their front door. Tom had a good look about to make sure the white-haired guy wasn't hanging around. Satisfied, they unlocked the door and quickly stepped inside. "That was a quick holiday," Jean complained. "I don't understand why you and my sister Molly don't agree. She went out of her way to make us welcome when you consider she didn't have much time to prepare for us coming."

"Why do I get all the blame? She was the nasty one saying those things about our sons."

"All she did was ask how Richard was getting on and whether he was behaving himself."

"It wasn't what she said; it was the way she said it, as if Corrie deserved what he got."

"I think you had better phone Richard and tell him we're home."

"And get an ear bashing from him? You can do it."

"I'll do it later," Jean said. "I'm going to make something to eat." After dumping the cases on the bed, Tom went into the living room, slumped down on the sofa, and turned on the television. Two minutes later, Jean could hear him snoring from the kitchen. She decided to call Richard, and at the last moment she changed her mind about telling him they were at home, knowing well he would come charging in demanding to know why. "Hi, Richard. We're having a quiet time down here. Your father hasn't said much since we arrived; that would explain why."

Barton carried Wilma out of the old factory and into the wooded area that surrounded it. He instinctively knew July wouldn't come back by her body language, so he wasn't hanging around to await her arrival. He had brought some of the bedding with him and placed Wilma in a sheltered patch of bushes and covered her. What he had to do next wouldn't take long, so she wouldn't suffer much of the cold. As he entered the factory, his mobile sounded and he saw his father's number; he was a little surprised when his mother spoke. After she had finished, he felt relaxed; now he didn't have that problem on his mind. He placed the gas bottle flat on the floor and surrounded it with the mattresses. The last one he placed on top so that it made an igloo shape. He had previously taken Wilma's plastic lighter from her jeans pocket; this he taped around the top of the container. It didn't take him long to cut strips of material from the remaining bedding. One end he attached to the trigger mechanism of the lighter; then he tied the rest and led them out the door like a makeshift rope. Back at his pile of mattresses, he reached under and opened the valve on the gas cylinder. Using the tool he had used to get in, he managed to get the door locked, and he then gave his material rope a gentle tug. He guessed he'd have about twenty seconds to get clear, but he was back beside Wilma and about to call it a failure when the explosion happened, sounding like a deafening whoosh.

The night sky lit up like a lightning flash. Even at that distance of about fifty yards, he felt a sudden wave of heat hit his face. He threw Wilma over his shoulder and was shocked at how light she was. *Must be the drugs*, he thought as he swiftly made his way through the rough wooded terrain and onto the road.

Only one vehicle passed, and he ducked behind a clump of bushes in case it was Declan and his mob.

She came to from her coma-like sleep and started to struggle from his shoulder. He dropped her on her feet, and for a moment she staggered back before he caught her. "Do you think you can walk?" he asked.

"Where am I?" She screamed, and she slumped to her knees.

He lifted her back onto her feet. "We need to get away from here." He slung her arm around his neck and dragged her on. He had to make a few stops to let her get her breath back, and soon they heard the emergency vehicles. He hauled her in behind a wall and sat her down. She began to whimper; then the whimpering got louder, to the point where she was screaming. The last thing he wanted was to strike her, but she was almost hysterical.

The blow he delivered silenced her at the same moment the fire services flew past, blue flashing lights illuminating the area. A moment later, more emergency vehicles sped past. She was beginning to help herself, making it easier for him to gain more distance from the emergency vehicles. At one point, she was almost walking independently, but that didn't last long before she collapsed again. In the distance, he noticed a faint light flickering through the branches of the high hedges that ran along the side of the road. He decided to set her down on the roadside behind a thick clump of bushes where any passing vehicle wouldn't notice her.

After a ten-minute jog, the light led him to a cottage. He crept up and around it, praying the owners didn't have a dog. At the side of the building, an old Land Rover was parked; it was similar to the type he was used to in the regiment. If no modifications had been made to it and it still had the muffled exhaust for silent running, he could drive it away from here with little sound from the diesel engine.

He had no problems getting the vehicle started and noticed no movement from inside the cottage. Slowly he eased it past the front door, and he was soon on the main road. Wilma was standing up but was bent over as if in pain. He piled her in to the passenger's seat and drove off using only the sidelights until he was a safe distance away.

"Maybe that guy left her to walk there and she wasn't able to make it," Badger said. "You know what she's like when she needs a fix."

Declan opened the door of the Range Rover, and before stepping out, he turned to Badger. "I get the feeling you have a soft spot for that whore."

Badger quickly responded, "Not any more than I have for the rest of the girls."

Declan gazed into his brown eyes. "if you want to keep your job, my advice to you is to ditch any feeling for these whores." He stepped out, slamming the door.

Badger got out and followed him into his house and into the lounge. "It's not the kind of feelings you think."

Declan slumped himself down on the sofa and looked up at him, grinning, "What kind of feeling do you think I think?"

"Well, I'm not fucking any of them," Badger snarled, "and have no intent of ever doing so. My feelings are just work related. We are supposed to look after them; that is our job." He sat on the armchair opposite. "Why do you think she never turned up?"

"I don't think that ape Barton is stupid enough to get her to walk to the club; he would know she was incapable. I'm thinking he has duped us into getting all our guys there and is up to something."

"The old mill!" Badger cried, and he shot up onto his feet.

Declan remained seated and shook his head. "Or the Westerner's Club." He snatched his mobile from his pocket. It rang a few times before the bartender answered. He asked how things were going, and the man seemed surprised at the call but reported that it was a quiet night and things were normal. He jumped up and joined Badger. "It has to be the old mill. Get the guys and get over there."

Badger was on his mobile as they rushed towards the Range Rover. "Pinkie's gathering them up and will be there soon."

"Don't rush," Declan ordered. "We don't want to get there before the guys. That big ape might have set a trap of some kind."

They could see the red glow in the night sky as they turned into the driveway. They didn't need to say a word; they knew what it meant. "Turn around and get to fuck out of here!" Declan cried. "I hope the guys up front do the same. Phone them and warn them."

Badger jumped on the brakes and snatched his mobile from his pocket, barked a few words into it, and cut the connection. "Just caught them in time."

Declan sighed. "That was lucky; had they driven into that yard, there would have been a lot of questions asked."

Badger, in a hesitant manner, said, "Do you not think it would have been better just to have given that guy the drugs and avoided all this?"

"And give in to a thug and a whore? No way! I don't care what it costs; I want that guy. I want to watch him die slowly and painfully alongside that whore and the bitch July."

Badger stopped the vehicle close to the club back door and followed Declan around to the front. "No damage done here," Declan said, and he pushed through the doors. Ignoring the greetings from the staff members, he entered his office, slumped down on the chair behind his desk, and gave Badger time to get seated at the front of the desk. "Do you think July's still with that guy Barton?"

"Where else could she be?"

"Her car has a tracking device. Do you know anyone with a tracer, or whatever it is they use to trace vehicles with them?"

Badger shrugged his massive shoulders. "Not offhand, but I could ask around."

"Trace her car, and we might find Barton and the whore as well." He watched the big neanderthal-featured man get up and walk out, gently closing the door.

Deciding to try his luck, Badger phoned July's mobile and got what he had expected—the operator telling him the person was unavailable.

On the monitor on his desk, Declan watched Badger standing at the bar and the barman shaking his head. Next on the screen came the tall, skeletal Pinkie, who nodded and stepped back from the bar with his mobile at his ear. Badger walked into the office with Pinkie at his tail. "We need the registration number," Badger said. "Pinkie here says he knows a guy who can get a trace on it."

Declan jumped up. "Good, no time to waste. Let's get to it now."

CHAPTER 12

Judd wasn't too concerned that the old couple had got into a taxi and left him standing. He knew where they were heading and was in no rush. He chose to let them get settled in and feel safe, stay out of sight, and let them think he had given up. Eventually the old man would venture out and head into town to his favourite bookmaker, a shop that was always crowded—an ideal place to administer the venom. He could have done it before, but that big oaf of a son made it difficult, with Judd not knowing when and where he might turn up.

When getting a taxi, Judd never got the driver to drop him off at his house, always getting off a few streets away. He didn't put too much trust in the drivers and always thought them to be friendly with the police. The only luggage he had was what he was wearing; he hadn't been expecting to travel so suddenly. He soon got to his home and into the shower and took a nap for a few hours to refresh his thoughts on how to get away from that bookmaker's shop without arousing too much attention.

The best disguise he had always used was to simply dye his hair. A nice common brown would be the best, and plain glass specs. No hat—people remember hats.

Sleep didn't come easy to him. He kept seeing people he had killed—people that had never done him any harm. Most of them deserved what they got, but a few were decent citizens who just happened to be in the wrong place and witnessed a crime—like this old man, who had walked into a club and been told to deliver a bag to an address on the threat of his only son's life. Judd had taken the contract and the money; now the job must be done or the next contract would be on him.

It was still dark when he climbed out of bed. After a mug of black coffee, he got to work on dyeing his hair. When the job was completed, he complimented himself on the difference it made. The reflection in the mirror showed a much younger man. With the glasses, he looked like a student home for a holiday. This role he played well; he would sling his rucksack over his shoulder and put a spring to his step. He stepped into his slit jeans and trainers, and the final touch was the duffel coat. He was ready to go, but the bookmakers wouldn't be open for a few hours, so he decided to have a recce around the area where the Bartons lived.

It took him over half an hour to reach the street. Some of the windows were lit; he assumed people were going to work. But the house in question was still in darkness. The street lighting was poor, and the side where he stood was almost in darkness. He stood for a long time watching the house, paying attention to the upstairs bedroom window, where he knew they slept.

Often, he had been asked why he didn't own a car. The simple answer to that was that cars were too easily traced and the walking kept him fit.

The shopping mall was starting to come to life, with shop workers rushing to their jobs. A few dog walkers were being pulled along by eager pets. Some late nightclub patrons were staggering home. The bookmaker's wouldn't be open for a while, but the little cafe opposite soon would be to catch the workers who were running late and needed their coffee fix.

After weeks of studying Tom Barton's routine, Judd guessed he would turn up at the betting shop around noon. He would havebought his newspaper from the shop a few doors up, and if the weather was good, he would sit on the public bench outside the chemist's and study the racing form. It was a bright, frosty morning, maybe too cold for the oldster to sit outside. Maybe he would enter the cafe and, over a cup of tea, bury himself behind his paper.

Judd ordered a breakfast at the counter and took a seat where he could watch the movements of the betting shop. An overweight man in a suit opened the door. A few minutes later, two middle-aged women entered. Judd put them down as being the cleaners. He had finished his meal and was on his way out of the cafe when he noticed the cleaners leave the betting shop. A quick glance at his watch and he decided that if the old man was coming, he would be leaving his home right now.

"Where are you going?" Jean Barton shouted at her husband.

"I've a few things I want in town," Tom replied, pulling on his jacket and placing his cap on his head.

"Bloody betting on the horses again. You were warned not to go out."

"That was when we were down in Cornwall, not here."

"What if that man's out there watching this house?"

"He won't be; he'll have given up when he saw us leave." He slipped out the door before she had a chance to continue with the argument.

Before he started his walk into town, Tom had a good look around, doubling back around the streets and ducking into corners. After a while, when he could see no sign of the white-haired stalker, he headed for the town centre.

The tall, thin woman behind the counter of the newsagent's shop greeted him in her usual manner, wishing him luck with the horses. She took his money for the paper and his tobacco. He had enjoyed his brisk walk in the cool frosty morning and thought it would be too cold to sit on the bench. He took up his usual seat in the cafe, placed his mug of tea on the table, and began studying the form on the racing page. Where he sat, he could observe the door of the bookmaker's. He could see it had been opened, but it was too early to go in; the staff wouldn't have had enough time to get things set up. By the time he had made up his mind what horses he wanted to back, he had finished his tea. He then got up and headed across the street to the betting shop. Before going in, he rolled himself a smoke and was joined by a few of the regular punters. They chatted about the day's racing until the cigarettes had been extinguished, and they then entered. Most of the clientele were regulars and all knew each other if not by name then by sight. On the odd occasion, a stranger would come in. This didn't cause too much attention, although some of the regulars would give them an extra glance.

When the tall, thin youth entered wearing glasses, nobody paid too much attention, although he may have got a few curious looks that didn't linger long. Tom Barton never noticed him; he was engrossed in the forecast of the first race until the stranger nudged his shoulder and asked for a tip on the race. Tom looked up into the man's eyes behind the thick-framed glasses and grinned. "I think the favourite could take this one." He didn't wait for a response from the stranger and returned his attention to reading the odds on the whiteboard. Having made up his mind on the horses he was going to bet on, he turned to the stranger, but the man had slipped away. Tom couldn't see him amongst the punters in the shop. He grinned, shook his head, and placed his bet at the counter.

Judd wasn't too far away, sitting at the same table as before in the café, observing the door of the bookmaker's. This was the unpredictable part of Tom

Barton's visit; he never left the shop at the same time. Judd thought it could depend on how the old man's luck panned out on the day.

Fortune wasn't with Tom; his first two horses fell before the finish of the race. He decided he'd had enough and left the shop before his third horse had started its race. *One of those days*, he thought, *when nothing works out the way I want.* He crossed the street and entered the cafe and instantly recognised the tall stranger sitting in the same seat he had sat on earlier. Tom sat across from him at the same table. "Did you have any luck?"

Judd grinned. "I didn't fancy anything." He drained his cup, stood up, and left.

After his tea and a sandwich, Tom returned to discover that his third horse had won, but his winnings didn't cover his losses on the first two.

"Not having a good day?" the man standing next to him asked.

Tom turned to see his regular betting buddy. "One of those days. You think you've picked a couple of certainties, and the buggers fall."

"Looks like your lucky cap is getting stale." His buddy pointed to Tom's cap, grinning.

Tom laughed. "I get the feeling you fancy my cap; you always comment on it."

"I think it would look better on my head than it does on yours." Tom lifted his cap off and stuck it on his buddy's head. "You can have it. See if it brings you any more luck."

Judd was fully focused on the man with blue cap standing at the bus stop. Although the man had his back to him, Judd was certain it was Tom Barton. Who else had he seen with such a prominent cap? He had the syringe strapped under his wrist so that when he clasped his hand on the man's shoulder in a friendly gesture, he could use his other hand to operate the plunger.

When the oldster turned to face the person who had placed a hand on him, Judd had already administered the venom. It was too late to do anything. He couldn't rush away; that would attract the attention from the crowd standing there. All he could do was stand and look unconcernedly around him. This he had plenty of practice at. He understood that it could take a few minutes to take effect, and luck was on his side, as the bus soon pulled up. He waited till everybody got on and stepped back as the vehicle drove away. All went smoothly; he didn't attract any attention. The only problem was that it was the wrong man.

Tom walked home, which took a good fifteen minutes. He was missing his cap and could feel the cold, frosty breeze on his head and regretted having given it away. His greying hair was fast receding, and he wished he had a replacement; now he would have to buy a new one. He knew it would be difficult to get one the same; he had bought that one a few years ago in Blackpool, mostly as a gimmick. He got a few laughs from his friends when he started wearing it. Jean, his wife, had threatened to burn it a few times, but she never did, and he became attached to it and would never go out without it. When he walked in the door, Jean was standing in the hall.

She looked at him with wide-open eyes. "What's happened to your silly cap?"

"I gave it away."

"Thank goodness for that," she replied with a grin.

CHAPTER 13

The headlights on the old Land Rover weren't very bright, and it took all Barton's concentration to keep it on the right side of the busy road. It tended to drift off to the left, and he kept thinking maybe one of the tyres was soft. Through the corner of his eye, he noticed Wilma twitching and kicking out her legs, and soon she began to moan. He pulled onto the grass verge and stopped, got out, and opened her door. "Do you need to be sick?" he asked.

She fell out into his arms, "I need some coke; that's what I need," she pleaded.

He eased her back inside. "Hold on a bit longer; I think I know where I might get something for you." Her head lolled from side to side and back and forward.

"Where are we?" she mumbled.

"We're heading home to my flat, only a few miles," Barton assured her, and he got the vehicle on the move. Before he got to his place, he needed to ditch this old vehicle and would have to do it a good distance from his house, which could mean getting a taxi into town to pick up his own car.

When on the run from a man like Declan and his mob, taking a taxi could be risky. The distant glow of streetlights in the night sky indicated he wasn't too far away from town. He pulled into a narrow lane he thought could be a farm road. After a hundred yards, he cut the lights and the engine. "Are you fit enough to walk a couple of miles?" he asked her.

"Get me some coke and I could run it," Wilma replied, her body shivering and her voice trembling.

"I don't have anything to give you just now, but if you can walk with my help, I might be able to get you something." He helped her out and put her arm around his shoulder, and for the first few yards he had to drag her. Eventually she found her feet, and he managed to pick up the pace. It was slow going; with every car that passed, they had to stop and hide behind what cover was available. They couldn't chance it, as the next vehicle could be one of Declan's or the police.

A trio of bungalows were a short way up ahead; two had lights outside the doors, and the middle was in darkness, with a car parked in the driveway. In a matter of minutes, Barton had hauled her into the passenger's seat and had it started.

He abandoned the car close to where his own was and handled Wilma into his vehicle. Again he had to almost carry her into his flat. She flopped down on his sofa and instantly stretched herself out on it. "I'll make some black coffee see if that will help." He got no response from her, and she curled up and began snoring. "Maybe not. I'll have some myself." He sat on the chair close to her, listening to her snore. He drank his coffee and decided that staying here wouldn't be safe. It would only be a matter of time before Declan and his gang found them. He had lost count of how many times he'd had to shake himself to avoid dropping off to sleep. A shower and then bed was his final decision; he would think about his problems in the morning.

Jumping out of bed, he realised he had overslept. He threw his clothes on and rushed into the living room to wake Wilma. He thought his eyes were deceiving him and had to get closer and physically place his hand on the leather cushion. They were cold. He realised she must have left some time ago. He made a rush search of the flat and soon discovered she had left. *She can't have gone very far in her condition,* he assumed as he rushed out. The only signs of life in the street were two elderly women talking by the side of a car. He apologised and asked if they had noticed a woman leaving his house. They looked at each other and shook their heads.

After searching through the local streets in his car, he decided the obvious place would be the club, where she could get her drug fix. The problem for him was that if he went near that place, they would surely nab him. He parked a few streets away and joined other pedestrians walking in that direction. A shop door offered an ideal observation point; the place had long since closed, and the doorway was in darkness. Anyone taking an interest in him standing there would assume he was sheltering from the rain.

She was standing at the club door when the daily cleaners approached. Barton guessed she was trying to explain why she wanted in. The door was suddenly opened by a man from inside, and they all entered. He could guess what Declan's next move would be, but he would be wrong; he had convinced himself that Wilma was beyond help, that she needed therapy that he couldn't provide, and that getting her that help would mean answering a lot of awkward questions.

On his drive back to his house, Barton's conscience started to prick at him. Could he really leave her to whatever fate Declan could inflict? Now that the old factory had been burned down, what would happen to her? His mobile sounded as he pulled up at his house. When he heard her voice, his heart skipped a few beats. "July," he managed to say, "where are you?"

"I can't tell you that at this time." Her voice seemed distant, as if she were on speaker. "I haven't found a place to live yet, but I need your help."

"What kind of help?" he replied.

"I need to get rid of my car. I'm sure Declan will have a way to pinpoint where it is; I think he's had a tracker device fitted to it. Will you drive it away somewhere and torch it?" A warning bell rang in his head. This sounded like a trick to get him. The moment he turned up to where she said she was, Declan and his mob could be waiting to jump him. "How do I know you are not with him right now?" A long silence followed before she replied.

"I can't go back to him; I know what will happen to me. I'm on the run from him, heading north. I've seen what he does with girls that cross him."

"But you haven't crossed him. I held a gun at you, forced you to cooperate with me."

"You try to convince him that was what happened. I know him; he'll have it in his head I was helping you."

"I'm leaving now; I'll phone you in about an hour and we can arrange to meet."

He could picture her features and perfect body in his mind and cursed his weakness for pretty girls. He was tempted to take her word, but somehow the warning bells wouldn't relinquish. He started his car and drove back into town, to the club.

As on the previous visit, he parked a distance away and walked. He had learned a good vantage point from the last few times he had been there, where he could see the front door and the car park at the rear. The Range Rover was parked on its usual spot close to the back door; the vehicle the goons had been using was next to it. A good ten minutes passed, and no movement came from the back door before he was certain that July was being honest and really was on the run from him. On his way back to his car, he began to wonder what could be happening to Wilma. She was in that club along with Declan and his thugs; he couldn't imagine what she could be going though, and didn't want to. He had tried to help, and the thanks he got was her retuning to the hell he had tried to get her away from.

He pulled into the first motorway services and phoned July. "Where are you?" he asked when she responded to his call.

"I've managed to hire a static home until I can find something more permanent," she replied, and she gave him instructions how to get there. It was dark when he arrived at the car park, and he had to call her again to find out where she was.

"I'll meet you there," she replied. "I'll only be a minute."

His heart jumped into his mouth when he noticed her pass beneath the lamp standard. He got out and went to meet her. He fought the temptation to throw his arms around her when she approached smiling. "So you really have run away from him?"

"I had no other choice."

"So what're your plans for your car?" he asked when they got into her static home.

"As I told you, I need to get rid of it as far away from here as possible. I'll make us a drink; then we can get started."

They sat on the small sofa, drinking jaw-droppingly strong coffee. "The best way to get rid of your car is to abandon it at an airport car park; that way when Declan tracks it, he'll think you've left the country."

She grinned and shook her head. "I don't think he'll fall for that old trick." She downed the dregs of her coffee, cringing at the taste, and placed her cup on a small shelf next to her. She stood up and gazed down at him. "But it could work; I could leave the keys in it, make it look like I've been in a rush to catch a last-minute flight."

"Do you have your passport with you?"

"Why?"

"Well, if he decides to search your belongings that you haven't had time to pack and he finds it, he'll know you haven't left the country."

"I don't have one; never had the occasion to apply for one."

"Does he know that?"

She shook her head. "I don't think so."

Barton stood up quickly and bumped his head off the ceiling, they both laughed, and he said, "I'll need to remember to duck my head in the morning."

She stepped closer and gazed up into his brown eyes. "So you plan to stay the night?"

"If that's what you want."

Stuffing his mobile back in his pocket, Declan jumped up off the sofa and waved to Badger, who was busy in the kitchen area making himself a sandwich. "The whore Wilma has come back to the club looking for a fix." They rushed out to the Range Rover, Badger biting at his sandwich on the run. "Get the boys to meet us there," Declan shouted as he jumped in the passenger's side.

As they burst in through the door, the bartender pointed to the back office. Wilma was sitting in one of the abandoned chairs and stood up when he approached. Declan grinned and slapped her on the side of her head, and she fell backwards over the chair. Badger dived forward and picked her up, but Declan was at his side and landed a kick to her groin. They watched as she doubled over in agony, holding her crotch and screaming. Another kick flashed past Badger; this time it landed on her ribs, and she fell, her head smashing against the old piano. She lay still as they stared down at her,

"I think she's gone, Boss," Badger said, and he stepped back as blood from her head began to flow close to his feet.

Declan pulled out his Renato Gamba Mauser HSc-80 pistol and fired a round into her skull. "Just to make sure," he said with a grin. "Get the boys to dispose of her."

Inside, Badger was seething. He wanted to rip the head off Declan's shoulders but managed to control himself, thinking, *One day, when the chance arrives.*

"Now to get that big ape and July," Declan said over his shoulders as he walked out, leaving Badger staring down at Wilma's body in disbelief, shaking his head.

Pinkie approached as Declan walked into the bar. "That mate of mine said his tracking device has only got a range of thirty miles."

Declan leaned on the bar. "So she must have travelled quite a distance. The question is, in which direction?" He looked at Pinkie. "if you were in her shoes, which direction would you go?"

Pinkie shrugged, thought for a moment, and then said, "Boss, I think I'd head for the nearest airport."

"The nearest one is Ringway, and that is well within thirty miles," Declan said, and he ordered a drink for them both. "I think we should concentrate on finding her car; we find that, then we'll soon know if she has left the country."

"How are you going to do that?" came the familiar voice from behind as Badger approached.

"Quite simple." Declan turned and stared up at him. "We travel to the limit of those thirty miles and try to track it from there. If we fail, we keep going until we succeed."

Pinkie interrupted. "That could take a long time, Boss."

Declan took a long swig from his glass. "I don't care how long it takes; I want that bitch and that big ape."

"What makes you think they are together?" Badger asked.

"I get this gut feeling that they are." He turned his attention to Pinkie. "Get your mate here and we can get started tracking them."

Pinkie was soon on his mobile and turned away while speaking into it. A moment later, he was back. "All sorted. He'll be here soon."

Marvin sat in the rear seat of the Range Rover with his homemade device. Pinkie was next to him, with Badger and Declan in front.

As they approached the suburbs of Liverpool, Marvin declared, "Nothing yet."

"Are you sure that thing's working properly?" Declan shouted back at him.

"I can guarantee it is," Marvin replied. "Checked it out this morning."

Declan's eyes had almost popped out his head when he first saw Marvin's device. The plastic casing was held together with an elastic band, and it had what resembled a miniature satellite dish on top of it that

Marvin kept turning and in different directions. A low buzzing sound came from it, which was beginning to get on Declan's nerves, and he noticed it was getting on Badger's as well. He turned to Marvin. "Do you have to keep that thing switched on all the time?"

Marvin nodded. "If you think the vehicle is within the thirty-mile radius."

"Switch the damn thing off for a while; I think she may have gone a lot farther." He turned to Badger. "Get on the motorway and head south, then, when we reach the limit of its radius, we can turn the damn thing on."

Badger gave Marvin the signal when it was time to turn his gadget on, but the constant buzzing never came.

"Are you sure it's switched on?" Declan shouted back at him. "I don't hear that racket from it."

"I need to change the batteries I think," Marvin replied, giving his device a shake.

"Well get on with it!" Declan barked back at him.

"I can't; I haven't brought any spares with me."

"For fuck's sake!" Declan shouted, and he slapped his hand on the dashboard. "What are we going to do now?"

"I think we should be able to buy new batteries from the services," Pinkie said nervously.

"Pull into the next one," Declan ordered the big driver.

As they waited for Pinkie and his mate to return from the services shop, Badger suddenly disturbed the thoughtful silence and asked, "Where did July originally come from?"

Jumping out of his revelry, Declan replied, "I think her parents come from Nottingham … Do you think she might have gone there?"

Badger nodded. "Worth a try, but we still have to depend on that piece of shit Pinkie's mate's carrying."

All they got from Marvin's device was the consistent buzzing as they toured around the streets of Nottingham. "If the vehicle has been parked inside a building like a garage, would it pick up the signal?" Declan asked.

"I'm not sure," Marvin replied. "I've never tried it for that."

CHAPTER 14

"That was another wasted day," Judd scolded himself on his walk to his rented house. He knew that in time he would have to report to Crow, but he didn't intend on telling him about the mistake and was more interested in whether the little man had got in contact with Tom Barton's son. He had made a promise to himself when he first got into the hit game never to kill for personal reasons. If this big son got in in his way, he might have to break that promise. He couldn't let the son live and have to spend the rest of his life looking over his shoulder. After a few cups of strong coffee, he opened his cabinet and lifted out his steel box. He had only two vials left, and one of them he had taken some out of, intending to administer it to Tom Barton. He had decided that after this job he would have to move on; he couldn't have two old men dying of the same symptoms so close to each other.

As for the son, a high-velocity round from a distance would soon put an end to that problem.

Crow told Judd he couldn't get in contact with the son, thinking he had changed his mobile. That was bad news to Judd, but in a way, he was pleased he hadn't administered the venom to the father. That would have alerted the big guy and have him snooping about again. This left him with no other choice but to deal with the son first. His choice of weapon would be important, as he didn't want to get close to this man but at the same time had to make sure he had killed him with the one shot. He knew he wouldn't get a second chance. He was confident that the son wasn't in the area; he had spent a lot of his time searching for him whilst stalking the father. But that was now a problem. Where was he? Would threatening the parents bring him back? In the mirror in the toilet, he studied his now brown hair and wondered whether he could get it back to the original white. That would surely panic them enough to call him. This he didn't want; he didn't need him snooping about, so how to get rid of the son without alerting the parents?

Judd was a natural loner; this was the reason for his success, and he never had to worry about somebody talking. But no matter how he tried to get around the problem, no matter how much time he spent thinking about it, the same answer always came out in the end: he had to get help. That help, he decided, could only come from Crow.

At the same moment Judd was trying to call Crow, the dapper little man was on his mobile, talking to Barton. "We need to have words" was all he needed to say.

"I'm not in the area," Barton replied, and he discovered the connection had been cut.

Barton and July awoke to a wet, misty morning after an exhausting night of lovemaking.

She decided that the best airport to abandon her car at would be in Edinburgh.

"Do you think he'll fall for that trick?" Barton asked.

She threw her arms around his neck. "Well, honey, it was your idea." They were sitting in the cramped kitchen, drinking tea and eating fried eggs she had made, when his mobile sounded. She was still in her nightgown, and Barton in his underwear. He had left his phone in the bedroom and sprang to his feet. Again he bumped his head off the metal roof.

She laughed. "They don't make these static homes for big guys like you."

"Tell me about it," he replied as he squeezed his bulk through the door. He regretted rushing for his mobile when he noticed the name that came up on it. He closed the bedroom door but never got a chance to ask Crow why or where before the call got cut.

"Get dressed!" he heard her shout. "The quicker we get this done, the sooner we can make plans to find another place to stay." She opened the door as he was climbing into his jeans. "We can shower when we get back," she continued as she began dressing herself.

Even after a night of lovemaking, his carnality jumped three notches as he watched her slip into her underwear. Her long, slender brown legs opened slightly as she pulled up her pants, her small firm breasts fitting snugly into her brazier. She glanced up to see him gazing at her and smiled. "Plenty of time for that later," she said, slipping into her tight jeans.

At the car park, she opened the door to the BMW. Before stepping in, she said, "Give me five; then you can follow. That should give me time to find the long-term parking place. I'll be at the pickup point as soon as I can; then we can head out and look for a place to stay."

He signalled a thumbs up at her and jumped into his own Volkswagen. This gave him time to phone Crow. A few moments later, July raced out onto the road, and he made the call. The little man took his time to answer, and Barton was about to cut the call off when his squeaky voice came on. "Why do we need to talk?" asked Barton.

"You'll find out when we talk!" Crow shouted.

"What's the bloody urgency?"

"Do I have to repeat what I have just said?"

"When and where do you want to meet?"

"As soon as." Crow gave a deep sigh. "It's for your own benefit."

"Okay," Barton finally said. "Can't leave right now; I'll have a few hours' drive before I get back. I'll give you a call when I get home." He cut the contact, not wanting to listen to any more orders from the little man. His five minutes were up, and he got on the move.

The motorway was moderately quiet, and July instantly got onto the fast lane. She loved speed, and her vehicle was more than capable of obeying her demands. She grinned as she glanced at the digital speed reading ninety-two miles per hour. When she glanced back on the road ahead, her whole life flashed in front of her eyes. She jumped on her brakes, but her car wasn't capable of stopping; a truck jackknifed, and the forty-feet-long shipping container capsized, blocking all the lanes. The last picture her eyes sent to her brain was her whole being thrusting towards a solid metal wall. Her car cannoned into the roof of the container, and a stream of following vehicles crashed behind, crushing her BMW. And moments later, they exploded into a ball of flames.

Declan's nerves were well beyond normality. He was getting tired, and his judgement wasn't working to any advantage. "Get us home," he ordered Badger. "We can start again tomorrow." It was 3.00 a.m.when Declan got out of the Range Rover at his house. Before closing the vehicle door, he said to Badger, "Be back here about seven, and bring these two with you."

An hour later, he was in bed and unconsciously turned to embrace July. He sprang up in a panic, and then the reality came to him. She was gone, probably sleeping with that big ape Barton. The things that ran through his mind about how he was going to torture that man kept him from sleep for hours. He swung his legs out of bed and padded barefooted into the kitchen, located his stash of cocaine, and set up a line. Still sniffing to clear his nostrils, he staggered back to bed and flopped down on top of it.

As if only a few minutes had elapsed, the alarm on his mobile sounded. He staggered from his bedroom still partially under the effects of the drugs. The most dreaded sight he needed to see was Badger standing on the doorstep. Declan pushed past him and on wobbly legs scrambled into the vehicle.

"Where are we heading?" Badger asked when he got into the driver's seat.

Declan wasn't paying much attention; his mind was in turmoil, he was beginning to realise how much he missed that girl, and the dope hadn't eased the pain of losing her. This made him more determined to find her—and to get his hands on the guy who took her away. "Try Yorkshire direction," he finally suggested.

On the way there, he turned on the radio rather than listening to the infernal buzzing of Marvin's device. The music was interrupted with a news flash announcing that traffic was tailing back for about ten miles on the eastbound carriageway on the M8. A jack-knifed lorry had overturned, causing a multi-car pile-up; six people were known to have been killed when their vehicles caught fire.

"Glad we're not in that area," Pinkie said. "We could have been stuck there all day."

He couldn't explain it, but something inside Declan set off a warning bell, and he turned to Badger. "Head up there."

Badger's body jerked as he turned and glanced at him. "You don't think … Surely not … It's a thousand million to one."

"I know," Declan agreed, "but I've got this gut feeling. I just want to be sure we can find what hospital the injured have been taken to and make enquiries."

Pinkie used Google to find the nearest hospital from the accident, and they headed there but got little information and were told to make enquiries at the local police station. Marvin, being of mixed race, was sent into Livingston Police Station on West Lothian Road. Claiming that his partner might have been involved in the pile-up on the M8, he gave the WPC the registration number. She wrote it down and headed along a passageway. When she returned, another two officers were with her.

Marvin got into the Range Rover and for a long moment remained silent. Declan could stand it no longer and shouted, "Well, what did you find out?"

"That vehicle was involved in that accident. The female driver was killed instantly."

The silence lingered for a long time, and finally Declan said, "Was she on her own?"

"Nobody else was mentioned."

"Take me home," Declan said. The last thing he wanted was to show these thugs he was hurting.

CHAPTER 15

*B*arton heard the news flash and decided to take another route to the airport. He realised he was running late and was worried should July panic.

She wasn't at the pickup point when he arrived, and he sat listening to the radio. Another news bulletin came on about the accident on the M8. That's when he became concerned. *Maybe she's been held up there?* He called her mobile but got no response. The worst-case scenario ran though his mind. *Was she involved in that accident? If so, how can I find out?* The only option he had was to return to the static home and watch it on television, thinking he might see her car among the queuing vehicles or as part of the wreckage.

He sat in the cramped space, watching the small screen, wishing he could spread his legs out, waiting for the news to come on. He called Crow, hoping to obtain some information about why he wanted words. But the little weasel was tight-lipped. "I'm not sure when I'll be able to meet you," Barton informed him.

"The sooner the better for your benefit," the high-pitched voice said, sounding like a military order.

The news soundtrack sounded, and Barton cut the call off. The national news had no information, and he had to wait for the local transmission. The scene was from above and showed total carnage; an articulated lorry lay on its side, blocking all three lanes. Cars and vans were crushed into one another, most of them burnt black as fire crews worked on them. Ambulances and police cars were all over the road, with blue light flashing from all directions. Barton tried again to call July's mobile but got the same results as before. It was then that he decided she must have been involved in that crash. The female broadcaster went on to announce that at least six people had been killed and many others injured, some seriously. The police were still trying to contact the relatives of those involved. The last thing he wanted to do was just leave it at that, but he was in no position to do anything else. As a wanted man, he couldn't march into a hospital and make enquires about a woman he hardly knew. The police would be there trying to identify the dead and injured, and too many questions would have to be answered. After a lot of thought, he decided that the only thing left to do was clear out of the area and get home.

On his long drive home, he couldn't shake the image of July from his mind. She was a beautiful woman; he could see her perfect brown body as she stripped naked to get into bed beside him. He pictured her smile, so genuine, with pure-white teeth and ebony eyes that could sink the soul of any man. The best he could hope for, and it was bad enough, was that she was among the uninjured.

He drove all the way without a break, got into his house, showered, and had a meal—anything to take his mind off that beautiful girl. But no matter how hard he tried, she was still there. His next distraction was to phone Crow.

"I'll meet you in the town centre car park in half an hour!" the little man shouted. "Don't be late."

Barton pulled up a few spaces away from Crow's huge black four- by-four, got out, and knocked on his window, but it wasn't the little man who was sitting in the driver's seat when the tinted window went down. Barton instantly recognised the tall black man who grinned at him. "Hi, Nevil. You got a new job?"

Nevil jabbed a large thumb at the rear. "Get in the fucking back."

"Only if you promise to be gentle with me," Barton said before opening the rear door.

The dapper little man grinned as Barton got sat beside him, but the grin didn't reach his cold grey eyes.

"You haven't changed your aftershave," Barton commented, returning the cold grin.

"I've got a job for you," Crow said. Ignoring Barton's comment, he stretched his hand over the front seat, and Nevil handed him a large manila envelope. "You'll find everything you need in there." He pushed it into Barton's hand.

"What if I don't want the job?" Barton held up the envelope, feeling the bulk of a package inside.

"When you study the contents, you won't be in a position to refuse." Barton was about to tear the flap open when Crow's his little hand shot over to stop him. "Take it home, read the instructions, and then destroy them."

The moment he got into his own car, Barton ripped open the envelope and tipped the contents onto the passenger's seat. The first item to fall out was a pack of fifty-pound notes. Next came a folder; he opened it to discover typed instructions on A4 sheets. He decided to go home before reading them.

The fifty-pound notes he wrapped up with tissues and placed in his fridge. He got himself settled on an easy chair with a mug of black coffee and opened the folder. The first paragraph on the first page was all he needed to read. No way could he follow the instructions. He was no chicken, but he knew when to run. The odds were against him surviving working for the owner of the Westerner's Club. But the odds of him surviving disobeying the orders from Crow were about the same. The big question that plagued him was, Where do you run when you don't know who's chasing you? *How many organisations is that little man involved with?* One thing Barton had learned was never to take the little man for granted. Often he thought he had Crow sussed out, only to find that was when the little weasel knocked him down. No matter what Barton got up to, Crow always seemed to be one step ahead. *This has to be a conspiracy. That club owner must have got in contact, and they have worked out a way to collar me.* Had Barton known that that owner was one of Crow's clients, he wouldn't have caused so much upheaval to his property and his goons. It all went back to the days of being gunned up and fighting back, trying to stay ahead of the game.

Halfway down the first page, he noticed a list of names; next to each one was a record informing him where the person could be found when not working at the club, whether this person carried a weapon, and what that weapon might be. Each one was described down to scars, tattoos, and prison records, if any. There were ten names; two were underlined with red ink. Barton took this to mean they were the most dangerous. This confused Barton. Why would Crow go to all the trouble of giving him the record of all Declan's thugs? The rest of the pages were about Declan and his business, and where he got his alcohol and drugs from, and most of that was through Crow's enterprise. The final paragraph was the stinger. The way Barton saw it was that Crow was hiring him to find out whether Declan might be purchasing some of his goods from someone else and doing deals, and not cutting the little man and the syndicate in on the shares. That decided how Barton would explain the cash.

Barton was sure the little man would know nothing about the immigrants in that old factory, but the only way to be sure would be to ask him. The call was brief, and he knew Crow wouldn't admit or deny any knowledge of it, but at least he knew about it now.

"Get over to that club first thing in the morning; you'll know what to say," Crow had said.

"We're not on good terms," Barton insisted. "It was me who burnt his old factory down, and he's after my blood." The signal went dead before Barton could explain further.

Judd was proud of his collection of weapons; he had them hidden in various locations all over the country. The one he had with him was his favourite and would be ideal for this job—the Heckler & Koch 33 (HK33 for short). He had bought it with American Litton night sights. With an old bath towel spread across the kitchen table, he stripped it down, cleaned and oiled it, checked the magazine was full, emptied the rounds out, and tested the spring. All was looking good. Carefully he packed it into the case he had made for this weapon, making it look like a guitar case, and pushed it under the bed.

Facing him now was the issue of how to locate this son of Tom Barton's. He thought of contacting Crow and asking whether he knew where this man was, but that thought soon dissipated, as he knew he would get no help from him. Crow had made it plain that he knew this man's son when he said he could get him a job out of the way. Judd eased himself down on the sofa and began working out a way of getting Crow to maybe accidentally drop a slight clue, and then it dawned on him. He grasped his mobile from his pocket. When Crow replied, it sounded as if he had rushed to reply, and when he discovered who the caller was, his voice dropped a few decibels.

"What's the problem now?" The little man finally asked.

Judd had to grin at the thought of the little man having to leave his lover boy. "I need an assistant."

"Well, go and find one."

"I don't know anyone I can trust; I thought you could recommend somebody." He went on to explain his requirements.

A long silence followed, and finally Crow came back. "Leave it with me; I'll call you, but this is going to cost you."

Judd could guess the little man would be calling around to the people he thought could be trusted, but the type of person he requested—finding one could take a while. He tuned into the news on the television to see whether the old guy he had accidently vaccinated with the venom had been mentioned, but after sifting through all the channels, he found that nothing had been reported.

It had probably been diagnosed as being a heart attack that killed him. Now Tom Barton had a few more weeks to live, but not his son. The shooting would be reported as a gangland killing and would soon be forgotten.

The response from Crow came faster than Judd had estimated. "I've got a girl—quite attractive, as you requested." The little man's voice came through crisp and clear. "She wants paid. She'll tell you how much; she works by the hour."

"Where do I meet her and when?"

"I'll get her to give you a call, and you can sort things out between yourselves."

Judd was about to ask how much she wanted, but the call ended abruptly, the way Crow always ended them. He got settled back down to watch the television and must have dozed off; the next thing he heard was his mobile. He scrambled for it from his pocket, and a woman's voice came on.

"Are you Judd?" she asked.

"Who wants to know?" he replied.

"A mutual friend of ours tells me you want to hire an escort for a few nights."

"That is correct," he assured. "When can we meet?"

"I'm free anytime you want."

"Where are you at this moment? If you're free, I can meet you there." No way was he going to have her come to his accommodation.

She was a real stunner and sent a stirring through Judd, but he knew better than to get involved. He sat in the restaurant at the table where she had instructed him to be. His heart skipped a few beats as she approached with a smile on her beautiful face. He could tell she had spent a lot of time on her make-up, and her long, coiling black hair hung over her naked shoulders. Her low-cut dress exposed most of her ample breasts, and her skirt just covered her navel and no more.

She sat opposite him and held out her hand. "I'm Donna, and are you Judd?"

Feeling embarrassment building up in him, and aware that his face was turning red, Judd lowered his head, afraid to make eye contact with the other patrons staring at her. Some of the women gazed at her enviously. He wasn't enjoying the attention; this was the last thing he needed. "We need to go somewhere a bit more private," he said.

"Okay," she replied, "but first let's have a snack and a drink first; let me get to know you a little."

The snack turned out to be a feast, as he watched her scoff down a plate full of chips and eggs, followed by a handful of biscuits and three cups of coffee. Judd reached over the table and gazed into her brown eyes. "I don't know what our mutual friend has told you," he said, his voice loaded with contempt, "but I'm hiring you to do a job,not to have sex."

She drained the last of her drink, smiled, and held up a hand. "I understand. As long as the money's good, I'll do what you want, providing it's not life threatening."

"It's safe enough, and I'm sure you can pull it off."

She stood up and smiled down at him. "Okay, I know a place where we can talk."

Judd got up and was shocked at how he towered over her. He hadn't realised she was so small when she walked up to him; maybe it was the way she dressed or the way she carried herself. He nodded. "Lead on."

She hooked her arm around his and led him to the car park, where she pressed the remote of a large silver BMW. "We can talk in my car," she said, and she climbed into the driver's seat.

Judd got in beside her. "I saw you restricted your mobile number when you called me. I need it if we are to get this job done."

"And I need to know what the job is about and how much you're willing to pay me."

"You'll get what you charge."

"I don't come cheap," she replied as she started up her car.

"I'm not expecting you to do a cheap job." Judd wasn't worried about what price she quoted. He had no intention of paying her; he had plenty of venom left.

"I need some money up front." She held her hand out.

"You'll get everything you deserve when you do this job; that way I know you'll do it right."

"No way!" she snapped at him. "Cash up front or the job doesn't get done." She waved her hand under his nose.

"That's fine," Judd replied, and he stepped out of her car. "Our mutual friend has recommended a few other girls; I'll get one of them."

"Okay … okay!" she cried. "But you had better pay up after the job, or I'll get someone to deal with you."

Judd smiled to himself, thinking, *How many times have I heard that threat.* "I told you, you'll get what you deserve. Now give me your mobile number." He stooped over, looking in her car window, and could tell she was reluctant to give him what he wanted, He could guess at the thoughts that were going through her mind. "If you don't give me the number, the job is off."

She hesitantly produced her mobile from a pocket at the back of her short skirt. "Okay, here it is." The moment his mobile sounded, she pushed her gear lever forward and sped off.

He stood there staring at his phone for a few minutes after her car had raced out of the car park. Judd briskly walked onto the main street and caught a taxi and, as he always did, got off a few streets from his accommodation. When he got in and settled, he phoned her. She answered instantly. "Tomorrow morning, we start," he instructed. "Be at the car park at zero eight hundred hours."

CHAPTER 16

*D*eciding not to go home, Declan instructed Badger to take him to the club. The place was in full swing when he arrived; patrons were crowded around the bar. Some were dancing to deafening rap music; others were sleeping over the tables. The fug of cigarette smoke stung his eyes, and he pushed his way into his office. Declan didn't want to be on his own; he was feeling the pain at the loss of July and was glad when Badger and the two others entered and also got seated. "I can't understand why that big bastard wasn't in that car with her," he said, more to himself than to the others.

"Maybe she pissed off from him as well," Badger said.

He glanced at the big man and then at the two others and nodded. "You could be right, but I still want him for what happened to the factory; I've lost a lot of money through that. Now I'm going to have to find another place." A long, uncomfortable silence followed between them; only the faint bumping of the music from the barroom next door could be heard. They all jumped when his mobile sounded. He grasped it from his pocket, noticed the name and number, and signalled for the three men to evacuate the office.

"Mr. Crow, how nice to hear from you again."

"I'm sending you that man in the morning, if you'll kindly be at your club when he arrives."

"As I have said, Mr. Crow, I'm not sure I need another security man." Declan replied, trying to sound pleasant.

"You'll be wanting this one; his name is Barton."

It felt as though all the weight had been lifted from his shoulders, and he had to fight the urge to jump for joy. Could his luck be changing? He got up and rushed to the door, jerked it open, and shouted for Badger.

Thinking something had gone wrong, the big man barged his way through the crowd. When he saw the grin on Declan's face, he relaxed and followed him into the office.

Still wearing the grin, Declan sat behind his desk. "Do you remember when Crow wanted me to take on another bouncer?"

With a confused expression, Badger said, "Yes, Boss."

"Well, that bouncer just happens to be the man we've been looking for."

Badger shared the grin. "You mean that big ape Barton?"

Declan nodded. "And he's coming here in the morning."

The grin faded on the big man's face as he sat down on the nearest chair. "I don't think he's stupid enough to turn up."

"If Crow has told him to, he'll know better."

"He'll come prepared if he does come."

"Then we'll be ready for him."

"We'll have to keep Pinkie out of the way," Badger reminded him, "after what Barton did to his face with that pipe."

"We'll have to plan a reception for him," Declan said, grinning, "and make sure none of the cleaners and day workers are in." He got up out of his seat. "I need some company tonight. Are any of the girls free?"

Badger nodded and got up. "I'll make sure one is free."

Bella was still in bed long after Declan had showered and got dressed. He pulled the duvet off her, but she didn't stir. He grabbed her arm and pulled her onto the floor. Her naked body bumped heavily on the laminate flooring; this shock opened her eyes. "What's happened?" she shouted.

"It's time you were up and out of here!" Declan shouted back at her, and he walked out of the bedroom without closing the door. She scrambled to get dressed and met him in the kitchen, where he was sitting at the table, drinking from a mug. "I've got a good job for you this morning," he said, drinking the dregs from his mug. "I've got a man coming to the club in a few hours, and I want you to entertain him, make him feel he's something special. Take him up to one of the rooms and keep him occupied, you know what I mean. I'll have a bottle sent up. Be sure he takes a drink out of it, and drop a couple of these pills into his glass. Be sure he doesn't see you doing it." He slid a card of pills across the table. "If you think it might need three, drop the extra one in."

Bella was a buxom girl with long blonde hair that always managed to fall over her blue eyes. She flicked her finger through it to clear her vision and grinned at him. "What does this man look like? Is he handsome and rich?"

Declan stood up. "He's a big man, tan complexion. He has long black hair that he ties back into a ponytail, and designer stubble. I would say some girls would describe him as being handsome." He pointed to the toilet. "Get your face made up; I want you to look your best. If you need fresh underwear, you'll find some in the wardrobe that used to belong to July."

Bella giggled. "July's underwear won't fit me."

"We'll stop and buy you some new ones on the way, but the cost will come out of your wages."

"I could drop the pills into his drink before it gets that far," she protested.

Declan shrugged. "Whatever. Now get into that toilet and get sorted out."

She turned at the door. "What if this guy doesn't fancy me?"

"You'd better make sure he does." He stepped over to her and pushed her through the door towards the toilet.

She stumbled, shouting back at him, "It's not my fault if he doesn't like me."

Declan threw himself at her, gripped her by the throat, and squeezed her against the wall. "You'd better make sure he does, or you know what will happen to you."

He had ordered the cleaning staff in early, got the place up to standard, and chased them out. Next he gave Bella a final check and instructed her where to sit. Pinkie and three others were hiding in the back office. Badger was instructed to conceal himself outside, and when Barton entered, he was to block his escape should he try to get out. Declan sat in his office and waited. At first the time on his office desk seemed to drag, but when the morning was almost over, time moved faster. It became obvious that Barton wasn't going to arrive. Declan jumped out of his chair, entered the bar, and called the three goons from the back office. "It looks as though he's not coming," he told them.

"Maybe he's hanging about outside; maybe he's on to us and knows we're waiting for him and is scouting about out there," Pinkie said.

Declan mulled this over for a few minutes and then said, "I've got Badger out there; surely he would have seen Barton."

Badger did see Barton, but he was too late to do anything about it when a flying fist struck him on his big chin, sending him reeling over the bonnet of a parked car. When he tried to recover, another punch landed on the back of his neck. On hands and knees, he tried to get away but didn't get far before a flying kick struck his groin from behind. The pain was so intense that he passed out.

Realising he had attracted an audience, Barton grinned at them and said, "Bloody muggers—the best way to deal with them." He got a few approving nods, and a woman applauded him. When the spectators moved on about their business, he lifted the big man's body by the underarms and dragged him behind a garbage skip. To make sure this big guy wasn't going to come round too soon, Barton landed a blow to his head with an empty glass juice bottle he found lying on the ground.

Before he walked away from the unconscious man, a mobile phone sounded. Barton guessed that would be the big guy's mates checking on him. He searched the big man's pockets and located it and decided the best way to confuse them would be to keep it and keep moving about so that every time they called, he would be in a different position. This plan, he hoped, would make them split up, making it easier for him to bring them down one at a time.

It was becoming annoying, the constant little tune from the big guy's mobile. But Barton persevered, even though it attracted attention from other pedestrians.

He knew that somewhere in the crowd, one or two of the club's thugs would be listening for it. The narrow lane was an ideal place to set his ambush. On both sides of the pathway, tall red brick walls cast a shadow from the midday sunshine. Halfway along, a group of wheely bins stood lined up on one side. Barton placed the mobile on the top of the farthest away one and crouched down behind the others.

He checked his watch. It had now been half an hour since he had left that big guy behind the garbage skip, and he knew they might have found him by now. From his vantage point behind the bins, he could see two men standing at the top end of the lane. They seemed to be having a conversation and looked to be undecided on what to do. He could tell by their reactions that they had heard the mobile. Maybe they hadn't found the big thug and were wondering why he was down this lane. Finally they split up, and one came towards him. It would have been an advantage if he had known where the other thug went, but it was too late to worry about that now.

The one who decided to search the lane was now level with him. Barton sprang up; the man's eyes almost popped out if his head at the sight of the bottle coming down at him. The thug stumbled but didn't fall, and he gripped onto one of the wheelie bins.

Barton had to strike him twice more before he went down. He dragged the thug behind one of the bins, picked up the mobile phone, and went in search of the other man. He wished he had paid more attention to what the other thug was wearing.

He found himself in amongst a crowd of shoppers and let himself be swept along with them, realising there was little chance of anyone picking him out. As he neared the Westerner's Club, he cut out from the group and stood in a shop doorway. The view of the club door was slightly obscured by a bus, but he could tell there was no movement from it. The big thug's mobile sounded, and he hastily shut it off and tossed it into a litter bin that was close by. He darted back into the shop door when the bus moved away.

A heavy built woman was standing close to the blonde man Barton recognised as being the boss-man. He was tempted to dart over and slug him with the bottle but was glad he had resisted when three men came out of the club door behind them. The boss-man started waving his arms and pointing in various directions. Barton guessed he was dishing out orders to the three men. A few minutes passed, and the thugs separated and departed, leaving the boss and the blond woman, who in turn went back into the club.

One of the thugs crossed to his side of the street and headed his way. Barton couldn't jump this man; there were too many witnesses. He decided to enter the shop. Two elderly women glanced up at him from behind a small corner counter. One smiled at him and continued studying what she was doing. The other, a smaller woman, approached him.

"Can I help you, sir?" she asked.

A quick glance around at the goods and he soon discovered he was in a charity shop. "Just having a look around," he replied, returning her smile.

"Anything in particular you are looking for, sir?"

Barton shook his head. "Just browsing; I might find something." He squeezed his way between clothes racks of second-hand shirts and jackets, all the while glancing out the window, watching for the thug to pass. A few people passed, but he never noticed him. He wondered whether the goon might have slipped by while he was talking to the lady. He pretended to be searching through the clothing for a while before thanking the ladies and leaving.

He delayed a moment and had a good look around but couldn't see the thug. He thought about charging in through the club doors and surprising the owner, but how was he to know how many more goons were inside waiting for him? It was the two youths jumping around at the opposite side of the street that drew Barton's attention; they quickly parted, and there stood the goon.

He wasn't a big man, but he had that hard-man demeanour, with a ball-shaped head, deep-sunken eyes, and a broken nose. He walked with a swagger, his broad shoulders swaying from side to side, his hands dug deep into his pockets and a cigarette hanging from his lips. Barton grinned to himself; he had run into this type before: so tough looking—but that is as far as the toughness goes. At a few steps behind, Barton was soon walking on the little hard-man's heels, pacing step by step with him, looking for a quiet lane or abandoned shop door to push him into.

The opportunity came sooner than he had expected, and Barton was quick enough to take advantage. He jumped at the goon, gripping him in an armlock. Two quick twists of his body, and he heard the man's skull snap from his spine. The tough guy was dead before his body slumped to the ground. Barton could only stare at the goon in disbelief; he hadn't meant to kill the little hard-man. In a panic, he decided to hide the body. With the body hidden behind an abandoned fridge-freezer, Barton ran back onto the street, heading back the way he had come, towards the Westerner's Club, with the thought that surely the head man couldn't have many more goons left to protect himself and his club.

CHAPTER 17

wenty minutes had elapsed, and Donna still hadn't turned up. Judd was pacing along the edge of the car park; twice he had called her, and he hadn't got a reply. He kicked an empty plastic milk carton and was about to thump his fist on a garbage skip when he heard a deep moan coming from behind it. He stepped back in shock when an ugly face appeared and growled at him. The man reminded Judd of a documentary he had once seen on television about ancient man, a Neanderthal, with deep-sunken brown eyes under a heavy overhanging forehead. Judd quickly turned about and rushed away. That was when Donna pulled up in front of him.

He jerked her car door open. "You're late!" he shouted.

"Only a few minutes," she said.

"When I tell you to be at a place at a time, you be there." He caught her arm and pulled her out. She staggered on her heels and jerked her arm free.

"That hurt, you bastard," she cried, rubbing her arm.

"Not as bad as it will if you're late again." He gripped her arm again and pushed her back into the driver's seat. He then rushed around and got in beside her. "Drive back to your house," he ordered. "Let's get you looking like a decent woman instead of the tart you look like now."

"I don't have any other kind of clothes," she protested.

Dragging her by the arm, he hauled her out of the car and pushed her into the charity shop that Barton had walked out of a few minutes earlier. The elderly lady stepped towards them.

"We're looking for ladies' clothing to fit this young lady," Judd told her.

The woman ushered her to a rack of clothing and looked at Donna, trying to decide on her size. After the woman had lifted out a selection of garments, most of which Donna said she wouldn't be seen dead in, Judd approached and whispered, "Make up your mind or you will be seen dead before you get into them." The threat didn't have much effect on her, so he took from the woman's hand a hanger that supported a dark brown trouser suit, and he pushed it at Donna's chest. "That looks about your size. Now get a sensible pair of shoes."

She was a transformed woman when she walked out of the changing room converted from a tart to what looked like a professional businesswoman, down to the briefcase Judd had handed her. On his instructions, she had wiped off most of her makeup and changed the style of her hair. Her tarty clothes she put into a plastic shopping bag. Judd took the bag from her, and together they left the shop. Sitting in her BMW, Donna complained about not being used to driving with high heels. "Well, take them off," he snapped at her. "Now get moving to your flat or house or whatever."

It was obvious that Donna she shared the small bedsit with another girl by the amount of underwear that was strewn about the room. They sat on one of the single beds, and she lit up what must have been her fourth cigarette since they met. "Do you have to do that?" Judd said, pointing to the cigarette.

"If you don't like it, you can fuck off," she spat back at him, blowing the smoke upwards.

He took hold of the hand that was holding her smoke. "If I fuck off, you won't get the five big ones I'm going to give you when and if you do this job right."

A broad grin dawned across her face, her eyes lit up, and she shuffled herself closer to him. "Tell me what I have to do."

Judd delayed a while, studying her eyes as if reading her thoughts. Finally, he said, "You knock on a door and ask for a Mr. Barton; he's an elderly man about sixtyish." He laid it out to her word for word over and over until she had it off by heart.

"It sounds a simple enough job for all that money," she said. "There has to be more to it."

"Oh, there is," Judd assured her, "but we'll come to that later."

As directed by Judd, Donna pulled up at the address and got out. Judd stayed inside the car and watched as she knocked. The door opened slightly, and the elderly woman peeped out from the narrow gap.

"I'm looking for a Mr. Barton?" Donna asked.

"Who are you?" Jean Barton asked, at the same time squinting over her the woman's shoulder at her car.

"I'm a solicitor representing a client who claims Mr. Barton bore witness to a crime my client is accused of committing."

"Why didn't you write him a letter or phone him?"

"I need to speak to him in person." Reluctantly Jean opened the door and nodded for Donna to enter. "He's in the living room, straight ahead." She pointed with a shaky hand. Jean squeezed past Donna and said to her husband, "There's a lady here to see you, says she's a solicitor, wants a word with you."

Tom, with a confused look on his face, jumped up out of his chair and stubbed his cigarette out on the ashtray sitting on the arm of it. His watery blue eyes stared at the young woman by his wife's side.

Donna stepped forward and held out her hand. "I represent Walter and Cousin, solicitors. My name is Anna Britons, but you're not the Mr. Barton I'm looking for; the gentleman I'm looking for is in his early thirties according to the description I have."

"Oh!" said Tom with a sigh of relief. "That'll be my son Richard."

"Do you know where I could get in touch with him?"Donna said, still holding his hand.

Jean cut in. "All we've got is his mobile number."

"We'll call him and tell him you want to speak to him," Tom interrupted before his wife gave this woman his number.

Donna smiled; this was what Judd had told her would happen. "Can you call him and get him to call this number?" She handed him a card.

Tom looked at the card, nodded, and placed it on the mantelshelf. "I'll call him later."

"Don't make it too late; this could turn out to be serious if it doesn't get sorted out soon."

Tom walked her to the door, leaving his wife standing in the living room. "What's all this about?" he asked her quietly at the door.

She took his hand again and held it longer than was necessary. "As I've explained, we're only interested in verifying what my client claims from your son; he's not in any trouble."

"That all went down as planned," Donna said as she got into the driver's seat of her car.

Judd smiled at her. "Good girl. How soon do you think they will phone him?"

Donna started her car and shrugged. "Probably doing that right now."

Donna's bedsit mate gawked open-mouthed at Donna as she walked in. "What's happened to you?"

Judd, walking in behind Donna, decided this was another tart. "She's on a job, and she has to change her wardrobe to succeed."

"You look as though you're going to church on a Sunday," the mate commented with a laugh as she sat down on her bed. "And who's this gorgeous-looking man?"

"He's business," Donna promptly replied.

"I thought you had given that up?"

"I have; this is real business."

Her mate laid back on her bed grinning and began playing with her mobile.

"I would appreciate if you didn't mention my visit to anyone," Judd said, and he caught her arm in a vice-like grip, knocking her mobile out of her hands. She yelped and struggled, but he tightened his grip and held it until she stopped.

"Okay," she whimpered, rubbing her arm. "You don't need to be so rough."

Donna could only stand there helplessly and watch, realising this was a dangerous man capable of torturing or even killing to get his way. She reached over and put her arm around her mate's shoulder and was about to say some comforting words to her when her mobile sounded. Judd was next to her in an instant, his head close to hers, listening to her phone. She had been told what to say when this man Barton called and had rehearsed it to perfection. When the call was over, Judd grinned. "Good girl," he complimented. "Now again, in case I missed something, tell me what he said and if he agreed to that proposal."

"I'm going to call Badger's mobile; you lot get out there and find him. Listen for his ringtone; I'll keep on ringing it until you locate him. He'll not be far away if he has to keep an eye on the club door." The moment he gave the order to the three men standing around him, they darted for the door. Declan stepped outside behind them in the hopes of catching a glimpse of Badger; the blonde girl was beside him. He watched the thugs cross to the other side of the street and split up before he returned inside with the girl. She took up her position on the seat as she had been instructed to. Declan returned to his office and began calling Badger's mobile.

Three failed attempts later, he decided Badger could have been a victim of this man Barton. He continued to call in the hopes that his goons might locate the ringtone. It wasn't shock that shook Declan; it was disappointment at the sight of seeing the blonde-headed girl assisting Badger in through the door of his office. The big man was nursing a massive lump on the side of his head with one hand, and with the other holding his crotch. the girl eased him into the chair at the front of the desk. "What happened to you?" Declan shouted.

"I'm not sure," Badger mumbled. "One minute I was standing across the street at the corner of that big building that is all boarded up, and the next I felt something like a sledgehammer hit me on the jaw. I remember flying over the bonnet of a parked car; after that it's all a blank."

The shock set in, and Declan sprang up from his seat sending it toppling back, knowing that if anyone could get close enough to Badger and hit him, that person must be good. "I've sent Pinkie and another two of the boys out to find you; have you seen them?"

Badger shook his head, still nursing the lump with his hand. "Sorry, Boss; I never noticed them among all those shoppers."

With his grey eyes bulging, and combing his fingers through his hair, Declan started pacing the length of the office. "You get out there and watch for this guy," he roared at the girl, "in case he turns up here." He gripped her by the shoulder and pushed her out the open door. "How can this one man cause all this trouble?" This time his anger was directed at Badger. The big man could only shrug his shoulders. His biggest problem was the pains in his groin. "I want that bastard. I want him now, so get your arse out there and find the rest of the gang and get them back here. I know he's going to turn up. He has to; he's been ordered to."

Badger struggled to his feet, feeling his legs wobble, and staggered out of the office. Bella rushed towards him when he fell against one of the tables. He held up his hand and said, "Thanks, but I'll be fine in a minute or so."

Ignoring his protest, she helped him onto a chair. "You can't take chances with a head injury like that." The entrance door burst open, and they both turned to see Pinkie stagger in holding his head, with blood gushing between his fingers. "You as well?" Bella shouted, and she rushed over to assist him.

Declan appeared at the office door, having seen Pinkie stagger in on the CCTV monitor. "What the hell's going on? I send you out to find Badger, he staggers in with a head injury and whatever else. Now you. What the fuck are we facing out there, a bloody army?"

"I wish it was a bloody army; at least we'd be able to see who we're fighting," Badger mumbled.

Declan came face to face with Pinkie. "What the fuck happened to you?"

Pinkie lowered his hands, looked at the blood, and staggered back. "I heard Badger's mobile down in Butcher's Lane. I told Tommy to carry on while I checked. When I reached the bottom, where the garbage bins are, all I saw was a bottle coming towards me. I tried to fight back, but the attacks kept coming, and then I blacked out."

"Where're the other two I sent with you?"

Wiping blood from his eyes with his blooded fingers, Pinkie shook his head.

Declan turned on Bella. "Lock the fucking door," he demanded. "The last thing we need is for that thug to get in here." They watched her rush to the door. "we need to get some guns," he told the two injured men, and he looked at Pinkie. "I don't want to use my collection; can you arrange to get some?"

"I'll see what I can do, but it's going to cost."

"I don't care," Declan said. "It can't be any worse than what that bastard has already cost me."

Bella had just managed to slide the final bolt when the banging started from the other side of the door. "Who's there?" she shouted.

"It's me, Gordon," came the reply. When she got the door open, Gordon rushed up towards Declan. "the bloody coppers are all over the place!" he shouted. "Tumour has it that a body has been found on that piece of wasteland at the bottom of the high street."

"What's that got to do with us?" Declan asked.

"I think it could be young Barry; I can't find him anywhere."

CHAPTER 18

*B*arton had just got his engine started when his mobile sounded. He frisked the pockets of his leather jacket, found it, and saw his father's name and number. "What's the matter?" Barton said before Tom had a chance to say a word.

"A woman has been to our door looking for you. She said she wants to ask you a few questions."

"What woman? Did she say who she was and what kind of questions?"

"She said she was from some legal company … I can't remember what the name of the company was."

"What made this woman think I was in Cornwall with you?" Barton shouted, getting concerned over his father's laid-back attitude.

"We're not in Cornwall; we came home early." Barton knew it would be pointless asking why, knowing it would start an argument. "Is this woman going to come back to talk to me or what?"

"No, she left a card with a number on it for you to call."

"Give me the number," Barton said, pulling a pen from his pocket. He wrote it down on the palm of his hand. As he wrote the number down, alarm bells sounded. This was a mobile, not the landline number of a legal firm. "You stay indoors," he said to finish the call.

"I've been to that club," Barton explained to Crow as he drove home to his house. "There were a gang of thugs waiting for me. I had to fight them off and never got a chance to get in." The mobile went silent, and he could almost hear the cogs in the little man's brain turning as he waited for the reply. When it did come, it shook Barton to the core.

"I've had the owner of that club asking me to provide him with a dozen thugs. Have you been killing off the ones he had?"

"Are you going to supply him?" Barton hastily asked.

"I need somebody inside that place; that's why I asked you."

"I gathered that from that info you gave me."

"The owner's name is Declan Craig," Crow informed him. "I've no doubt you know that by now. I've been getting some info on him that I'm not too happy about—that's why. So now I shall have to find someone else to get inside. I suspected something was going on, and when you informed me about that old mill, that convinced me."

Barton didn't know whether it was relief he felt or upset for letting Crow down. He knew that this wasn't the end and the little dapper man would have an alternative job for him. He drove past his house, checking that there were no suspicious vehicles parked close by. It turned out that every car parked was looking dodgy—or was he getting paranoid? Nevertheless, he parked a way off and cautiously walked back.

As he was about to shower, he noticed the number he had written on his palm and decided to call it. A seductive, oily female voice answered. "I was given this number to call," he said.

"And you are?" she asked.

"I'm the person you came to my parents' house looking for."

"You must be a Mr. Barton?"

"What do you want?" He quickly cut in.

"We need to talk."

"What about?"

"Can't discuss it over the phone; we have to meet."

"Where?"

"Somewhere private. Are you familiar with the area?"

"I know most of it. Why?"

"There's a big lay-by just past the Kings Hotel on the A34 after Alderley Edge. Can you find it and be there about one o' clock tomorrow afternoon?"

"I was led to believe you had offices; can't we meet there?"

"Too many snooping ears there."

"This sounds very private."

"You just try to get there on time," the female voice insisted.

Don't worry, Barton thought after the call ended, *I'll be there in plenty of time.* He knew that area quite well. He had visited that hotel a few times on dates but couldn't remember exactly where that lay- by was. He remembered the surrounding landscape as being forested by young conifers. That was His kind of terrain, where he felt at home, and where he had done most of his training with the regiment in similar areas around the country. He lay awake and reflected on the times when he had visited that hotel. He remembered driving along the A34 on the long summer nights with a girl sitting beside him and seeing the young trees that had been planted on the rolling pastureland. They must have been about man- size then. That was a few years ago; if they were still there, they were likely nearly fully grown.

The plan was set. At first light, he would drive out and find that lay- by, park his car, and head off into the forest and do a recce. This woman may not be expecting him to be there first, giving him time to see whether she was alone. There were no doubts on his mind that this was a setup, but by whom? Could this be another of that club owner's schemes to get hold of him? This club owner had discovered he had parents; who else would have sent thugs to where they lived. If that was the case, what else had he discovered?

The game looked good. It had gone to plan. Crow grinned as he studied the chessboard in front of him. Three pawns had been taken—two white and one black. Both kings and queens hadn't been moved, but the game was young. The black bishop was being threatened by the white king's knight. It would be simple enough to take the knight, but that wasn't in his plan. This was his delight, to play the game with real humans; each piece had a name. After every move, he would turn the board around and become the opposition, so he was 100 percent in charge. Judd's name was printed on a paper sticker and placed at the bottom of the white knight, which was now threatening the black queen's bishop. He stretched back on his chair with his hands behind his head. Before he could attack the bishop, the knight of the black king would have to be taken. The pawn he had dedicated to that job he adorned with a sticker bearing the name "Donna". He turned the board around and moved the piece. *Not just yet*, he decided. He studied the game for a while longer and concluded that it would stay that way.

Stiffly he got up off his chair, wincing at the pain in his leg from a wound he sustained during his army days. This in the end made the report official and got him a medical discharge. He told his friends and family in civilian life that it was a war wound. But if his unofficial medical records were ever displayed to them, they would soon learn that he got it trying to rape a young private. The soldier was charged for assaulting an officer to make it look good for the records. Lieutenant Colonel Crow was later advised to resign his commission, but he refused and forced the high-ranking officers to have him medically discharged and save the good name of the regiment.

Martin smiled at Crow when he entered the lounge and sat next to him on the sofa. Crow nodded towards the television. "What are you watching?"

"Oh, just some old movie," the young man replied combing his fingers through his dyed blond hair. "I like the old ones," Crow replied, "I think they're more down to earth than the modern ones."

Martin stood up and reached for the drinks cabinet. "What would you like to drink?"

Crow held up his hands. "Not for me, darling; I need to keep my head clear. I have a few problems to sort out." He admired the tall, well-groomed young man as he set about preparing himself a drink. He had close-cropped hair, wide-set blue eyes, and a warm smile. Still, there were times when this young man infuriated him. Martin went away often, insisting that it was his job. "You don't need to work," Crow had told him. But Martin was the career type and was ambitious. He had worked his way to becoming a detective constable and would have been promoted farther had it not been for his young age. Crow had known from the start, the night they met in a gay bar when Crow lived in the big city, that Martin was a copper.

The tall young man had introduced himself but wasn't honest about his occupation, and Crow wasn't expecting him to be. This was the kind of challenge he couldn't resist. They had moved up north when Crow inherited his family home, which meant Martin had to commute. This arrangement didn't last long; the travelling was wearing the young man down, and he decided to find a flat near his job and come up on his days off. Keeping his criminal activities from this young man was much easier with their current arrangement, although it was not the challenge he expected. The first few months were exciting trying to keep his lifestyle from Martin, but after a while, the challenge fizzled out. When his young lover came home in the evenings, he was so tired that all he did was sleep on the sofa. Another advantage he enjoyed from Marin was in listening to tales about his employment. The young man would often come home with a few stories about his daily work—nothing specific, but enough for Crow to work out the bigger picture. "Have you applied for a transfer yet?" he asked, edging himself closer.

"These things take time," Martin replied. "I have requested it with my boss, but nothing has come back."

Crow frowned, but it was all show; he didn't want his lover living here. He was beginning to realise that this young undercover detective was a lot smarter than he had given him credit for, and it would only be a matter of time before he began to find something that would expose Crow's involvement with the syndicate.

Because of his sexuality DC Martin Penn was assigned to go undercover in the Crow organisation. But after a year, he hadn't discovered anything that would incriminate the little man enough to get him convicted. He had, however, succeeded in sending a few other crims down that were connected to this syndicate. But the higher command wanted the top men, and his time limit was running out. It made it more difficult when Crow moved out of London, and it would have blown his cover had Martin moved with him, according to his superiors, who said it would look too obvious if he were to be transferred. A chance had to come for him to hunt the house for evidence. So far that hadn't happened; he needed the little man to be out. But Crow never left him alone long enough to do a proper search. Detective Constable Martin Penn had a list of names connected to Crow and the syndicate. These names he had handed to New Scotland Yard for closer investigations, in hopes that they would come up with a positive result. Maybe then they could get a conviction.

CHAPTER 19

*I*t was still dark when he got out of bed although it was after seven. The winter mornings did not see sunrise till about eight. *Time for a shower and a good breakfast*, Barton decided, *then a steady drive to the rendezvous with this woman.*

A half mile past the hotel, he found the lay-by. Things hadn't changed much since his last visit here, but the conifers had grown. He reckoned they must be about twenty feet high and dense, making it almost imposable to pass through them. This wasn't good; he would have no place to take cover and observe without being too close. He got out and locked his car, and he strolled back the way he had come, keeping close to the treeline. A few cars passed in both directions, sometimes blasting their horns at him—mostly girls and women, with the odd man waving and puckering his lips at him. Not wanting to be remembered, he stepped into the darkness of the overhanging conifer branches.

There was only one car parked in the hotel car park—a silver BMW. He guessed it could belong to this woman. But how to be certain could be a problem, as most hotels open early for guests wanting a quick start, but not with only one customer; and if his guess was right, she wouldn't be in a hurry to leave.

His guess was spot on; she walked out the hotel doors at twelve thirty—a slightly built woman with a long black ponytail that almost reached her hips, which swayed as she walked to her car. She wore a slim brown trouser suit with high heels that she seemed to struggle walking in. He formed the opinion that she was more used to wearing trainers or lower-heeled footwear.

She let out a yelp when she tried to close the car door and saw a man standing jamming it open with his body. The gun in his hand was just a few inches from her nose. "Slide over to the passenger's seat," Barton snarled at her.

"Who are you?" she whimpered when she got settled in the seat.

"I was about to ask you the same question. I'm the man you're to meet at one o' clock in the lay-by down the road."

"You're early," she said.

"So are you," Barton replied, pushing his gun closer to her temple. "Now, who's hiring you?"

"You wouldn't dare fire that thing here; the people in that hotel would hear the shot and have the law here in a few minutes."

"Yes, and in that few minutes I'll be gone, and you'll be dead, so answer the question."

"And soon after that you'll be joining me! You don't think I'd come here without backup, do you?"

"I've been recceing this place for over two hours; if you had any backup, I would have found it."

"Not if the backup was in the hotel with me."

"So where is this backup?" Barton asked, glancing around the area.

"I'll put it to you this way, Mr. Barton: the man who has hired me is a lot smarter than you. He guessed this would be the first place you would come to; that's why he picked this place to meet."

"So where is this smart man?" A few moments of thoughtful silence passed, and then he jumped out of the car and ordered her out. "Open the bonnet," he shouted, and he admired her shapely buttocks as she reached in and pulled the catch. He lifted it up and called her to the front. "You see those wires leading from the ignition unit? If you follow them, you'll find explosives. This device was meant to go off the moment you started your car, so your backup was meaning to kill us both." It was pure bluff; he was gambling that she didn't know anything about the mechanics or electronics of a car.

She stepped back, uncertain. "How could a bomb have been planted? If this car had been tampered with, the alarm would have gone off."

Barton caught her arm and guided her away from the car. "We're dealing with pros. These guys would have guessed I would jump you here and would have no problems deactivating an alarm." He walked back to her vehicle, leaving her standing there, and closed the bonnet. "We need to get away from here," he said, and once again he held her arm and led her out of the car park and onto the road. She stumbled along beside him as he still held her arm for support.

"Where are you taking me?" she said, trying to free herself from his grip.

"My car is just a short way down the road in that lay-by," he explained, tightening his grip on her arm.

"You're hurting me, you bastard!" she yelped.

"Well, stop struggling." She did more than stop struggling; she rammed against him from the impact of a high-velocity round as it smacked into her skull. Barton instantly dropped to the ground, pushing her body off the top of him and crawling in amongst the trees. He didn't get far before he heard the crack of a second shot whipping past his ear. He snaked his way into the thicket of the conifers, but no more shots had been fired. Time seemed to drag, and he had no idea how far he had crawled and wondered whether the shooter was giving chase. He lay still, listening intently for telltale sounds, but all he could hear was the gentle breeze through the trees. He realised this shooter had to be a hired professional and knew he wouldn't give up. And if anyone around heard the shots, they would think it was a farmer or a hunter.

He had been crawling for an hour when he made a time check. Although his progress was slow, he knew this plantation must come to an end soon. It was no use standing; the tree branches were too close. Progress would be almost impossible and would rip the skin off his face. He carried on crawling below the lower branches. For all he knew, he could have been going round in circles; it was so dark the sunlight never penetrated this far down.

As he progressed, he noticed that the trees were thinning out and more light was coming through. Here he risked standing, and soon he stumbled onto a grassy track that snaked through the plantation.

He wondered whether he should risk following it and maybe get caught out in the open if the shooter was in pursuit.

Badger, with a bandage around his head, sat at the other side of Declan's desk. "If I get my hands on that bastard, I'll rip his head off."

"You'll have to wait your turn," Declan said. "And by the time I'm finished with him, he won't have a head."

"He didn't have to kill young Barry," Badger said. "According to the medical report, his neck was snapped; that had to take some strength to do that."

"Well, he sneaked up on you and gave you a thumping, and you never saw it coming."

"What are we dealing with here? Maybe there's more than one of them."

"No," Declan said, "there's only one. I've done a bit of checking on him; like every one of us, he has to have a weakness."

"Do you know what that is?"

Declan nodded and grinned. "He has family living close by."

Badger could guess what the next move was going to be and said, "Do you want them picked up and brought here?"

"That would be a good idea," Declan replied. "He would think twice about burning this place down if he knew they were here. But no, I want to get two guys into his parents' house and hold them there. Get them to phone him asking for help, and when he turns up, we jump on the bastard."

"I don't think he's going to turn up unprepared," Badger said.

"Then we anticipate that and be ready for him."

"When do you plan to do this?"

"A couple of Crow's men are on their way; as soon as they arrive."

"You're sending a couple of strangers to Barton's parents' house. Do you think that's a good idea?"

Declan shook his head. "I know it's not a good idea, but I don't have a choice; I don't want to take the chance of losing more of my guys to this bastard."

"Boss, I want to have a crack at him after what he's done to me and my friend Barry."

"We'll all get a crack at him," Declan assured him. Badger had just stood up to leave when a knock came to the door and a young woman pushed her head in.

"Two men here to see you, Mr. Craig," she announced.

Declan stood up. "Show them in, Ashlie."

They were about the same size as Badger; one was shaven-headed and tattooed from his neck over the top of his head and half his face. Declan didn't like tattoos, as they made people too easy to identify in a line-up, but considering the job he was about to give them, it didn't matter. The other had the stance of an ex-copper or a long-serving soldier, with a ruddy complexion, long blond hair, and a droopy moustache that required trimming. "I've got an easy job forboth of you," Declan said, grinning and walking round his desk while holding out his hand. "It's a sort of babysitting job, but these babies are old—but just as easy to handle."

After a detailed briefing, the two men got bundled into the back of the four-by-four, Badger driving and Declan sitting next to him. The men were dropped at the door and told to barge in and jump the couple. "Give them a bit of roughing up, but not too much that they can't make that phone call."

"What next?" Badger asked as he drove them back to the club.

"Next comes the tricky part," Declan said, "Barton's going to come prepared, as you pointed out, so I don't expect him to drive up to his parents' door. We get a few of the guys with their cars parked at likely locations where he might leave his vehicle to sneak his way to the house. When he's spotted, they get on their mobiles and everybody moves in."

Badger pulled up at the back door of the club. They both got out, and he said, "That sounds too simple. You don't think he's going to fall for a trick like that?"

"That's exactly why it should work," Declan explained. "He's a wily bastard and will be expecting something a bit more complex than that."

Badger opened the door and let Declan pass in. "That's going to take a few of our guys, and that will leave the club short of bouncers."

"I've got a few more men coming later," Declan said, grinning. "We'll use them for the job of nabbing this goon."

"They'll need to be good," Badger said, closing the door.

"Strength in numbers," Declan replied, and he headed back to his office.

Badger didn't follow but instead went and sat on a stool in front of the bar. His head was throbbing as though he had a toothache, and he asked one of the cleaners to pour him a large whiskey. After a couple of mouthfuls, his headache had improved enough to see that Declan's plan was going to be a disaster.

Tom and Jean Barton were watching television but not paying too much attention to it, and the volume was down low, or they wouldn't have heard the diesel engine at their front door. Tom jumped up and ran for the door. On the way, he picked up a heavy brass candlestick from a pair that adorned the shelf in the hallway. Jean managed to get the other one, and when the door flew open, they launched themselves at the two men who barged in.

The attack was so unexpected and vicious that the two men turned and ran out, blood blinding them. They took most of the blows on the face and head. "What the fuck's happened?" Bald Head cried as he crumpled to his knees on the pavement.

"They were waiting for us," the blonde man said, his nose seeping blood onto his moustache.

"I think that bastard set us up."

"Why? What have we done to upset him?"

"I think he sent us in to test the waters, as the saying goes." The blonde man helped his mate to his feet. "We'd best make ourselves scarce here before the neighbours start getting involved, wanting to know what's going on." But before they got on the move, the neighbours were at their doors—and so were the Bartons, shouting for help. Tom was pointing at the goons, yelling that the two had broken into their house.

They attacked from all directions. The two men were pinned to the ground, and a barrage of kicks and punches landed to their heads and bodies. It stopped only when a police car came screaming to a halt at the mob. The two constables rushed out, and soon another patrol car came rushing in. They got the neighbours separated, and statements were taken, and the two thugs were cuffed and bundled into the back of one of the cars.

Deciding on which direction he should take along the open track delayed Barton for a few valuable moments. Although he had got down on his knees, he realised he could still make an easy target. The decision made, he charged along the grassy lane until he was stopped by a barbed wire fence. At the other side was an old brick building, and there was about fifty yards of open ground to get there. The risk had to be worth taking and would give him the advantage of spotting this shooter before he got within shooting distance.

The structure looked as though it was originally built to shelter sheep or cattle before the trees were planted, and the only opening was the doorway. This didn't offer much advantage; he could only observe in the one direction. Barton was certain this shooter was no fool and wouldn't attempt to approach from the front. Hoping the shooter was behind him, he decided to continue using the building as cover and find a vantage point at the far side of the open ground. At this time of the year, the grass had gone to seed and was lying flat, making it easy to cover the ground quickly, but it didn't offer many places to hide.

Fortune was on his side when he stumbled into a deep ditch with only a few inches of water trickling down it. This, he decided, was the best cover he could find, and he crouched there and waited for the shooter to stumble into the ditch the way he had; then he would launch his attack.

As the day wore on, a blanket of mist hovered over the treetops and soon rolled its way in his direction until he could no longer see the old building. This could be an advantage or a disadvantage; it could mean that the shooter couldn't get a bead on him, but on the other hand he might not see the gunman coming and lose the advantage of surprise. All Barton had to depend on was his hearing; visibility was down to a few yards. What disturbed his senses was the faraway sound of traffic, which made him wonder how far he was from the road. Had he been going round in circles in the dense forest?

Judd cursed himself for his own stupidity for not setting the sights for close range when he observed the wooded terrain. He knew he wouldn't get a long-range shot at Barton here. He had followed Donna out of the hotel and darted back in the door when he saw his target approach her car. He wondered what was happening when he saw them look under the bonnet. He next noticed them walking down the road towards the lay-by. He gave chase and decided to take the shot at the point where the road made a sharp right turn.

Both the girl and Barton dropped from his shot, and he thought the round had gone through her and into him. *Two birds with the one stone?* he wondered. But he soon found out he was wrong when he discovered the girl was lying on her own with half her skull blown away. He was about to pull her body into the trees when he noticed movement a short distance away, thought he saw something low down on the ground beneath the lower branches of the conifer trees, and could hear twigs snap.

He then let fly a wild shot in that direction, as sometimes the shot hits the target, and soon after, he tried to fight his way in. But he soon found that impossible when the sharp needles and rough branches tore at his flesh and clothes. Judd could see that the only way to make progress through the trees was to belly crawl, and no way was he going to attempt that. He turned and pulled Donna's body as far in as he could manage and headed towards the lay-by and Barton's car.

At about a hundred metres past the car on the opposite side of the road, he found a narrow break in the conifers and decided this would be the best place to take the shot when Barton finally returned to his vehicle. He paced out the range and set his sights, perched his rifle on a low branch, and waited.

With the mist thickening and darkness beginning to fall, Barton decided it was a waste of time waiting for the shooter. If he did turn up, and that was unlikely now, he could walk past unseen. His only means of working out which direction to take was to follow the sound of the traffic, which didn't sound too far away. He walked along the bottom of the ditch. His feet were quelching with water, but the steep sides offered some protection should the mist lift as quickly as it had come down.

The traffic sounds were getting closer, and the glare of headlights flashed as the darkening sky blanketed around him. This he was glad of; if the shooter had night sights, the beams would distort his vision through them, and the mist would be to his disadvantage. Like magic, he was out of the mist patch and up ahead was the silhouette of a building against a low red moon—the effect of the mist rising in the early evening sky. Barton realised he had come across the hotel from the rear. He climbed over the low stone wall and found himself in the car park. A few cars were parked along the side of the building, and he crept from one to the other, keeping his head down, taking no chances in case the shooter was also creeping about like him or might be inside the building.

He couldn't believe his luck; the next vehicle in the line he recognised as the silver BMW the woman had been driving. Amazingly, the doors were unlocked and the keys were still in the ignition. He hadn't given her time to grab them when he steered her away from it. Before getting in, he had a good look around; and when satisfied the car park was deserted, he stepped in and got it started.

His own car was still parked in the lay-by, undisturbed, when he drove past, and he couldn't see the shooter—not that he was expecting to see him, but sometimes a little bit of luck came his way. He had decided that since the mist and darkness had come down, the shooter would have given up the chase and would be watching the vehicle in hopes of him returning, to take a shot at him there.

There were no doubts in his mind that the shooter was a pro. Who had hired him was the question. The only suspect he could think of was the club owner, Declan. The thing that put the damper on that thought was that Declan seemingly had no reason to hire a shooter when he had a bunch of thugs that could attempt to do the job.

The first thing Barton did when he got home was put on the kettle and phone a breakdown service. He informed them where to come and collect the keys and where the vehicle was. There was one problem, though: he didn't know whether this shooter had a car. He hadn't noticed any other vehicles in the car park when he'd approached Donna's and could only hope she had given him a lift and he wouldn't be able to follow the breakdown truck. With the arrangements for his car sorted, he sat down to a coffee and a sandwich and phoned his parents. His mother answered in a distraught voice, blabbering about what had happened to them. This got his adrenalin going again. "I told you both to stay in Cornwall!" he shouted at her. She returned with the same story as before, about his father not getting on with her sister. "Are the police still there?" he asked her. This time it was his father who answered.

"I don't see any of their vehicles in the street; I think they left when they bundled those two thugs in one of their cars."

"Did you have to give a statement?"

"There was not much we could say, just that two thugs barged into our house, and we managed to fight them off."

Barton knew this wasn't a one-off break-in; must have been planned, and he had a good idea by whom. It was time to take the fight to them, and their nerve centre was that club.

CHAPTER 20

DC Martin Penn slouched back on the huge white leather sofa. A large flat-screen television was on the wall opposite. An old western movie was showing. He had the volume turned down so he could hear when Crow flushed and left the toilet. He reached over to the small low table at his feet and lifted the lid on the laptop. He typed in a few passwords, but none of them were accepted. He hastily shut the lid and entered the failed ones into his notebook. He was still writing when Crow walked in.

The little man hadn't flushed the toilet and hadn't been there; he had said that was where he was going, but instead he had entered a small box room next to it, where he had a multiscreen monitor and could observe the young man's every move. Concealed cameras were in every room; they were the most topical and expensive pieces of technology of the time. Some could be very small; he had a ring that contained one, imbedded in a diamond, which he wore on his index finger. In places a camera couldn't cover, he took the ring off and placed in a position where he could see what his associates and lovers were doing behind his back. Every room was bugged with microphones no bigger than a pinheads. He even had them in the toilets. He delighted on inviting people to his house for the purpose of getting to know their dirty little secrets and using them to his advantage. "What's this you're writing?" he asked, and he sat next to his lover.

"Just a few ideas I can use at work," Martin explained, putting his notebook back into his pocket and smiling.

Crow held out his hand. "Let me see; maybe I can suggest something."

Martin shook his head and withdrew himself. "You really need to be on the job to be able to come up with something that would be considered."

"I'm a retired lieutenant colonel; have been for many years. If I can't come up with an idea, I don't know who can."

"I've no doubt you can, but it wouldn't feel the same knowing that it wasn't my own idea."

Crow smiled, reached for the remote, and turned up the volume on the television. The film was about a father, wife, and son and their stormy relationship. This brought on thoughts of the Bartons. For weeks he had been having trouble with the son, and Judd hadn't yet dealt with the father. He decided to maybe get Judd to deal with the offspring at the same time. Then he dropped a few clues on Martin's lap about the identity of the shooter. The ability to do this without incriminating himself was the reason he tolerated this young detective.

"A penny for them," Martin said, disturbing Crow's thoughts. He moved in closer to him.

This was one of the little man's pet hates, but he forced a grin. "They're not worth that much."

Martin stiffly stood up yawned and stretched. "I'm off for a shower and an early bed; got an early start in the morning. Do you fancy joining me?"

Crow shook his head. "You go ahead, and I'll be in soon. Want to see the end of this film." When he heard the shower running, Crow crept into the bedroom and found the notebook in Martin's pocket. He discovered three pages of what looked like codes or passwords, each one with a score through it. It didn't take a genius to work out what it all meant.

The sound from the shower stopped, and Crow replaced the notebook and headed back to the lounge. Martin pranced in wearing only a towel around his waist and sat beside him on the sofa. Crow turned and put his arm around his bare shoulders. "Maybe I'll join you." He slowly got up and left.

As on his previous trip out of the lounge, he entered the box room. Once again Martin lifted the lid of the laptop and began swiftly tapping at the keyboard. Crow afforded himself a grin, knowing that the password would take years to discover at the rate the young man was attempting. When the time came, he would drop a hint and let Martin work out the rest, and the names that would come to the fore would be those people he wanted to dispose of.

Badger downed the last of his drink when Declan shouted from his office and waved him in. "Those two bloody idiots I sent to the Bartons' house, have been lifted by the coppers," he said as Badger sat on his usual seat in front of the desk. All Declan got in return from the big man was a shrug of his shoulders and a grimace. "You don't look surprised or shocked?"

"Judging by the look of those two," the big man said with a grin, "why should I be?"

"You might have told me what you thought of them."

"I tried to warn you."

"I'll get onto Crow and tell him what I think of his two men."

"I think the last thing you need is to fall out with that cunning little fox. Remember: he controls the stock that come into this place. If he finds you have been dealing outside, I think you know the consequences."

"How's he going to find out?" Declan asked, picking up the phone.

"By getting someone inside."

Declan threw him a curious look, and then, after a moment of thought, he grimaced. "By sending one of his guys here to work."

Badger adjusted the dressing on his head and stood up, "You've been asking him for quite a few of his boys lately, but most of them have been dumbos. Except for that guy Barton."

After a couple of shakes of his head and a shoulder shrug, Declan said, "I never gave it a thought," still holding the phone to his ear.

"After you tell Crow about the two clowns, bring that subject up. See if he knows what happened—why Barton never turned up."

"Crow never gives out information on the guys he sends; it puzzled me when he mentioned Barton's name. That's the first time that has happened. He'll know what went down that day, and that big shit will have to explain why he never arrived here." A long moment passed as Declan let the big man mull this over. He then added, "The minute the police let those two clowns out, get them and bring them here," Declan said, and he waited till Badger was out the door before phoning Crow.

It was as though the little man knew about the two goons, almost as if he was expecting it to happen. Or maybe Declan's message was second-hand. He was surprised when he asked about the guy Barton, and Crow was forthcoming with information and gave the name and description in detail. He wasn't sure whether he was happy with what he had learned, because this was the thug at the root of all his problems. In the years he had worked with Crow's organisation, he had never known him be upfront with information about the criminals he had sent. This was confusing; what was the little man up to?

Badger was in conversation with an elderly man at the bar and became concerned when he noticed the expression on Declan's face when he sat next to them.

Badger politely asked the oldster to excuse them. "You look like you have aproblem."

"When do you think those two clowns will get released from the nick?" he asked.

"They can only hold them for a limited time before they have to charge them; after that, the clowns will get out on bail."

"How long's that going to take?"

"That depends on what the judge decides—whether they are a danger to the public or not." He pushed his half-drunk beer glass away and stood up.

"I think we'd better discus this in your office, Boss; you never know who's listening."

Declan glanced around the room and agreed; the place was beginning to fill up with patrons—too many ears. Back in the same position as before in the office, Declan leaned over the desk. "We can't let those two clowns talk to the coppers; they could land us all in it."

Badger grinned. "I heard they got a good kicking from the neighbours and that the old couple thrashed them with heavy candlesticks." His grin widened. "That means they'll be in hospital under police escort."

Declan returned his grin. "And the coppers will have to take them there first, and we know who their nurse will be." He snatched the phone up and was soon giving instructions to the receiver of his call. "All sorted," he soon informed Badger. "All we have to do is go there and pick them up."

"Did he give you a time?"

"In about an hour—give him time to get the stuff and administer it to the two coppers that are escorting them."

Dressed in porter's overalls, Badger and Pinkie pushed a wheelchair each into the compartment, slipped past the sleeping constables, and dragged the two men out of their beds. They came willingly, knowing this was their way out of trouble from the law. But little did they know the police were the lesser of their troubles. They confidently pushed the chairs out past the reception and out the main doors. Not once did they get a second glance from the hospital staff or the security. They abandoned the wheelchairs in the car park, gagged and bound the two men, and bundled them in the back of a stolen van.

As arranged, the scrap dealer was working late and opened the gate to let the van in. Pinkie handed him the envelope, jumped out, sauntered to the four-by-four, and got in the rear seat behind Declan. Badger, in the driver's seat, nodded and received the thumbs up before driving away. "By the time that crusher is finished, the van won't be recognisable," Declan commented as they sped down the motorway. "And two bodies won't be distinguishable from the twisted metal."

Barton was enjoying driving the silver BMW and got it parked where he could watch the club doors and the entrance to the car park at the rear. He didn't have to wait long before the familiar vehicle drove in. He couldn't identify who the driver was but guessed it would be the big guy who always did that job. The one he thought he had broken his hand on when landing a few punches to the guy's face. The kick to his groin he'd delivered would have crippled a normal man for a few weeks.

It looked like the Westerner's Club was in for a busy night by the amount of people entering. *Could be here for a while*, Barton decided, and he got settled down to listen to the radio. He didn't have time to tune into a classic station before the same four-by-four drove past him. This puzzled Barton when he followed them driving into the hospital car park. *They're not here to visit a patient; that's for sure.* The answer came when only two men got out and walked to the entrance. He drove past the four-by-four and recognised the club owner sitting in the passenger's seat and another man in the back.

The parking facilities were quiet, with only a few cars spread out over the area. Not wanting to draw their attention, he pulled into the first vacant spot. The two men loitered at the entrance door. Barton recognised the tallest as being the driver and could see he had large a plaster on his head. They seemed to be waiting for something or someone to arrive, judging by their body language. His judgement proved to be spot on when, moments later, a small white van pulled up in front of them, blocking Barton's view.

He was at the point of starting up the car and driving round to see what was going on behind that vehicle when the two men appeared, each pushing a wheelchair with a patient in it. The driver of the van got out, and a tussle started between the people in the chairs and the thugs. Barton could only guess what had been going on when the van screeched away and the wheelchairs were abandoned at the front doors.

The big guy with the plaster and his mate ran back to the four-by-four and soon drove off, probably to follow the van.

It was no easy job tailing the four-by-four; they seemed to be zigzagging through dark, narrow streets. At one point, Barton was sure they had doubled back on themselves. This was a ploy to confuse anyone who might be following, and they almost succeeded.

In a stroke of luck, Barton almost ran into the van as it came out of a side street. He slammed on his brakes and let the two vehicles pass. He didn't need to drive any farther when he noticed the four- by-four's brake lights come on and the vehicle pulled to the side of the road. The van carried on and turned in through a set of open steel-sheeted gates.

All lights were extinguished, leaving only a single streetlamp which cast shadows off the high metal fencing. Nothing moved for what seemed like half an hour, and then a man ran out of the gates and got into the four-by-four. Barton sat there until the vehicle turned onto the main road before he got out and edged his way to the gates.

The van was parked a few yards from where he stood looking in a scrapyard for vehicles. As he edged closer, he heard banging from the back of the vehicle, as though someone was kicking at the door.

"What the fuck do you think you're doing?" A gruff voice shouted from behind.

Barton swung round to be confronted with a burly man in a high-vis jacket carrying a crowbar in his hand, ready to use it. He shouted the first thing that came to his mind: "This is my van; it's been nicked." Even in the dim light, he could detect panic on the man's face, and he saw his shoulders droop slightly.

"Have you reported it?"

"Yes, and I'm just about to call the police." Barton snatched out his mobile and held it up.

"You don't need to do that," the man said with a nervous quaver in his voice. "I'll give you the keys and a few quid for your inconvenience." At that moment, a loud thump came from inside the van. The scrap man opened the back door, and a guy rolled out, kicking and moaning behind a taped gag, his hands fastened behind his back and his head and neck bandaged. A moment later, another tied victim fell out in much the same condition.

Barton jumped forward and gazed at the men lying at their feet, and then up at the scrap man. "What have you been doing with my van?" he shouted.

"I had no idea they were in there!" the scrap man shouted back. "This guy came in and asked me to scrap this vehicle, gave me the paperwork. I paid him, and he left."

"At this time of night?" Barton said, looking at his watch. He flicked up his mobile again. "I wonder what the police will have to say about all this." Although it was dark, the high-vis jacket was in plain sight, reflecting off a distant lamp behind the metal fence. The man's movement was fast, but not fast enough. Barton side-stepped in a split second, and the crowbar swished past his ear. At the same moment, one of the injured men rolled over, tripping the scrap man. He fell at Barton's feet and received a hard kick to the head. The crowbar slipped from his hand, and Barton quickly retrieved it and thumped it into the man's back. With the scrap man out cold at their feet, Barton cut the two men free and told them to get into the van and drive as far away as possible, "if I ever see either of you again, you're dead!" he shouted as they scrambled in the front, got it started, and screeched their way out of the yard.

Behind him the scrap man started to moan, and Barton hooked the crowbar around his neck and yanked it up. The man yelled when the sharp claws dug into his flesh. "Who paid you to scrap that van?" Barton yelled.

"I don't know," came the garbled reply. The crowbar got another yank.

"I'll not ask you again. If you don't tell me what I want to know, I'll smash your skull in with this."

The scrap man made the mistake of trying to scramble to his feet and was rewarded with a hard kick to the ribs. He gasped and slumped back down.

"Okay," Barton said, "Say goodbye to the world."

"It was one of Declan Craig's guys," the scrap man groaned. He lay still for a while, expecting the final blow. It never came. He lay still for a few more moments before he struggled painfully onto his feet to discover he was on his own, relieved yet puzzled at how this stranger could have disappeared so quickly. As he hobbled back to his small office, he decided there would be no more dodgy late-night deals.

CHAPTER 21

Judd was cold, wet, and hungry with scratches all over his face and neck when he got into his accommodation. His first job was a long shower to get all the irritating pine needles off his skin. The meal he sat down to was one of those tasteless prepacked frozen things he had purchased for quickness. After eating, he drank three cups of black coffee whilst sitting in the lounge on an easy chair. The last thing he wanted was to drift into a deep sleep. He needed to work out where he had made the mistake when he'd failed to make the hit on that big guy. How could a man of his huge physique simply glide through those thick pine branches? Judd convinced himself that this son of Tom Barton's was a pro. And knew he had to be extra careful should the tables turn on him. There was only one man who could confirm this, and after careful consideration, he made the call.

After telling the Crow the problems he was having to go through, to get a hit on Tom Barton, he was surprised at how cooperative Crow had been. "You do what you have to do to get the job done," Crow said.

"You sound as though you want this Richard Barton out of the picture?"

"That's up to you if you think it's necessary," Crow replied after a few moments of silent thought. "By the way, did that woman do the job?" he asked. Judd had almost forgotten about the girl he had shot accidently.

"There was a little mishap. That guy Barton must have killed her; I found her at the roadside. I dragged her into the forest and hid her body."

"That won't do!" Crow shouted. "Somebody will find her, and the law will connect her to my organisation. If that happens, you can be sure I'll point a finger at you. You'll have to dispose of her so that her body can't be found."

"Get some of your thugs to do that; I've not got the time."

"That will cost you."

"That's fine, we can sort things out later." Judd put his mobile back in his pocket and lay back, content in knowing what he was up against now. His funds were running low, and the quicker he could get this Tom Barton hit over, the sooner he would be able to do some of the other jobs that had been piling up. Admittedly he'd made too many mistakes with this job; possibly three people had been killed, and still he hadn't carried out the contract. All because of this son of Tom Barton's. He realised that if he went ahead and killed the father, his son would retaliate, and the best way to get peace of mind would be to get rid of his offspring first.

"Appeal to Barton's carnal instincts," Crow had said. "He can't resist a pretty woman."

Judd sensed the humour in the little man's voice. *If only I had known that, that girl would still be alive.* Now he would have to find another, but without Crow's knowledge. The nearest place he could think of to hire a whore for a day or so was the Westerner's Club. He had noticed the place whilst stalking Tom Barton and had taken a glance at the tarty girls entering and guessed what their job description entailed. The problem was getting to know the owner of the place. Would this person hire out one of his girls, and for how much?

The black coffee wasn't doing its job, and he was fighting to stay awake. In the end he had to give in, and he flopped into bed with a last thought, and that was to accost one of the whores before she went into her job and make her an offer she couldn't refuse.

The taste of the coffee still lingered in his mouth after six hours' sleep. The bedroom was aglow with the early-morning sunshine blasting directly into his face. He shielded his eyes with his arm andslowly eased out of bed. A loud banging from his front door stopped him abruptly on his way to wash and shave. "Who is it?" he shouted.

"Never mind who it is; just open the fucking door or we'll kick it in!" a deep, throaty voice shouted.

"Hold on a minute; I need to get the key." Still in his underwear, Judd rushed into his bedroom, stuck his hand under the mattress, and fished out his favourite weapon, the Astra A-80 pistol. With the weapon stuck in the waistband of his underpants, his right hand on the grip, he slowly opened the door with his left.

The moment he turned the key, the door flew open, knocking him off balance. He staggered back but managed to pull the pistol out and point it at the three thugs who charged in on him but was too slow, and the weapon got knocked out of his fist. In the flick of an eyelid, he found himself on his back on the floor with three heavy bodies pinning him down. "What's going on?" he cried. Vice-like fingers gripped both his arms, and he felt himself being lifted onto his feet. "What's going on?" he repeated. "Who are you? Who sent you? What do you want?" Another set of hands gripped his legs, and he was being lifted and hefted into the bedroom and tossed onto the bed.

"Get dressed." A man with a big face towered over him; he had no teeth, and greasy black hair was falling over his eyes. Another man stood at the other side, pointing the gun. The third person stood at the foot of the bed; this one looked much younger than the other two and appeared to be in charge. He picked up Judd's clothes from the floor, where he had stepped out of them, and threw them at him.

Judd decided that resistance would be futile and dangerous, and he complied. They didn't give him a chance to put shoes on; this, he guessed, was in the plan so he wouldn't make a run for it if he got the opportunity. He was made to walk to the other side of the street, heading in the direction of a line of parked cars. Another long walk down the line and the soles of his feet began to tear, and he could feel the blood oozing out of them. A car door burst open in front of him, and the vice-like grip from the goons behind forced him inside it. The driver started the car while two of the three goons crushed in beside him, one on either side, in the rear; the youngest goon sat in front.

The youngster turned around and stared at Judd. "Take us to where you dumped that girl's body."

"We could have sorted that out without all the rough stuff." Judd grinned and began to relax now that he knew what it was all about.

"Do you think so?" the youngster snapped back at him. "That girl was a good friend."

"Well, you'll have been told who killed her. I found her and pulled her off the roadside before someone else discovered her body and got the law involved."

"We haven't been told who killed her," the youngster said. "We decided it must have been you." He turned to the driver and nodded for him to move off. "Where are we heading?" He snarled back at Judd.

A group of bikers were parked in the lay-by, and the driver was told to carry on past. "Hope they don't go in too far amongst the trees if they've stopped for a piss," Judd said, and he glanced back to see them smoking and pranking about.

"Give them five, and we can turn and go back," the youngster said.

The bikers were mounting up when they returned. The driver carried on and turned around in the hotel car park. The lastbike was justpulling out as they drove in. They quickly got out, and Judd ledthem to where he had dragged the body. He gazed in disbelief; the girl's body was no longer there.

"Are you sure this is where you left her?" the youngster shouted.

"Do I look stupid?" Judd barked back at him.

The big, greasy-haired toothless goon stepped back. "This is creepy; let's get to fuck out of here."

"Hold on," the youngster said. "All those trees look alike; it would be easy to mistake the exact spot where you dragged her to."

"Well, it was quite misty and was getting dark," Judd admitted.

"Okay," the youngster said, "spread out and start looking."

Judd was pinning his hopes on these goons not being able to tell the difference between a hit from a high-velocity round and one from a pistol, for there was no way he could make a run for it on his bare feet.

The thug with his gun was a clearskin with tight, curly dyed blonde hair who permanently displayed a sardonic grin. He chirped in for the first time: "If she was dead, she didn't get up and walk away, so somebody must have found her."

The youngster frowned at him and shook his head in a ridiculing manner. "Let's get started," he said, and he led the way along the edge of the trees. An hour later, they headed back to the same place where they had started off. Judd was limping; his bare feet looked like something that might be found lying on a butcher's slab. The others were scratched and sweaty. Judd couldn't manage another step; he had to get off his injured feet and sat down on the grass edge, nursing his injuries while the others carried on.

When they reached the car, they found it locked, and the driver was nowhere. "What the fuck's going on?" the youngster shouted. The answer came a second later when a group of armed police officers rushed at them from the trees at the other side of the road.

Judd witnessed this and crawled back into the forest. He lay for what seemed like hours before he heard the police vehicles drive away. He knew they wouldn't abandon the scene without leaving officers behind in case the public started rubbernecking and walking all over the area.

CHAPTER 22

is mobile sounded when he got back into Donna's silver BMW. Barton was informed that his car had been uplifted and was on its way the pre-arranged drop off point. This was the tricky part; he didn't know whether the shooter had a vehicle and could have followed the breakdown truck. Luckily, he turned up first; this gave him enough time to recce the deserted wasteland area, and he found a space between two ruined buildings that offered cover, should the shooter decide to try his luck.

"What's all the cloak-and-dagger stuff?" the driver asked when he turned up and was directed into the darkness between the old buildings.

"I'm hiding it out of the way," Barton replied. "Divorce problems." The driver grinned and soon offloaded the car and got on his way. Barton waved and got into his own car. He slowly drove around the rough area, searching for signs of the gunman, half expecting a shot to be fired at him. When nothing happened, he drove past Donna's car, where he had abandoned it behind a pile of rubble, and headed home.

The shock came when he phoned his parents later. They described the two men that had tried to get into their house. There were no doubts in Barton's mind that they were the same thugs that had been gagged and tied in the back of that van. The shocking part was the thought of him letting them go. But now, thanks to the scrap man, he knew who had sent them. "None of this would have happened if you both had stayed in Cornwall," he said, finishing the call.

He settled back on the sofa with a can of beer, content in the knowledge that it wasn't that club owner who had hired the shooter. His mind was in overdrive as he lay struggling for sleep when a sudden flashback struck him about the death of his younger brother and his mate Danny. *It had to be the same shooter.* He scolded himself for being so slow on the uptake. How could he have mistaken that tall, slim, sick-looking guy with the prematurely white hair? Although Corrie's body was never found at the scene, Barton knew he had met the same fate as Danny.

After a few glasses of orange juice for breakfast and a long spell of deliberation, he decided to call his old boss, Billy Benson, to see whether his little bird could come up with some info about the shooter.

"I'm not going down that road," Billy said in a gruff whisper. "That's getting into the real heavy stuff, way over my head."

"This guy has been contracted to hit my family," Barton appealed to him.

Billy took a long time to reply, and when he did, he said, "You're ex-army, so hunt this shooter down."

Was this direct advice or a subtle hint? The word "ex-army" lingered long after the call was over. If his thinking was on track, this would test his tenacity to the limit. It was the way Billy expressed the word "ex-army" that confused him for a moment. His immediate thought was of ex–lieutenant colonel Crow,the only ex-army personnel he knew who was involved. But why would Crow go to the expense of hiring a hit man to knock off his father, a grey-haired old man whose only fault was doing as he was ordered under the threat of his son's life?

The reasoning behind Declan Craig sending goons to his parents' house was obvious, and he was feeling quite proud of them and their quick thinking in fighting the thugs off. This brought on the thought of Wilma. *What has happened to her? Why hasn't she called?* The last he remembered of her was her entering that club. He promised himself to find her again.

As a precaution, he never parked his car on the same street where he lived, and he constantly changed the locations. When he located it, it was surrounded by firefighters aiming jets from extinguishers at it. "What's going on?" he asked the nearest firefighter when he approached.

"Is this your car, sir?" the man asked. Barton nodded. "It looks like it's been torched."

A police constable approached and asked, "Do you live in this street?" He went on with his notebook and pen at the ready.

"No," Barton replied. He was left with no other choice but to give the policeman his details, knowing that the truth would surface when they checked the registration of his car.

"If that's where you live, why have you parked your vehicle here?" The young constable asked, his pen scribbling on his pad at top speed.

"I ran out of fuel." This was the first thing that came to Barton's mind.

"Well, there seems to have been fuel in it," the fireman interrupted. "That's why it exploded."

Barton shrugged. "The engine stopped firing, and I thought it was fuel starvation." He watched as his charred vehicle was lifted onto a transporter and turned to head to where he had abandoned Donna's silver BMW. He waved a taxi down and regretted doing so, for when he arrived at the wasteland, he found the same scenario— firefighters and policemen standing around the charred remains of the car.

He stopped and about-turned; he didn't want to be questioned at this scene. When he approached the street, a youth was standing with a girl, watching the activity. Barton asked what was going on.

The girl volunteered and said, "A car has caught fire, and we saw them remove what looked like a body from the boot."

"Could you tell if it was a woman or a man?" he asked, trying not to appear too concerned.

They both shook their heads, and the youth said, "There were too many emergency crew members around it; we couldn't see for sure."

Barton walked away wondering whether he had been driving around in that BMW with a corpse in the boot, and the next question was, Whom did the body belong to? His first reaction was to snatch out his mobile, and he sighed with relief when he heard his father's voice and was assured that his mother was with him. When he finally got a taxi and got back into his house, he decided it was time to move, time to find another place to live. This house was getting too familiar. He knew that the club owner—and possibly the shooter— would have discovered where he lived.

Certainly the police now knew his address, and he must be on their wanted list. Whilst preparing a drink in his kitchen, Barton heard a loud crash from his front room. He instantly knew his window had been smashed in—a sound that was all too familiar to him—and didn't rush into investigate. Instead he dashed out the front door and was out on the street when the explosion came. His instinct had cut in, and he had resisted rushing to the other side of the street; experience told him that flying glass would blast out like water from a high-pressure hose.

From a distance, a voice was echoing strange words he couldn't understand, Barton opened his eyes, but all was black. He began to realise he could have been left blind from the explosion. Panic took over, and he needed to reach for his eyes, but a pair of hands caught his wrists and stopped him.

"It's okay, sir," a female voice said, still sounding a long way off. "You've had an accident, and we have bandaged your eyes; the doctor says your sight will come back when we remove the dressing in a few days."

He had no concept of what time or even what day it was; he could sense she was still close to him. "How long have I been in here?"

"You were admitted yesterday. Fortunately your injuries are superficial, and as soon as we get your wounds cleaned and your eyes examined, you should be able to be discharged." A moment later, he heard a door close and guessed he was alone. Being mildly claustrophobic, he wasn't coping too well, and it took all his willpower to stay calm. He remembered how simple it was to pretend to be a visitor, so anyone could come in here and he would have no idea who it could be. The more he dwelled on this, the more panic began building up and overwhelming him. He had to get out of here. His mind was racing ahead. He could feel he was in a hospital gown. *Where have they put my clothes? Could they be in a small cabinet next to my bed, or folded on a chair?* He had to find them.

Gently he prized the dressing up from his eyes. Something tugged at his eyelids like stitches and sent a sharp, stinging pain through them. He gave it a few more minutes for the pain to subside and tried again; this time the stinging wasn't so severe. He eased the dressing up until it was clear of his eyes, but his vision was pure white, with no shapes. Gradually the white became grey and dark silhouettes formed. He guessed it must be equipment or furniture.

"No! No," he heard the female voice ring out from his side. "You must keep the dressing on."

He felt cool, soft fingers take his hands away from his face and replace the padding over his eyes. "I need to get out of here," he pleaded.

"Why? What's the urgency?" A male voice said from a long way off.

"This is a police officer," the female voice explained. "He wants to ask you a few questions."

"Have you any idea what caused that explosion in your home, sir?" The male voice asked.

Barton shook his head.

"You must have known it was about to happen for you to get out on time?" the officer continued.

"I heard the widow smash and ran out the door to see who was responsible."

"Can I have your name, sir?"

Barton had established an alias he had used often; he had gone to the expense of getting false papers and always managed to pull it off. "Norman Brown," he replied.

"How long have you lived at that address?"

"Not long."

"What was your previous address?" Barton filled him in with what he could remember from the information on his false papers. He sighed when he heard the officer close his notebook. He then heard him thank the nurse, and his footsteps trailed away.

"You keep that dressing on your eye, Mr. Brown," the female voice scolded, and soon after he heard the door close. This time when he eased the dressing up, he could see colours and shapes. Although out of focus, he recognised what he was looking at. He swung his legs out of the bed and stood up, but he soon had to get back down when everything started spinning around.

Strong fingers dug into his shoulders and began to shake him. Barton swung out at this intrusion and heard a male voice telling him he was here to take the dressing off. "Although," the voice went on, "it looks as though you've tried to do that yourself."

Barton realised he must have dozed off. "What time is it? What day is it?" He asked, and he could feel the hands working at the dressing. The sudden daylight hit him like a camera flash. He shut his eyes, but the glow didn't go away. "What the hell's wrong with my sight?"

"It's okay, Mr. Brown," the voice replied. "Give it a few more hours, and things will gradually return to normal."

He was a despicable, sleazy-looking little man. Even Declan's skin crawled at the sight of him. But he got the job done and was cheap to hire. "So what have you got for me?" Declan asked.

Paddy Barnes grinned, exposing toothless gums. His eyes lit up as he dumped the package on the desk. "This should do the job."

Declan jumped back; his chair almost fell over backwards. "Bloody hell, Paddy, I hope that's safe!"

"Oh, it sure is. You have to press that little trigger; then you have ten seconds to get to fuck."

"You know where the guy lives," Declan said, feeling more relaxed. "When he gets home, give him time to relax before you lob that thing through his lounge window; that way you can be sure that's where he'll be."

The little Belfast man grinned again. "You can be sure of that. Nobody survives Paddy's bombs." He held out a dirty little hand. "That'll be fifty quid for each car and a hundred for the house—two hundred all in."

Declan watched the little creep gather up the notes and the device, dump them all into a plastic shopping bag, and leave without closing the office door. Badger almost knocked him over on his way in and slammed the door. Jabbing his thumb over his shoulder, Badger said, "What's he doing here, Boss?"

"Doing the job that everyone else has failed to do."

"If you don't mind me asking, Boss, what job would that be?"

"Putting an end to that bastard Barton."

"I thought you wanted to do that personally."

"I did, but time is running out. I don't want him messing about to fuck things up again. I've got another shipment coming in soon."

"Gives me the creeps every time he's around," Badger said, sitting down in front of the desk.

"Has all the equipment been set out in that new warehouse?"

"I've instructed Pinkie to supervise that lot of guys Crow has sent over. He knows what's required."

Declan got off his seat and headed for the door. "That little creep has managed to find out where

Barton lives," he said over his shoulder as he walked out.

Badger got up and followed him. Paddy was downing the last of his pint and waving to Declan as he left. "Be careful of that creep, Boss; he's a friend of no man. Would plant one of his bombs at the slightest offence or for the highest bidder."

"Don't worry; I know him. He'll get the job done and be drunk for a week. He's going to phone me when it's done, and soon after, he'll be done." He picked up his glass and headed back to the office, indicating for Badger to stay behind to keep an eye on things.

Badger was on the point of dozing off while watching the monitor when his mobile sounded. He jumped and snatched it from his pocket, and he immediately noticed Paddy's number.

"Did you get the job done?" Paddy assured him that the bomb had exploded in the front room as instructed, but the big guy had got out. "Was he injured in any way?" Declan shouted.

"He was shipped off in an ambulance."

Declan disconnected, tossed the phone on the desk, rushed to the door, and waved Badger in. "That big ape has survived; he's in hospital," he panted. "We need to find out which one they have taken him to and get in there and drag him out."

"What, right now?" Badger said.

Declan nodded. "Let's get moving. Get one of the boys to help when we find where they have taken him."

Badger grinned. "Are we going to do the wheelchair trick again?"

"We need to phone the hospitals, tell them we're relatives." Declan retrieved his mobile and was informed by all the hospitals that a Mr Barton hadn't been admitted. "He must be using a false name." Declan sighed and dropped his mobile back on the desk. "We'll just have to go round them all and look for him."

"That could take a while," Badger said, not looking happy about the idea.

"If you've a better idea?" Declan snapped. "We could go to the site and ask there. Somebody will have an idea where they have taken him."

Tom and Jean Barton were at the site, asking the officers what had happened to their son, and they were informed of the event. They were given the details on what hospital he had been taken to, and Jean in turn passed this information on to Pinkie, who was posing as a newspaper reporter.

Pinkie, with a wide grin, returned to Declan's silver four-by-four. "Got it, Boss, but couldn't find out what name he's using."

Convincing the girl at the reception that he was a reporter and wanted to interview the man who had been admitted following an explosion at his home was simply a matter of holding up his notebook. He admired her pretty features as she spoke to someone on the phone. After a few words, she turned to him. "A porter will show the way." Pinkie smiled and had begun to walk towards the seating area when he turned and asked, "Do you have a name for this man?"

She nodded and punched a few keys on her computer. "A Mr. Norman Brown."

Declan's face was a picture of joy when Pinkie waved at them from the door. Badger wasn't sharing his enthusiasm; he felt this was too easy. Side by side, they pushed through the glass doors and joined Pinkie. At the same moment, a porter arrived, nodded at them, and waved at them to follow.

They seemed to walk though endless corridors and made a multitude of left and right turns before arriving at the ward. Badger was lost; he couldn't remember how they had got to where they were.

But that wasn't his real worry; he knew this wasn't going to be as simple as the last time. This place was inundated with security cameras and staff members, most of them in various uniforms.

The porter opened the door to the room and let out a deep sigh. "Looks as though the patient has been discharged."

Leaving the three men standing in the corridor, he rushed to the nurses' station. They could do nothing but watch the man talking to a nurse in a heated conversation. "Now what?" Declan said, and he strode towards the nurse's station; the others followed.

The porter and the nurse turned as they approached. The nurse said, "It appears this patient has just walked out." She rushed past them into the room and stood at the bottom of the bed, staring in disbelief and waving her arms at the sheets on the floor and the hospital gown hung over the chair. "How could he have got past me?" she cried.

The porter answered that question. "The fire door—it should still be open. It can only be closed from the inside." Followed by the nurse and the three men, he ran out of the room and rushed towards the fire exit. He stopped a few feet away; he didn't need to go farther to know the door hadn't been tampered with.

They all gazed at the nurse, who shrugged and shook her head. "He didn't get past me."

"If you're sure of that," Declan said, "Then he has to be here somewhere."

Badger began searching the rooms, and the others all followed suit. When they finally met up at the nurses' station, he said, "He's a tricky bugger; he must have slipped out. Did you leave here for some reason, even only for a minute?"

"I had to go to the toilet," the nurse confessed, "but that's just behind my desk. With the amount of people working and visiting, somebody must have noticed a big man like that with a dressing on his head. We could check the security cameras, but that might take some time."

Declan signalled the two goons, and they rushed out, following the exit signs. It took them five minutes to get out to the parking area and found that the four-by-four's tyres were all flat. "Not again!" Declan shouted.

Pinkie was in a state of panic, prancing about kicking the wheels, while Badger stood back, secretly grinning.

Declan slammed his fist down on the roof of the vehicle. "When I get my hands on that bastard, I'll squeeze his eyes out and piss into the empty sockets!"

If he doesn't get to you first, Badger ruminated while calling the breakdown services on his mobile.

CHAPTER 23

Two elderly ladies giving the impression that they were out for a leisurely drive in their old car noticed the man limping along the roadside and stopped to offer him some help. Judd smiled as they both got out to help him into their white Citroën estate. "What's happened to your shoes?" they asked, putting tissues under his feet as he got sat in the rear.

The only reply he could offer was "I seem to have lost them." They glanced at each other, and it was the look in their eyes that made him decide to play along. "My wife and I were staying in that hotel; we had a falling out. She packed all our clothes, including my shoes, and left."

"You poor thing," the one who got into the front passenger's side said. "Go home, Marge; I've still got some of my Martin's clothes and footwear; I'm sure he was about the same foot size—nine, I think it was. It's so long since he passed away I've forgotten."

Between them they got him into the house and onto the sofa. Marge made tea while her friend wiped his feet and bathed them in a bowl of water and disinfectant. After gently drying them, she left and returned with several pairs of shoes and socks. No matter which ones she tried, he couldn't tolerate the pain.

"You'll have to rest up for a few days," said Marge, carrying in the tea tray, and her friend nodded willingly.

"I'm not sure I can stay that long," Judd said, taking a drink from the cup Madge handed him, "and I wouldn't want to impose on you."

"Well," Marge said, "you won't get far with your feet in that condition." She smiled at her companion. "What do you think, Hannah?"

"Don't worry, young man; you're not imposing on us, and we will enjoy your company,"

Hannah grinned and stood beside her friend. "Finish your tea, and we'll make up a bed for you in the spare room."

He watched the door close behind them and finished his drink. He then lay back with his head on the back of the sofa, gazing up at the ceiling, and slowly the light shade above his head started to spin. At first it turned slowly, but it soon gathered momentum until it was just a blur. Then, as if a black blanket had dropped on him, all went dark.

A severe cramp in his legs abruptly woke him. He tried to move them and found he had no power over them. He was aware of lying on his side, his face on cold slabs. His surroundings were out of focus; he could make out only a dark greyness that shimmered. He shouted, but his lips wouldn't move, and he could feel the tape pulling at his stubble. A creaking sound came from somewhere, and the greyness turned to a bright yellow. The female voice he recognised as being Hannah's said, "How is your feet today?"

Judd tried to move and discovered he had been bound from head to foot with duct tape, leaving only his nose and eyes free. Another voice came at him; this time it was Marge, saying, "He's a lovely subject, perfect for our purpose."

This time the struggling was driven by panic, but no matter how hard he tried, Judd couldn't move. He was still trying when he heard the door being closed. With no more energy, he resigned himself to the fate of what was about to happen. He'd spent all those years outwitting and out-fighting the best, only to be held hostage by two old ladies.

The cramps returned to his legs, and the attempt to stretch them failed. He couldn't even wiggle his toes. Perspiration from his forehead ran into his eyes, stinging them. Cold from the stone slabs chilled his body. That's when he realised he was naked beneath the tape. How could these two old ladies have managed to carry him to this place, which he had decided could be a cellar? How could they have managed to strip him? He remembered the difficulty they'd had getting him into their car and into the house. The realisation then struck him: *There has to be a third person.*

Thinking that person could be a man, panic kicked in, and he began to struggle. The door hinges creaked, and yellow light filled the room. Padded footsteps approached and stopped. For a moment, nothing stirred. He could hear breathing above his own gasping. It happened that he wanted to scream, but the tight gag restrained him.

The needle went deep into his buttocks, the point piercing his pelvis. Soon after, the door closed and the place returned to grey darkness. Above the cramps, he could still feel the piercing stab of that needle. Gradually the pains eased; he felt his whole body slump, his eyelids became heavy, and the darkness blanketed him.

The purring of an electric fan aroused him. He flicked his eyes open, and still the grey darkness surrounded him. A biting cold breeze filled the room, and horror struck him. Could this be a chiller he was locked in? He had witnessed the results of hypothermia on one of his victims. Frostbite had ensued, and all the extreme limbs turned black, and the death was a slow, painful end. A surge of panic struck again. This time when he wriggled, he discovered that his limbs were free and the tape was gone. At the first attempt to get up, his legs buckled under him. The second time, he supported himself with his back against the wall and slowly rose and stood there for a while, feeling the rush of blood to his limbs and the persistent stinging pains on the soles of his feet.

The purring stopped, the door creaked, and the room filled with the yellow light. A blast of welcoming heat hit his naked body. The two women stood in the opening. Marge had a shotgun in her hand aimed at him, and Hanna was at her side. They parted, and a bald man stepped between them. He grinned at Judd and came forward. "Do you have a name?"

Judd shook his head. "Fuck off." He pushed himself from the wall and attempted to rush at them, but his legs gave way.

On the floor, his back against the wall, he looked up at this man in green hospital garments who was armed with a syringe, bending towards him. Timing and distance never entered his head; it was a natural reaction that paid off. Both his feet contacted with the man's pelvis, sending him careering backwards into the two women.

The blast from the shotgun was deafening in the confined space. He felt the hot fluid splash onto his naked body but didn't take the time to see what it was. His attempt to roll to the side, away from the man staggering back towards him, failed, and he was once again pinned down. By the time he freed himself, the two women were standing over him, the gun a few inches from his forehead. Hanna gazed at his naked torso, turned, and vomited. Judd glanced down at his chest to see the man's entrails splattered over him. His reaction was to wipe it all away, but the gun jabbed into his head.

"Make another move and you'll be next," Marge snarled. Hanna, although not recovered, gripped Marge's arm and cried, "What have you done? This wasn't supposed to happen."

Marge shrugged her arm away. "Well, we've achieved what we wanted to do; now all we have to do is make it look like this idiot did it."

"How do you intend to do that?"

"A burglary gone wrong."

"The police are not going to believe that!" Hanna whimpered. "He's hardly fit to stand up, never mind shoot someone with a bloody shotgun."

"By the time they come, he'll be dancing and singing when I shoot him up with the cocaine mix that piece of shit has concocted," Marge said, nodding at the body on the floor.

They both glanced at the remains of the shot victim. This was all Judd needed—a split-second distraction. He snatched the barrel of the gun and tore it out of Marge's hand, at the same time kicking her legs from under her. She screamed in pain and fell against Hanna; they both stumbled back and tripped over the dead body. Judd got up on wobbly legs and staggered towards them, swinging the butt of the gun at their heads. Marge got the first blow and lay still, her eyes still staring at him in shock. Hanna tried to get up but was slipping on the blood from their victim. It sounded like a thin layer of ice breaking underfoot when the butt made contact on her skull. He hastily dropped the shotgun on top of the man's body; it was a weapon he had sworn never to use—too noisy and too messy.

He hobbled to the door, and it creaked as he closed it behind him. He turned the big iron key and heard the metallic mechanism clang into place. On hands and knees, he climbed up the stone stairway. At the top stood another door, this one much lighter, and it opened easily. A modern kitchen faced him; the bright tubular lights hurt his eyes. Shielding his eyes with a hand, he limped to the door at the opposite end of the room, lifting a large kitchen knife on his way and holding it ready should he be faced with another occupant.

A long corridor with closed doors on both sides faced him. The lights were dim here, and he made his way to the end using the wall for support. He found himself in front of a large window that looked out onto a field. This would be his escape route, but first a shower and some clothes. He felt as though he was never going to get to the last room. He had to be sure no one else was in the building. He had left all the doors open.

The last door led to a staircase to an upper floor. Again on hands and knees, he climbed, hoping to find a bathroom. His search was a success, and he took a quick soak in a bath of cold water, followed by a search of the bedrooms, looking for the one that the bald man had used, hoping to find some clothes. He remembered that this man was short and had a pot belly; this became obvious when he tried on the trousers. The legs were short, well above his ankles; the waist—he could have tucked a pillow down the front. The shirts and jackets hung loose, but Judd wasn't too perturbed by all this; he was glad to have something to cover his nakedness and get the hell out.

The window where he had planned his escape was stiff. He returned to the last room and found a heavy glass vase, which he hurtled through it, shattering the entire pane. Climbing over the sill gave him a great deal of pain in his legs and buttocks when he crawled through. When things don't go well, the slightest unexpected thing becomes a disaster.

Shards of broken glass lay on the gravel path beneath the window, the sharp edges pointing upwards. Taking all his weight on his hands when he fell, he received multiple stab wounds; one pointed piece went all the way through his right palm, exposing a good six inches of bloodstained glass. He struggled onto his feet and gazed in horror at the wounds on his hands and at the blade-shaped shard still stuck there.

This had to come out, but how? No way could he go to a hospital; too many questions would be asked that he didn't have answers to. Although the woman Hanna had cleaned his feet, they had removed the dressings with his clothes. The bald man's shoes were too small; all he had on his feet were socks. Trying to walk was a painful task, and he couldn't assist himself with his hands. It was a relief to get off the gravel path and onto the grass verge, but after a few yards that became almost unbearable. A rustic bench seat was a welcome sight, and he made his way towards it. It was wet, but that didn't bother him; he was pleased just to get off his aching feet. He studied his bloodied hands and worked the fingers on his left hand, but when he tried the right one, he screamed from the pain. Somehow that shard of glass had to be removed without causing further damage. In his line of work, he needed good, steady hands. There was only one person he could call on for help; but with no phone, how could he do that? Even if he could get one, how could he operate it with his hands in this condition?

He couldn't believe his own lack of observation, one of the things he prided himself on. At the corner of the building, he could see the tail end of the white Citroën estate. No matter how much pain this was going to cause, he would have to steel himself against it. As he hobbled towards the car, he prayed that it had been left open. Using the tips of the fingers on his left hand, he operated the door handle; in other circumstances, he would have grinned with the success when the door opened, but pain prevented that. He did, however, spare himself a smile when he noticed the ignition keys had been left in.

Driving with one hand and injured feet was no easy thing to do; his only hope was that he didn't have to make a sudden stop. He discovered that the old car drifted badly to the right and changing gears had to be done lightning fast; this caused excruciating pain in his foot. The steering wheel and the gear lever soon became stodgy with his blood.

Twenty miles per hour was as fast as he dared go; this earned him a lot of blasting horns from other road users on the motorway. He was glad to turn off the motorway, and he drifted onto the slipway, which ended on a badly repaired road. The potholes and bumps caused him to lose control a few times, but finally he came to the lane that led up to the house.

In his study at the rear of the house, Crow's attention was drawn to the monitor screen. The white estate car drove up to the front of his house and stopped. He didn't recognise the figure that struggled to get out yet felt this was no stranger. On his way to the door, he called Martin, who was sitting in the lounge, engrossed in a movie on television. "There's someone at the front of the house," he explained to the young man. "Just pulled up in a car and got out. Come with me to see what he wants."

The young detective opened the door, and the first thing his eyes fell on was the bloody shard of glass protruding out the back of Judd's hands. He threw the door open. "What's happened to you?"

Crow stepped out from behind him, and despite the colour change to his hair, he instantly recognised Judd. "Get something to wrap that up," he told the young man. "I'm not having his blood over my carpets."

"He needs to go to a hospital," Martin said.

"No hospital," Judd protested, backing away from the door.

"Just get something to wrap that up," Crow interrupted. "I'll make a few calls."

They left Judd standing at the door, and a few minutes later Martin came out with a wad of cotton wool and some towels. "You'll need to wrap it yourself. I'm frightened I might cause further damage."

After a time of cringing and screaming, Judd finally got the wound wrapped up so that the blood was being contained within the dressing. Martin led him into the kitchen and sat him at the table.

"Got it sorted," Crow said as he barged in. "I've got a friend in the medical profession; he's on his way. But it'll cost you."

Judd was in no condition to argue. He shook his head and nursed his injured hand.

The little man glanced at Martin. "Do you mind giving us a few moments?" Martin instantly left, closing the door. Crow opened it slightly to make sure the young man was out of hearing distance and then quietly closed it. "You won't be able to hold a rifle with your hands in that condition."

"There's more than one way to make a hit."

"Well, you'd better make it quick, or the contract is off."

"Don't worry; I'll get it done soon."

"What happened to get yourself into such a state?" Crow took the seat opposite and pointed to his injured hands.

"It's a long story; you don't want to hear it."

Crow nodded. "What I find hard to understand is that you succeeded with that undercover policewoman in that forest. You did a good job with that idiot Lumpy. You made the killing of Damston look like a child's prank, not to mention the two thugs in that old house. Yet you're having trouble with this old man?"

Judd stared into his eyes as if trying to come up with a feasible excuse. "That old man is living on his luck, and as you know, luck always runs out."

"Well, it had better run out soon; Randel is pushing me to dispose of him; he wants to return to this country but says he can't until we get rid of some people, this old man being the first."

It was on the point of Judd's tongue to ask why, but he held back because it was against his rules to. He didn't want to know his intended victim. He never got involved but just did the job and moved on. This way he could sleep at night; this way they weren't people, but just targets.

A soft knock came from the door, and Matin stuck his head in. "The medical person is here."

After a polite greeting, Crow left the medic to deal with Judd and headed to his secret room to watch the action on the monitor in multiscreen and to keep an eye on the young detective who had supposedly returned to his movie on the tele.

Martin hadn't returned to the lounge; he held back until the little man had gone upstairs. He heard a door softly close and returned to the kitchen. He needed to get a good look at this stranger with the injured hands, had to get a sample of his blood for DNA before this medic disposed of it all, for he had no doubt that this would be protocol for the dodgy medic.

CHAPTER 24

$\mathcal{B}$arton dumped his head dressing into a laundry tub as he followed the exit signs. His eyesight was still not 100 per cent, hence the reason he walked slowly. He didn't want to collide with other people who could remember the incident and identify him.

The ground was wet, as though it had just stopped raining. He had to step around a few puddles as he walked between vehicles in the car park. There in front of his eyes, although he had to get closer to be sure, was the four-by-four that belonged to the club owner. After a good look around, seeing that no one was paying him attention, he got to work on the tyres. In his rush to get out of the house, he had left his jacket with his wallet and mobile in the pockets. Now he stood watching the vehicle sinking lower as the air gushed out from the tyres, and he realised he had no money, nowhere to live, and only the clothes he had on. Sleeping rough was no problem; he had done it a few times. The problem was that he could get picked up and dumped in a cell for the night. The last thing he needed was to go anywhere near a police station. A glance at his reflection in the window of a car—with his long hair hanging loose, his stubble continuing to grow, and his clothes dirty and ragged, confirmed that he looked the part.

He didn't want to do it but had no other choice. The man looked drunk or under some influence as he came towards him on the footpath. Barton ducked behind the bushes, and when his victim staggered past, he sprang out at him.

The man let out a howl. Barton gagged him with one hand and with the other dragged him into the bushes. A few sharp punches and his victim lay silent. Barton crawled out of the bushes wearing a dry- cleaned set of clothes and in possession of some money, though not a lot, a debit card, which he hoped was contactless, and,most importantly, a mobile phone. Before he left, he made sure the man wasn't seriously injured but just out cold, mostly through the influence of booze or drugs.

It wasn't until he was in the B&B that he noticed the name on the card and smiled to himself. *Billy Bunter.* Barton handed the card over to a nervy, seedy little man behind the desk with eyes that flicked from side to side. Holding it in his scrawny little fingers, he scrutinised it and processed it on his electronic gadget. He then slapped a key on the desk, told Barton where the room was, and returned to his porno magazine.

Barton climbed the creaky stairs with pile-bare carpets. As he ascended, the smell from the toilets got stronger. By the time he reached the room, he was gagging. He found the door ajar and noticed a set of women's underpants under the unmade bed. The stench of cheap perfume accosted him, and he rushed to open the window, but it was jammed with years of multiple coats of paint. He closed the door, deciding that the cheap perfume was better than the smell from the toilet. A precarious-looking wooden chair next to the bed almost gave way under his weight. He fished out Billy Bunter's mobile and called the only person he knew could provide him with a job and money up front.

Though not being of a very excitable nature, Crow felt his heart jump a few beats when he recognised Barton's voice. "You sound as though you're in a bit of trouble, old boy."

"Trouble … that's an understatement. My house has been bombed, my car torched, I've been shot at, and I've nothing but the clothes I'm wearing—which, incidentally, I had to mug someone for."

"What do you want me to do?"

"I need a job and cash upfront."

"I offered you a job, but you didn't turn up for it."

"Because the owner of that club is after my blood." There must have followed about two minutes of silence, and Barton was beginning to think they had lost contact when the little man came back saying, "Call me back in an hour."

Crow cut the contact, looked at the monitor displaying the performance going on in the kitchen, and noticed Martin standing close behind the medic. He grinned and diverted his attention to the chessboard and reset the pieces in preparation for a fresh game. "Looks like the black knight has retreated to fight another day."

Barton lay on the bed fully clothed, looking up at the bare light bulb hanging from a long brown cable. His eyesight was still not back to normal, and the bulb appeared to be swinging back and forth. He jumped when Billy Bunter's mobile rang at his ear. He looked at the screen and saw the out-of-range number and knew it was Crow.

"Did you forget to call?" Crow asked.

"I must have dozed off." Barton said, swinging his legs out of the bed.

"We need to have a meet, old boy," Crow went on. "Do you remember that cafe where we first met? Be there at nine tomorrow morning."

Barton decided to give the toilets and washroom in the B&B a miss, and he rushed out the door. A glance down the street convinced him that no taxi driver would be on the hunt for a fare here. It was an area of total neglect by the council; most of the terraced houses were boarded up. Wheelie bins lay strewn and toppled on the pavements. If the clock on the church steeple at the end of the street was accurate, he had only ten minutes to get to that cafe.

Crow was drumming the long nails of his effeminate fingers on the table and constantly glancing at his watch when Barton walked in. "You're late," he complained, and he waved Barton into the seat across from him.

"Sorry; I couldn't get a cab. Had to come by a bus that stopped at every stop along the way."

"We can't talk here, so let's take a walk in the park," Crow said, getting to his feet.

The area was deserted, save for a few dog walkers. They came to a bench that was located out in the open so that anyone approaching could be spotted. Crow took out his handkerchief and wiped the seat before sitting. When Barton got settled, not too closeto him, Crow noticed and said, "I have a job for you. It involves that club owner. He joined our syndicate a few years ago. The agreement was that no member should be trading without the knowledge of the others, so that all would have an equal investment.

"Wasn't that the idea you had when you asked me to go there in the first place?" Barton said.

Crow appeared to ignore his comment and went on. "This club owner, Declan Craig, according to my informant, has been involved in bringing in illegal immigrants and earning a great deal of money on the side. He rents or buys old warehouses and furnishes them with bedding and other facilities to accommodate these people until they find permanent living quarters."

"I guessed that when I set that old factory on fire."

"That's part of the job I have for you—to find out where his next place is and destroy that one as well."

"What do you mean 'part of the job'?" Barton said, jerking his head back.

"One step at a time, old boy," the little man said, holding out a cautioning finger.

"So how do I find this other place?"

"You found the last one, so do the same with this one."

"That could take some time," Barton quickly interrupted. "And I need a car and cash."

"A car is no problem; I've anticipated you would need one, and it's been arranged. But for the cash, you can use what I gave you for the last job that you didn't do." Crow promptly stood up, dug his hand into his breast pocket, and handed Barton a piece of paper. "You pick up the vehicle there."

Barton remained seated and cursed at the little man as he marched his way to the park entrance. He took a mental note of the address on the piece of paper, tore it up, and followed Crow out of the park. He wasn't in time to see whether the little man got into the car, and Nevil waved as he drove past in the large black Range Rover. The rear windows were tinted, so he didn't know for sure whether Crow was in the vehicle—one of his cunning little tricks he had played in the past for security reasons. He would have another car following behind the one he got out of, and when the meeting was over, he would fake jumping into the one he had arrived in, and at the last minute jump into the following car.

It took Barton the best part of an hour to find the address, and he almost buckled at the knees when he was shown the vehicle. A tall, gangly young man handed him the keys with a broad grin and bounded back into his converted caravan-office. He climbed into what he reckoned was a 1950s Land Rover, ex-military, with a large petrol engine that drank fuel as though there was a gaping hole in the bottom of the tank. To make matters worse, it had been painted pink with yellow wheels. "This is going to attract so much attention," he grumbled. How in the hell's name am I going to follow that mob in this? He pushed the key into the ignition and remembered he also had to press a button to start it. Another point that struck his memory before attempting to get it going was whether this old vehicle had been converted from leaded fuel to unleaded. The engine fired at the slightest touch of the button and sounded noisy, with maladjusted tappets. This was what Barton had been expecting, and he cursed as he pulled out of the forecourt.

After a few yards of chugging along the road, he noticed that the fuel gauge was registering zero. *Has Billy Bunter had time to call his bank and cancel his card?* was the first thought that came to mind. At the last moment, he remembered that the fuel tanks were under the seats at the front. He could feel the assistant's eyes on him from the window as the pump started filling the huge tanks. This was going to cost well over a hundred quid, and the limit of a card was usually thirty on contactless. It took a good five minutes to fill both tanks, and a few other vehicles were queuing behind to get in. Barton signalled the female assistant that he was going to pull away from the pump to let the others in and come back and pay when he had done so. He got a thumbs up from her and a smile.

That would be the last she would wear that expression that day, as Barton drove out and sped his way down the main road with both tanks full.

A group of people were standing talking in the car park close to the Westerner's Club. They turned to look at the multicoloured Land Rover with awe. This was Barton's fear; he didn't need the attention. But it was too late to do anything about it now, and he jumped out, slamming the door. The parking area behind the club was empty. Barton thought this unusual, remembering that during his last visit at about this time, a few cars had been parked there.

He decided to risk taking a walk to the back and see what the rear door looked like in case he ever needed to break in. It was made of steel sheets with an iron barred gate against the front of it, secured with a huge padlock. *Little chance of getting in there in a hurry.* He noticed the security camera above the door and another high on the corner of the building. He cursed himself for his lack of perception; he should have known there would be cameras here.

At the entrance to the way into the club car park, Barton had noticed a large pothole; it was this that alerted him. He heard a vehicle hit it, and he headed for the only cover, behind some large green wheelie bins. It wasn't the four-by-four he was expecting. When the car pulled up next to the door, a thin little man got out. Barton recognised him as the barman who had served him that night. The man tapped on the metal door, and soon after, he reached his hand in between the bars of the gate. Whoever was inside must have handed out a key, and the little barman fumbled with the large padlock.

Barton decided it would be only a matter of minutes before the person who was inside looked at the security monitors and noticed him prowling about. At the sound of the metal doors closing, he began to make his way back to the street, trying to avoid the cameras. He had got halfway up the entrance road when the four-by- four swung in.

CHAPTER 25

Sleep was the last thing Declan wanted to think about. Pinkie dozed on the sofa, snorting and grunting as a result of the injury he'd got from the pipe Barton stabbed him with. This disturbed Declan's train of thought. "Give that fucker a kick," he ordered Badger.

The big man gladly complied.

Two hours it had taken the breakdown truck to arrive. They had huddled in the vehicle with the engine running to keep warm as they watched the torrential rain run down the windows. Declan had said when they got on the move, "Go back to my place; I've got some guns. Hunt this bastard down and be rid of him."

The kick was more powerful than Badger had intended it to be, and Pinkie let out a chilling howl and jumped up, his fists in fighting position. But the blow had struck him on his inner thigh, and he buckled over and landed back on the sofa whining and nursing his injury.

"Calm down!" Declan shouted. "You were making a hell of a noise; I couldn't think." Declan left the two men arguing and returned with a black metal case. He opened it on the floor in front of them, and they gasped at the contents. Bedded in black foam rubber were six handguns. "HK, mod. P9S, Heckler & Koch" was printed on the sides of the breeches.

"How did you get hold of that lot?" Pinkie managed to say through the pain in his thigh.

"That doesn't matter." Declan grinned. "Take one each; they have full magazines of nine rounds of nine-millimetre shells. I'll show you how to operate them."

Badger was a natural and soon picked up on how to handle the weapon. Pinkie was a lot slower, and Declan was about to give up on him when it all suddenly fell into place. "Don't put that loaded magazine in until you have to fire that thing," he warned, thinking of his own safety, "and make sure you point it in the right direction before you pull the bloody trigger."

In Badger's opinion, Pinkie didn't look too confident handling the weapon and agreed readily with his boss. "Maybe"—he cleared his throat—"he would me more useful staying behind to guard the vehicles to make sure the tyres don't get let down."

Unsure whether to take that as advise or just a nasty dig, Declan shook his head. "I don't plan to leave the car unattended, but to locate that bastard and shoot him on a drive past."

"An opportunity like that could take quite some time," Badger promptly replied.

"Not if we set a trap—set up a situation where he has no other choice but to comply."

"How do you intend to do that?"

"By grabbing his parents."

Badger shook his head and shrugged. "You tried that before, and it failed."

"That was because of those two clowns; this time we nab them ourselves."

"They'll be on their guard; you won't be able to do it at their home."

"I wasn't intending to," Declan said with a grin, closing the metal case after Badger choose a weapon, "we get someone to invite them out for a meal and a few drinks, slip a few pills into their glasses, and when they're out cold, we call the son."

Tucking the pistol in his belt at the back of his jeans, Badger asked, "Who do you know who is friendly enough with them for them to accept an invitation like that?"

"I don't know such a person, but we know a good con man who could soon get friendly with them."

It didn't take Badger long to realise who he was talking about. "I don't trust that little maggot."

"We don't need to trust him; he'll do what he's told for a price."

Pinkie followed them out of Declan's house, feeling put out at not being offered one of the guns. He climbed in the rear seat of the big vehicle and listened to them making plans on how to kill Barton to the point of where they should dispose his body. It was when they mentioned the name of the little Belfast man that Pinkie's nerves gave him a jolt. Like the rest of Declan's mob, he didn't feel safe around him; all it took was a slip of the tongue to offend Paddy, and boom, your house was a pile of rubble. Why Declan seemed to protect the little creep was beyond his understanding. All his mates had good reason to get rid of Paddy at one time or another; they had even got together to work out a plan, but Declan stepped in objecting. Badger had been the inspiration of the plan and wasn't too pleased and had let his feelings be known. "I've got plans for that little sleaze," Pinkie remembered Declan saying. "After that, you can all do what you like with him."

"Keep an eye out for any suspicious-looking vehicles following us," Declan said, disturbing the silence. "We don't want this new place getting burnt down." The old barracks had been lying empty for many years, and trees and shrubs had taken over. The buildings had been vandalised, all the windows had been smashed, and the walls were splattered with graffiti. The only building that had been preserved was the gym hall. Declan had spent a fortune on getting it ready for the next assignment of immigrants, who were due in a few hours.

"It won't be hard to find this place," Badger commented as they entered the double doors. "It's pretty close to the road. People living in those houses"—he nodded towards the high-rise buildings across the field—"will be able to see what's going on."

"That's why we have to operate in the dark," Declan said.

"A truck won't be hard to see or hear even at night."

Declan ignored his comments and turned on the lights; the interior resembled that of the previous building, with mattresses rolled up down both sides of the floor. "This will hold a few more than the last place. I've got ex-army single beds getting delivered today." He led the way to the bottom of the hall and opened a door that led them into a fitted kitchen with modern facilities. Next to it was a small bedsit, and beyond that a toilet and shower room.

"A problem I noticed," Badger continued. "A truck would have to reverse in; that would mean holding up the traffic on the road. A passing police patrol will want to know what is going on." They made their way to the double exit doors, and still he got no response.

"The truck driver should give me a call when he is about an hour away," Declan said as they got into the four-by-four "That will give us time to get back here and get organised."

Pinkie leaned forward. "Who's going to look after this place and the immigrants?"

"That's been sorted," Declan mumbled.

One of Paddy's downfalls was that he had a regular drinking pub. Declan knew when he would be there and where he always stood and what his drink would be.

The Fox Bar was as usual: dim lighting, smelly carpets with cigarette burns, and a strong odour of stale beer. Only the few regular customers accustomed to it would enter. Gabby was more than pleased to see him walk in with Badger. "Paddy in yet?" Declan asked.

Gabby turned and looked at the clock behind the bar. "Be here in a few minutes. Can I get you anything?"

Declan declined and sat at the nearest table. Badger remained standing at the bar; he knew that the moment Paddy spotted his boss, he would sit next to him in a flash. If the little Belfast man were a venomous snake, Badger would have had more respect for him, even a little sympathy. As it was, he regarded Paddy as one of the most evil and unpredictable parasites on the planet.

No sooner had the door closed than Paddy headed for Declan's table. He carried his toothless grin all the way, his small, close- together blue eyes showing surprise at both sides of his owl-beak- shaped nose. He held out a scrawny little hand that Declan ignored.

"What brings yourself to a place like this?" he asked as he got seated and leaned across the table.

Declan sat back a few inches, away from the odour from Paddy's breath. "I've a job for you."

Paddy grinned. "Would you be wanting to discuss it here or somewhere more private?"

Pushing a few ten-pound notes across the table, Declan stood up. "Be at my club at six tonight; come into the office. Be there on time, or I'll get someone else."

Paddy scooped up the money and saluted. "Have no fear; Paddy's always on time." He counted the notes while at the same time studying Declan heading for the door. He jumped when a big hand clamped on his shoulder, and he found himself looking into the deep- set brown eyes of the giant of a man glaring down at him.

"You be there," Badger growled, "or I'll ram my fist down your throat and pull your arse out your mouth the next time I see you."

"I've never had that done to me before" Paddy shouted after him as Badger headed for the door. "Might be quite a thrill!" He giggled and stuck up a two-fingered gesture at the big man after the door closed.

Declan was standing at the passenger's door of the vehicle as Badger opened the driver door. "Having words with Paddy?" he asked the big man as they climbed in.

"Just a few words of friendly advice."

"You need to be careful what you say to that piece of shit."

Badger fired up the vehicle. "Where are we heading?" he asked.

"The club," Declan said, and he jumped when Pinkie patted his shoulder. He had forgotten about leaving him in the car to guardit.

"I saw that little bastard slink in the door," Pinkie said. "He had a good look at this car; must have known it was yours." A big grin was dawn on his milky features.

Declan gave him a quick glance and then turned to Badger, "I don't like the sound of that; I think it would be wise to swap this over very soon." He turned to Pinkie. "You take this back to the house and swap it over; we'll wait for you in the club."

"It would be easier just to get rid of that little shit," Badger said, getting the four-by-four on the move.

"Not just yet." Pinkie pushed himself back on his seat and said, "I shit myself every time he's around."

With his arm pumped full of who knows what drugs, Judd lay still as the medic finished dressing his hand and sprayed some antibiotics onto the soles of his feet. Judd was pain-free for the time being. It was the young man standing close to him that became a concern. It was obvious he wasn't medically trained, so why was he here? The glances the medic gave the youngster made it seem he was asking the same question. It was when the young man offered to clear away the bloodied dressings that Judd got into a panic. With his good hand, he grabbed the medic's arm. "What's hedoing?"

The grey-haired medic lowered his head, looked over the rims of his glasses, and frowned. "Supposedly helping to clean up."

"Well, stop him." Judd struggled onto his feet. "Get that stained dressing off him and burn it."

The medic pushed him back down on the sofa, "You should stay off your feet for awhile."

Judd jumped up and limped out of the medic's reach and threw himself at the young man as he was about to open the door. But young Martin was too quick and managed to get out and slam the door in Judd's face.

From his room, Crow watched the performance on his monitor. He smiled and moved a pawn on his chessboard. "Not an important piece," he whispered to himself, "but playing a strong attacking position." He laughed as the medic pulled Judd back from the door, and his laughter got stronger as Judd elbowed the man in the face, knocking his glasses off.

The struggle lasted a few minutes, and Judd managed to break away and get out the door. The youngster had gone, and Judd hobbled as best he could along the passageway to the large front entrance. A chilly breeze whistled through the trees as he looked out into the darkness. The only sounds were from a nearby road. The white estate car was still where he had abandoned it, and the keys were still in it. He assumed the youngster must still be inside.

When he turned to go back in the open door, the medic and Crow were standing there.

"You shouldn't be walking about with your feet in that condition." The medic approached and gripped his arm. Crow was at his other side, supporting him, and together they steered in him back through the door. He was in too much pain to resist, and with only one hand, he couldn't fight back. Roughly they dragged him back into the lounge and pushed him down on the sofa. "I need you to get back to fitness and get that job done!" Crow shouted at him. By this time the medic had left and softly closed the door,

"I don't know when I'll be able to use a gun," Judd said.

"That's why you have to rest up and get back as quickly as possible."

"So where do I do all this resting up?"

"I know someone who has a few rooms for let; you can use one for a few days."

"I could go to my own place and rest up there."

Crow shook his head. "You need someone to look after you, help you stay off your feet, and let your hands heal."

The youngster stuck his head around the door, and Judd tried to jump up, but Crow managed to get a hand to his shoulder and restrain him. "What's he done with all that bloodied dressing?" Judd cried.

"I've bagged it and I'll burn it in the morning," young Martin replied, referring mostly to Crow.

Crow smiled at the young man and turned to Judd. "Was that what all the fuss was about?"

Judd sat back on the sofa, "I don't want any of that getting into the hands of the police and have them find my DNA on it."

"Don't let that worry you," Crow assured him. "I'll make sure it all gets burned." The conversation seemed to get the young man's undivided attention; Judd noticed his head jerking back and his demeanor stiffening. He noticed that Crow had also became aware of it. The little man turned to the youngster. "Go and see what that medic's doing."

Appearing disgruntled, Martin left, slamming the door behind him. But it was all an act; he had hidden enough of the soiled dressing for the lab to do the testing. The problem was how to conceal it, and how to get it out of the house and into the car without Crow detecting it when he got a lift to the railway station. All he ever carried was a small briefcase with a few papers inside. He had learned that the little man lived on his gut feelings and would see that something wasn't right. The medic was putting his coat on. Inside the front door, he handed Martin an envelope.

"Give that to Mr. Crow," he said, and he left.

The envelope hadn't been sealed. Martin smartly headed for the smaller lounge, got seated on the sofa, and read the contents. It was an account of all the drugs that had been used on the casualty and the time the medic had spent treating him. This was a dream come true to a young detective—evidence of an NHS medic moonlighting, treating criminal gangs with stolen drugs. Would this be enough, with the soiled dressing, to bring this organisation down? Maybe,

maybe not. He decided he needed more. He had to find out who this injured guy was and what was his connection to this cartel? He had overheard the name "Judd" mentioned as he approached the large lounge door, but that could be a code name or a short version of his real name.

Crow had left Judd on his own, stretched out on the sofa, and entered his secret room, where he soon found the video feed of Martin sitting reading a piece of paper he had pulled from an envelope. He watched him replace the paper and tuck the envelope into his hip pocket. He grinned to himself. "You won't be leaving with that, young man. Maybe the same envelope, but not the notes." A flick on the remote gave him a view of the large lounge. The shock of seeing that Judd was no longer on the sofa sent an icy chill through him. There could be only one conclusion as to his whereabouts; he was hunting down Martin.

Not taking the time to close the door behind him, Crow rushed to the small lounge and was in time to catch Judd about to enter, armed with a large kitchen knife. "You were told to rest your feet!" he cried. "And what do you intend doing with that?" Crow pointed to the knife.

Startled, Judd swung round, striking his bandaged hand on the wall. He groaned in pain and dropped the knife from his other hand. He stooped over to recover it but was too slow and watched as a highly polished shoe kicked it away, out of his reach.

"I need to see for myself that those soiled dressing are burned," he moaned.

Crow bent down and picked up the knife. "With this?"

"I need to make sure *all* the dressings are in that bag."

The little man gripped Judd's arm and steered him back to the lounge. "I told you I would make sure of that."

Judd resisted a moment. "I don't like the look of that young guy; he has that arrogant look of an informer."

"If he was, I think I would have rumbled him by now."

Judd wasn't convinced, he had long since learned not to trust this little man any farther than the length of his nose. He eased himself back onto the sofa; it felt good to be off his feet. "I would still like to check the contents of that bag. I've evaded getting caught by being careful, and I'm not about to change that now."

Crow stepped back, holding up his arms. "We can do that first thing in the morning; then we shall arrange that place for you to rest up for a few days."

His independence was his survival; he made his own rules. He didn't like this little man making plans for him. "I need to go to my own place and rest up," Judd persisted.

Shaking his head, Crow said, "I need to get you back on your feet in a day or so. That won't happen if you have no one to look after you."

Holding up his injured hand, Judd complained, "This'll take more than a day or so."

"You might not need that hand to do the job," Crow grinned as he headed out of the lounge. "I've heard of your other methods," he said, closing the door. He realised he had left the door to his secret spy room open and quickly made his way there. The moment he entered, he knew someone had been there. Even for a rush out, he would never leave his monitors on. Whoever had been in here must have darted into the large lounge and decided he had no time to switch them off. He had no doubts who this person was; the only other person was Nevil, the driver, and he was confident that the tall black man wouldn't prowl about his house; he would have no reason to. Seated on his padded chair, he studied the chess game. A second later, he made the move, grinned, and stood up. *Now let the fun begin*, he mused, and he turned off his monitors and locked the door. He signalled to Nevil using a buzzer that had been used in the past to call the servants, and the tall man was at his side in moments.

They both searched the house and failed to find the young man. Outside, they discovered that the car Judd had abandoned at the front door was gone.

Judd heard the shuffling going on and slowly got off the sofa, listened again at the lounge door, heard them going out, and, inch by inch, eased his way into the hallway. Up ahead the front entrance lay open; he made his way towards it. He instantly guessed what the problem was when he heard the tall black man ask Crow whether he had any clue where Martin had gone. "Heading back to his job in London; we can't let him get there," came Crow's reply with an edge to it.

Judd had to hobble back to the lounge when he heard them return from the front door, but he managed to hear the little man's reply. "What is his job in London?" he heard the tall driver ask, and he just managed to get back onto the sofa as the door opened. With his eyes closed, pretending to be asleep, he felt a hand shake his shoulder.

Crow's face was a few inches from his. He tried to edge back, but the face came closer. "What's wrong?" he said.

"That car you drove in here—can you remember the reg number?"

Judd shook his head. "I nicked it from two old ladies."

"That youngster has just run off with it," Nevil the driver said from behind Crow.

With a wide grin, Judd said, "He won't get far with it; I just got here running on fumes."

The words were hardly out of his mouth when the little man turned and charged out of the room, the tall driver at his heels. Judd was too slow and in too much pain, and by the time he reached the front door, the Range Rover was chasing down the avenue.

A painful search around the grounds revealed that the garage doors were down and locked, and no other vehicles were parked on the drive; Judd could do nothing but return to the lounge and hope they caught that youngster.

Martin put up a good fight, but Nevil was too large and strong. He had only got to the end of avenue when the vehicle spluttered to a halt. He made a few attempts to restart the engine, got out and grabbed the bags and the bloody dressing, and made a run for the main road. But he had wasted too much time, and the big black hands grabbed the back of his neck. He struggled and landed a few punches, but it was like an egg against a wall, and he felt himself being toppled to the ground, and blackness enveloped him.

Nevil dragged the young man's body back up the avenue while Crow followed behind them in the vehicle.

"Take him down to the cellar," Crow instructed when they got back into the house. "Tie him up and gag him; then come and help me with Judd."

CHAPTER 26

There was no place to hide; the large black four-by-four was only a few feet away from him when it pulled to a sudden halt. Barton wasn't sure whether he was surprised or shocked to see Nevil behind the wheel, but he was relieved that it wasn't the big man who drove Declan's vehicle.

The rear passenger's door opened and Crow stepped out. "I'm not surprised to see you here," Crow said, grinning as he approached.

"I can't say the same about you."

"I have a little business to discuss with the owner. I see he's not here yet. If I were you, old son, I'd make myself scarce."

Barton made no argument and bolted to the end of the lane. When he reached the pink Land Rover, he noticed that a few pedestrians were paying quite a bit of attention to it and decided to walk on past. Most of these people wouldn't forget the man with the badly fitted clothes jumping into an oddly painted vehicle—a vehicle the police would have been informed about after his performance at the filling station. He wondered whether he had overdone it with Billy Bunter, for his debit card hadn't been cancelled. There wasn't a lot of cash in the account, and Barton withdrew it all. It was enough, he decided, to buy an old banger of a car, just to last a fewdays.

It took him over half an hour's haggling with the constantly smoking owner of the clapped-out BMW. Barton was doubtful it would last a few days by the sound of the engine.

"It has a nine-month MOT," The dealer said, lighting another cigarette. "A good little runner. The last owner was an old lady."

Barton drove out of the yard, noticing a cloud of black smoke in his wake. The fuel gauge registered zero, and he was fortunate a filling station was just a few yards away. When he went to pay for the petrol, the guy behind the till grinned.

"I see Slicker has finally sold that piece of shit." He nodded towards the B.M.W.

As Barton drove on, the black smoke continued behind him; he could hardly see vehicles following. He dared not put his foot down in case the engine cut out or it belched out more smoke. The last thing Barton wanted to see just happened to be waiting to turn out from a side street a few yards ahead—a patrol car. He didn't need to glance in the mirror to know they would be after him. He made a quick swerve into a narrow lane, almost side-swiping the wall.

Ahead was a succession of large green garbage bins. He jumped on the brakes, but they were ineffective. All he could do was brace himself for the impact. Luckily the bins were empty, and they gave way under the impact. He squeezed himself out at the same moment the police car rammed into the rear of the BMW.

The patrol vehicle had got jammed in the narrowest part of the lane, and the policemen couldn't open the doors wide enough to get out. Barton grinned, gave them a wave, and ran along a footpath hidden behind the bins. He ignored their shouts and continued onto another side street, where a bunch of black youths were standing smoking. "The coppers are coming!" he shouted on his way past them.

They soon caught up with him, and they ran into a busy shopping mall and soon separated. Or that was what he thought until he stopped and one of the youths gripped his arm. "What's your game, man?" the youth asked between gasps.

Barton grinned and pulled his arm free. "No game, I just don't like coppers." He continued walking and mingling with shoppers. He sensed that the young man was following close behind and picked up his pace. When he reached the end of the shopping mall, he stopped and turned around; the youth almost collided into him. "What's your game?" he repeated, gripping the young man's jacket front.

Stepping back and freeing himself from the big man's grip, the youth said, "I recognise you, man; I've got your pic on my phone. My sister sent it to me. You were with her when she got killed in that crash up in Scotland."

The vision of July hit him like a sledgehammer. He could see her getting dressed that morning; her perfect body had turned him on even after a night of lovemaking. "There must be some mistake," he said.

The youth shook his head." No way, man." He fished his mobile from his jeans pocket, fiddled with it, and then held it up to Barton's face. "That's you, man." Barton glanced at the photo.

"I didn't know she had a brother … didn't know her that long."

"She worked in that club. The owner had some kind of control over her and other girls. She wanted to get away but needed help to do that. She said you helped her."

"The owner must have been supplying them with drugs and booze," Barton replied, walking away.

"July wasn't really into drugs, not in an addictive way. She tried them a few times, but never enough to become addicted," the youngster said, pacing behind.

Again Barton stopped, and he looked down into the youth's brown eyes. "What is it you want from me?"

"I want you to help me get my hands on that club owner." Shaking his head, Barton continued walking. "He's got an army of goons protecting him at all times."

"That's why I need your help, man."

"I'm not just talking muscle; they are all gunned up." He held his mobile up at Barton. "Is that the owner of that club?"

Without stopping, Barton looked at Declan's photo and nodded. At that moment, four black youths stepped out from behind a building, blocking Barton's path. He looked at the youngster at his side. "What's going down?"

"These are my mates; we want you to get us into that club."

Barton shook his head. "You're out of your depth; these guys are the real deal—I'm talking shooters.

Pros. They will blow you all away. Me with you … I'm not what you would call on friendly terms with that guy. He has cameras all over that place. The moment I'm spotted, they'll jump on us like flies on shit." He edged his way past, leaving them in a heated debate. After a few yards, they chased after him and again surrounded him. "Look, man," the tallest of the bunch said with a cigarette hanging from his mouth, "This guy held one of our members against her will, tried to turn her into a druggie so she would whore herself …"

"What do you mean, one of your members?" Barton cut in.

"Just a little gang of friends." This time it was the youngster who spoke.

"I strongly advise you not to go near that club," Barton said. "I could give you his home address, but you can be sure that will be secured—but maybe not as much as the club."

A few moments of acrimony went on as they grouped together. The youngster broke away and asked, "Could you take us there?"

"You need to get transport; it's out in the sticks and a few miles from here."

"Not a problem," the tall smoker cut in with a wide grin, and he pranced over, glided past Barton, and disappeared into a narrow passage.

"He'll be back in a moment," the young man said with a grin. No sooner had the words left the youth's mouth than an old rattling Transit van came up the lane and stopped a few feet away. With a cigarette dangling from his lips, the slim figure jumped out and waved a hand at the vehicle. "Sorted!" he cried.

Barton had to grin. Shaking his head, he said, "That's going to look suspicious driving along that respectable area. The noise of it will bring the residents to their windows, and the next thing you know, a squad of police cars will be pulling you in."

The youngster interrupted. "We could park it a distance away and walk the rest."

Barton had been detailed to drive; he felt it was the least he could do for July. The youngster was beside him in the passenger's seat, and the rest in the rear. The interior had been boxed in, so he had no idea how many youths had filed in before he was ordered to drive. He guessed most of them had been inside before the van arrived; he could feel by the way the vehicle reacted that a lot of bodies were in the back.

The parking place where Barton pulled into was, in his opinion, too close to the target house, but he could find no other suitable places. He gave the youngster instructions on how to get to the building, and the young man jumped out and opened the rear doors, and the gang bounded out.

"Keep this thing ticking over," the tall smoker said, knocking on the side window, "in case we need to make a quick run for it."

Barton grinned at the tall, thin smoker climbing over the hedge to join the others. He heard them make their way through the thick shrubs like a herd of pigs stampeding through a supermarket. Soon they were out of his sight in the darkness of the moonless night. As he had been instructed, Barton let the rattly old engine tick over. Time seemed to drag. He felt as though he sat listening for their return for hours, but in truth only fifteen minutes had elapsed when a blast and fireball lit up the night sky and almost lifted the van off its wheels.

Barton could see the windscreen flying towards him, could feel his face being ripped by flying particles of glass. He found himself still sitting in the seat, but he had been blown through the wooden panelling into the back. Later he realised how lucky he had been that the panelling was made from thin plywood. The first thought that came to him was to get out of this situation. That blast must have been reported, and emergency services would be on their way.

What had happened to the gang of youths was the least of his concerns. Ironically, when he managed to get out the rear doors, he heard the old engine still ticking over, and it continued doing so as he reached the main road.

His eyes were still not 100 per cent after the blast at his house; now he had the problem of his blood running into them. He stumbled along the road, listening to a chorus of car horns, and the slamming of brakes, and tyres screaming on the road surface. He had to get off this road before a police car turned up and dragged him into it. On both sides, high, dense hedges cast dark shadows that seemed to reach the sky when the beam from his headlights hit them. Barton realised he hadn't the will or energy to force his way through this barrier and decided to rest up in the grass verge and, he hoped, remain out of sight until the traffic quietened down, before moving on.

The last person Declan wanted to see in his club was standing leaning against the bar, talking to a tall black man. He rewound the tape to see how Crow had entered. It hadn't been by the front door. *Must have come in the bloody back door. Who the bloody hell let him in?* He slapped his hand on the desk; this got Badger's attention.

"What's wrong, Boss?" the big man said as he sprang up from his chair, almost spilling his coffee.

Declan returned the recorder to the present and pointed to the two figures standing at the bar. "That's what's wrong."

The instant Badger recognised the little man, he said, "Trouble."

Declan stood up. "Only one way to find out." Side by side they stood at the bar, looking down at the dapper little man. "What brings you to my humble little establishment?" Declan asked. Like boxers at the start of a championship fight, Badger and Nevil glared into each other's eyes, only a few inches apart.

Crow grimaced at the two and then turned and smiled at Declan. "I need a small favour."

Instantly Declan got on the defensive and took a step back,knowing what Crow's small favours could lead to. "What kind of small favour?"

Crow's grin widened, and he held up both his hands. "Nothing too dangerous or expensive. I've got someone who needs a place to bed up for a few nights; he's injured and needs nursing."

"Well, I don't have a spare room or a nurse."

"I'm sure you can find a bed for him. He's willing to pay. Any one of your girls could look after him; just make sure he doesn't injure himself further. All they have to do is bring him food and generally help him with his toilet—"

"And make sure he doesn't bugger off," Declan interrupted.

It was Crow's turn to step back. "Nothing like that. He's not a hostage. I want him back in a few days, fit to do a job."

Declan fought the urge to ask a lot of questions, knowing that it would be dangerous to do so, but he needed to know who this person was. "Could you give me a clue as to who and what this injured person is?"

"As I have said, nothing too expensive or dangerous; that's all you need to know."

"When do I expect this person? I'll need some time to get all this arranged."

Crow took another step backwards and turned towards the main door. "That's not what I've been informed. According to my information, you're very good at accommodating people."

Declan was struck dumb and could only stare open-mouthed at the little man as he and his large black bodyguard left.

"What was all that about?" Badger asked, shaking his head and drumming his fingers on the bar top.

"That little bastard knows about the immigrants; we've got an informant."

Badger interrupted him. "Don't forget about that guy Barton; he's been out there and has seen what was going on."

A broad grin dawned across Declan's face. "You're right, and that little man sent him to me to give him a job. So they know each other. We need to get Paddy to move quicker and get a grip on Barton's patents." He dug into his pocket for his mobile, but it started ringing before he got a hand to it. He snatched it to his ear. "What?" he shouted into it. "When?" He slapped the phone down on the bar top and gazed at Badger, his eyes wide open and his lips trembling. "My other car has just been blown up. My house is on fire; the emergency services are all there."

"That little creep Paddy?" Badger asked.

Declan shook his head. "I'm his meal ticket; he's not so stupid as to do something like that."

"Nothing would surprise me with that shitbag."

"We need to get out there!" Declan shouted as he rushed for the back entrance. "Don't want the coppers coming here asking questions."

On the drive to his house, Declan had visions of the worst scenario of the damage that could be possible. But even that was nothing in comparison with what faced him. His home was a blackened shell. He waded in ankle-deep water from fire hoses and burst pipes. His garden and courtyard were crawling with firefighters, ambulance crews, and policemen. The acrid stench of burnt material sent him into a fit of coughing he couldn't control, and a paramedic rushed over and handed him a mask. He noticed that Badger already had one on.

The worst was yet to come when two police officers and a fire chief led him to the back of his house, where six burnt bodies lay on the back lawn. "I understand this is a horrible shock to you, sir, but we need to know if you can identify any of these bodies?" one of the officers asked, leading him by the arm and flashing his torchlight at the nearest one.

Declan stared at the long, thin body close to his feet and slowly shook his head. The youth's black features were miraculously intact. This wasn't so with the rest of the bodies; Declan could only shake his head and step away from the odour of burnt flesh.

"Have you any idea what they would have been doing here?" the same voice asked.

"Breaking in is all I can think of," Declan replied in a voice that seemed distant.

A tall figure stepped into his field of vision, silhouetted by the vehicle lights behind. "It's unusual for a group of six or more to do a break-in. Normally one or two—three at the most, in my experience." The figure came closer. "Do you have any idea what they might have been after?"

Declan shrugged his shoulders and shook his head.

"According to the fire chief," the detective went on, "there was an explosion. He said some of the neighbours were almost blown out of their chairs. Another had a window shattered. And as you are aware, the closest house is about fifty yards from here. That must have been a powerful explosion. Have you any idea what could have caused it?" He shook his head when all he got was the same reaction as before. "Give your details to the constable; I'll be wanting a few words with you in the morning, so get to the station early." As the tall detective walked away, Declan sighed in relief, but the feeling didn't last long, as he noticed two uniformed constables step in front of tall figure. He watched as quite a few words were exchanged. They glanced in Declan's direction, and finally they approached him.

"An old Ford Transit van has been found," the detective said, "just the other side of your garden hedge. It too has been damaged. Do you know anything about that?"

Shaking his head again, Declan said, "Maybe these guys came in it … abandoned it for the insurance and decided to escape through my back garden. It's a farm track into the fields—an ideal place to hide a van."

"We'll talk about it in the morning when you come in." The detective flicked up his arm glanced at his watch. "Be there by nine o' clock."

CHAPTER 27

The dampness and cold were beginning to creep into his bones, but the years of training in the special forces had taught him to ignore this discomfort. He knew to stay low and still, as it's movement that gives one away; movement attracts the eye even in the dark. But here that didn't last long, as vehicle headlights flashed in his eyes every few seconds. If any driver did see him lying at the side of the road, they ignored him. Although this was a country road, the traffic was relentless.

Barton could feel the cramps in his legs and arms and knew he would have to make a move soon. Painfully he eased himself onto his knees but had to dive back down on his stomach when the blue flashing lights of the fire services screamed past; he counted three in all. Soon after came a fleet of police cars, and then a few ambulances. *Bloody hell, this is worse than*

I thought. When the pandemonium quietened down, he climbed to his feet. *What the hell have those kids done?* He wrangled with his thoughts as he stumbled along the grass verge, trying to avoid being caught in the beams of headlights.

It wasn't a car's headlights that discovered him; this light came from above, and he could hear the constant throb of a helicopter engine hovering over him. Barton knew it would be useless trying to run or hide, as they would be equipped with heat-seeking devices. He decided to brave it and pretend to be thumbing a lift. Wearing these badly fitting dirty clothes, he would look like a bum trying to get a free ride.

A big vehicle's brake lights came on, and the indicators flashed. It pulled into the grass verge. The front passenger's door flew open, as did the rear offside. The two dark figures rushed at him. The stiffness in his limbs from lying on the wet ground slowed him, and they grabbed an arm each and fought him into the rear seat.

"What the fuck's going on?" Barton shouted.

The two figures struggled to get in but barely managed to get the doors closed before the vehicle shot away at such force that Barton's head struck the headrest. In the lights from the oncoming traffic,

Barton noticed the man sitting beside him wiping his nose with a tissue that was drenched in blood. He remembered landing a few wild punches and quietly grinned to himself. "What's going on?" he shouted again. "I'm only trying to get a lift home." The only response he got was the bleeder snorting to clear his air passage.

In silence, the drive went on for miles. He knew it was a waste of time trying to get answers, so he decided to whistle an unmelodic tune that would last and, he hoped, get on one of their nerves. About an hour later, he had still received no response. The tune was beginning to annoy him and his whistle was beginning to dry up when the vehicle turned off the motorway.

They passed through a village and turned into a rough track. A few yards along, the driver turned off the lights. The sheer blackness enveloped them, the track became bumpy, and Barton banged his head off the roof, as did the man sitting beside him, but still no sound came from them. The vehicle made a sudden stop, and the man in the front passenger's seat sprang out and jerked the door open. Barton lunged at him, but the goon sitting next to him pushed him out and followed through, jumping on him and grabbing him in a stranglehold from behind. His mate soon joined in the struggle, and Barton felt himself being dragged backwards, his heels rubbing on the gravel surface. This continued for a few yards before he was pinned to the ground and another pair of hands pushed a bag over his head. This other goon, Barton guessed, must be the driver. They struggled him over onto his front, and he felt his hands being secured with cable ties. Painfully he got jerked to his feet and pushed forward and against a solid wall—a building, Barton assumed.

A creaking door opened. Strong hands pushed him forward, and he tripped. With his hands secured, there was no way of recovering his balance, and face first he hit the stone floor. He heard the hinges protesting again and a securing bolt being pushed home. His attackers had made one big mistake by failing to secure his legs and feet. How to get onto them, could be a problem for him, though, as he did not know what this place was they had thrown him into. It could be a small stone cubicle, like a cellar, or a large barn or something of that nature. To get onto his feet, he decided, he would need something to jam his back against. From there he could push himself up. It took a lot of struggling to get from face down onto his side, but after numerous attempts, he succeeded. By digging his heels against the stone floor, he got himself moving and was fortunate that after a few pushes he came against what he surmised was a brick wall.

Getting onto his feet proved to be painful on his shoulders, but it didn't take long. His next move was to get rid of the black plastic bag from his head. If successful, the goal was then to find a sharp corner to cut the cable ties from his wrists. Before he made the attempt to shake off the bag, the door opened with a noisy grind from the hinges.

"Back to your old tricks," the familiar voice said.

Barton couldn't place it at that moment, but the smell from the cigar smoke soon gave it away. "Randel. I thought you had fled abroad somewhere?" He heard footsteps approach, and the bag was ripped from his head. It took only a moment for his eyes to adjust to the dim light, and his first sight was of the big man sitting close to the doorway on his wheelchair.

"I could have had you bumped off a long time ago," Randel said, blowing smoke in Barton's direction. "Now I'm glad I didn't."

Barton made to walk towards him until a set of hands gripped his arms. "Can I ask why?"

"In due course," Randel chortled, and he swung his chair around and steered his way back through the door, followed by the two goons that had grabbed Barton from the roadside. The door was once again slammed and bolted. He was relieved that the bag had been removed and he could now see what his surroundings consisted of. But his relief was short-lived when the dim light from high in the rafters was switched off.

One thing that he had noticed was that the bricks supporting the door frame had sharp edges to their corners. He wondered whether these would be sharp enough to cut the cable ties.

It was no simple task locating the edge in the dark. When he finally succeeded, on his first attempt he slashed his hand and soon felt the blood running down his fingers. He was fearful that his blood would lubricate the cutting edge, making it more difficult to saw through the plastic strip.

It took a long time and much effort to finally get his hands free, and as he was massaging his wrists, a thin blade of light appeared from under the door. He jumped into the nearest corner with his hands behind his back, making them appear to be still secured. When the door creaked open and the light shone across the stone floor, he noticed the cut cable ties lying where they had fallen.

Barton had no idea how many goons were about to walk in; all he could do was charge at them before they noticed the cut cable ties on the floor.

Having put so much effort into his attack, he failed to stop and stumbled onto the wheelchair, knocking it over, sending the big man crashing onto the stone floor. Barton landed softly on top of Randel, who screamed like an injured animal. The goons charged to the rescue, and they, too, stumbled and fell on top of Barton and the big man. A free-for-all struggle took place, with feet and fists flying in all directions.

"Get off me, you bastards," the big man screamed.

After a few more moments of wrestling and gouging, Barton felt himself being dragged by the neck and finished on the floor with heavy bodies holding him down. Because of the angle his head was being held at, he could see Randel being helped up and into the wheelchair.

After wiping the hot cigar ash from his clothing, he steered the chair over, looked down at Barton, and shouted, "you haven't changed, Barton! Always the idiot, not knowing when to give up when the odds are against you!"

Barton felt himself being jostled onto his feet and pushed face first against the wall as fresh ties were fastened to his wrists behind his back.

"Don't injure him too much!" he heard the big man shout. "I need him for a job."

Hands gripped him by his upper arm, and he was being pushed towards the open door, where he stumbled and fell into a small room where he tripped over a metal chair and landed head first on the floor. The hands gripped him again, lifted him, and forced him onto the chair. The light in this room was brighter, coming from a tubular bulb on the ceiling. Barton took it in turn to study the faces of the four goons that stood around him. He thought he recognised one of them. At that moment he wasn't sure, but he was confident that it would dawn on him who this person was later.

The wheelchair entered, and Randel was holding a pistol in his fat, dumpy hand, pointing it at Barton's head. "I need you for a job," he snarled, "but if I have any more trouble from you, I won't hesitate to shoot you."

It was on the point of Barton's tongue to tell him to fuck off, but he remembered that this fat man always did what he said he would do.

He spat blood and grit from his mouth. "What job?"

Randel held up his other hand. "A job I'm sure you'll be glad to do; and you will be well rewarded if you succeed."

"And if I don't?"

"You're a dead man." Randel grinned, his fleshy cheeks almost forcing his small, deep-set blue eyes to close. The pistol got jabbed closer, now an inch from Barton's nose.

"I get the message," Barton said, and as he tried to move away from the barrel of the weapon, a hand gripped the back of his neck. Strong fingers dug into his flesh, holding his head in place.

"In my absence," Randel said, "a little maggot has been trying to muscle into my business. Rumour has it that you were responsible for burning down this piece of shit's warehouse."

Cringing at the pain at the back of his neck, Barton made an unexpected twist and felt the fingers relax, "You know what rumours are," he grunted, twisting his head from side to side. "Ninety per cent lies."

Randel's grin faded, and he moved the weapon back. "Not this one; that's the job I have you for. This little maggot has gotten himself another place. I want you to destroy it—and the maggot with it."

Eyeing the goons standing around him, and still breathing heavily from the struggle, Barton replied, "You have plenty of thugs to do that job for you."

The big man shook his head, the flesh on his jaws and neck wobbling in the opposite direction. "I don't want a connection. If the rest of the syndicate discovers that it was my boys, it could cause complications."

It was Barton's turn to shake his head. "Why pick me for the job?"

Randel withdrew the weapon and rested it on his lap. He wheeled his chair back, stopped at the door frame, and said, "You were friendly with a whore named Wilma. I got it on good authority that this little shit put a bullet in her head. I also know he is out for your blood for the job you did on his warehouse. If you succeed, I can get the contract that is ongoing on your father called off. If you don't, well … you know what the end results will be; these shooters never give up."

The tall white-haired man appeared in Barton's mind's eye. He had guessed from the first time his father had complained about being followed by this guy that it could be a hit. But why? What had his father done to deserve this? Nevertheless, it sent a chill through him at the confirmation of it. He made to take a step towards the big man but was soon restrained by the goons. Shrugging free, he said, "You call off that contract, and I'll do my best."

Randel shook his head and continued to reverse his chair out the door. "You do the job first." A dark figure appeared behind him, took hold of the handles, turned the wheelchair around, and pushed him along the passageway and disappeared into the darkness. Simultaneously, the remaining goons jumped on him, and after a brief struggle, they pinned him on the floor. Above the agony at the way they had his body twisted, he felt a needle prick on the back of his neck. The heavy bodies trapping him down gradually moved away. His remaining energy and will made him want to battle on, but first he needed to rest and wanted to sleep. His eyelids were heavy,as if made from lead. Visions in his head started to spin; the faces of all the people he had known were in a vortex that picked up speed until he could no longer distinguish their features.

CHAPTER 28

"If you're sure that it wasn't Paddy who bombed your house," Badger said, steering the four-by-four onto the high street, disturbing Declan's thoughts, "all I can suggest is that it must have been that big guy, Barton."

Declan's thoughts were on the same line as he watched the closed-up shops, lamp posts, and pedestrians drift past his passenger's-side window. "You read my thoughts again; we should have killed that bastard when we had the chance."

"Where are we going to kip tonight?" Badger asked as he stopped the four-by-four at a traffic light.

"We won't be sleeping tonight; we're on the hunt for that bastard Barton. I'll phone Paddy, see if he's had any communication with the parents."

At the change of the traffic lights, Badger looked at him and asked, "Did you recognise any of those black youths?" He slammed the vehicle into gear, and it jumped forward.

"There wasn't much left of them to recognise, except for one of them, and I'm sure he was July's younger brother. I can't see them being involved with bombs. If they were I'm sure they would have had the sense to get away before it went off."

As he pulled the vehicle up at the rear door of the club, Badger said before climbing out, "What were they doing at your house?"

Declan could only shrug. "You can be sure I'm going to find out." He slipped out of the vehicle and skipped up the steps to the door. With Badger at his heels, he went on. "I hope they weren't looking for trouble because of his sister's death."

"They must have learned that that was an accident," Badger said when they got seated in Declan's office.

With his phone at his ear, Declan gave him a nod before turning his attention back to his mobile. "Paddy, where are you? Have you been in touch with that couple?" He gave a thumbs up signal to Badger and jumped out of his chair. "Paddy got Barton's number from his parents, but the bastard's not answering. But we know who'll know where he is."

Shaking his head slowly, Badger said, "If you're referring to that little Mr. Crow, I doubt you'll get anything out of him."

"If he wants us to nurse that injured person, then he's going to have to tell us."

Badger eased himself up, hearing his knees crack, and joined him as he walked through to the bar. "Where do you intend on nursing this person?"

"He can sleep in one of the flea-infested semen-crusted beds upstairs with one of the whores," Declan replied, at the same time scrolling through his mobile, searching for the number Crow had supplied him. It took a few attempts before he got a response, and as usual the voice that replied wasn't Crow's. Declan knew it was Nevil's; this was one of the little dapper man's security measures, "I need to talk to your boss." Another of the little man's measures was never to mention names on the phone. A long silence elapsed, and he wondered whether they were still connected.

The deep voice boomed in his ear and came back saying, "I'll pass the message on, and he'll get back to you."

Declan let out a deep sigh and shouted, "I need to talk to him now!" stabbing his finger at the phone. He slammed the phone down when he realised he had been disconnected. Badger picked it up and had a good look at it to make sure no damage had been done. When its ringtone sounded, Declan snatched it out of his hand. "Is that you, Mr. Crow?" he yelled into it. He could have eaten his words at the mention of the little man's name.

"I hope you have a good reason for this intrusion!" the high-pitched voice yelled at him.

"We need to meet."

"Give me a hint why?"

"It's about that nursing job you offered."

For a moment, Crow's voice sounded distant. Declan realised he was talking to someone else in the room where he was.

"Where are you now?" the little man came back.

"The same place where we met the last time."

The response was quick. "I'll be there in an hour," the high-pitched voice sang out. "I'll bring the patient with me; give you time to clean a room up for him."

In his experience with Crow, Declan knew that the little man's hour could be five hours or five minutes. He nodded at Badger. "He's on his way, and he's bringing that injured person."

Badger glanced around the lounge. Most of the tables were vacant, and the patrons looked sober, deep in conversation. "I don't see any of the girls; all the rooms must be occupied."

"Give it five. If none of them are finished, we need to get up there and chase one of them out."

"The john might want his money back."

At dead on the hour, Nevil pulled the Range Rover up at the back of Declan's club. Crow watched from the rear seat as the big man got out and banged on the door. Judd, sitting next to him, soon let him know he didn't like the look of this place and had seen the comings and goings of dodgy people. The door quickly opened, and the barred gate got pushed out. There was no mistaking the person who stood in the light from inside. The two men faced each other for a moment before Badger stepped aside.

A nod from Nevil was enough to assure Crow it was safe to enter. Seated in Declan's office, with Nevil at Crow's side and Badger standing at the door, Declan was quick to offer his conditions before agreeing to accommodate this injured person.

The dapper little man grimaced and pointed a threatening finger at Declan. "You don't dictate to me. One call from me and you're no longer on this planet. You take good care of this injured person; if you don't, you know what will happen to you and your establishment." Before Badger had the chance to intervene, Nevil had his gun out, pointing in his direction. The big man froze and took a step back when he heard the click from the safety catch. "Barton is a fellow solider," Crow went on, holding up his hand to appease the two big men. "Not from the same unit, but we did some time in the same conflict. Brothers in arms, as the saying goes."

"Time passes; that means nothing to guys like Barton now!" Declan barked.

A smile dawned across Crow's face, and he jumped to his feet. "You would say that. Not having served, you wouldn't understand. We'll bring that injured man in and leave you to it. In a few days, we'll come and collect him. For your sake, we hope he hasn't any complaints."

She jumped up off the bedside, where she had sat wearing only a bra and pants. "Get some clothes on," Declan shouted at her. She rushed for the door and had to squeeze past the men standing behind him. This caused Judd to whine in pain when she tried to pass him in the doorway. "This is the best I can offer," Declan said, walking to the far side of the bed and nodding down at it.

"I'm not sleeping in that flea pit," Judd whimpered, not having recovered from the pain caused by the girl, and not looking comfortable with Nevil's grip on his shoulders.

Declan turned to Badger. "See if you can find some clean bed linen."

Badger stormed out, slamming the door; they heard him swearing and cursing as he descended the stairs.

Sniffing around the room, Crow pointed at the bed. "I don't think I would be best pleased sleeping on that."

"As I have said, this is the best I can offer."

"What about that big house you own?" Crow asked, now holding a tissue to his mouth and nose. "Surely you must have a spare room there."

Red in the face and with froth dripping from his mouth, Declan shouted, "I don't have that house anymore! That bastard Barton bombed the fucking place!"

Wide-eyed, Crow dropped the tissue from his face. "When was this?" he asked, and he noticed Nevil drop his support of Judd.

"A few hours ago."

Before replying, he helped Nevil to put Judd on a creaky wooden chair at the side of the bed.

"So this is why you're desperate to get your hands on Barton?"

"That and a few other reasons," Declan sharply replied, his voice still three octaves higher than normal.

Crow knew the other reasons, but to show his ignorance, he asked, "Could you explain what other reasons?"

At the moment Declan was about to reply, Badger burst in. "I can't find any clean linen, Boss; the girls say there is none."

"Well go out and buy some!" Declan shouted.

By the look in this big man's deep-sunken eyes, Crow was convinced Badger was about to explode and was getting prepared to make a sharp exit. But just as quickly as the anger appeared in the big man's eyes, they mellowed. Crow sighed as he watched Badger's extensive body turn, closing the door softly behind him.

Declan returned his attention back to the little man. "Personal reasons," he retorted.

With a fresh tissue in his hand and holding up the other, Crow said, "I don't know where Barton is at the moment. Even if I did, I wouldn't tell you. So if you want to keep your little racket going on, look after this man, and have him ready to do the job I have for him." With a mock salute, he turned on his heels and waited until Nevil opened the door, and they bothleft.

Declan soon charged down the stairs and caught them at the back door. "I need some recompense for the loss of one of my rooms and a whore."

Crow nodded to Nevil, who quickly snatched the gun from his pocket, cocked it, and put it to Declan's temple. "This will be your recompense if you don't carry out my orders," he whispered, reaching close to his ear.

Declan wasn't surprised, when he slammed the back door on the men, to see that the patrons had stopped amidst their conversations to take in what was going on. Giving them a grimace, he held out his arms, saying, "All is in order." In truth, that was far from being the case. He was walking on a slippery slope. One wrong move, and it was curtains for him and his business. His first glance was at the man serving behind the bar; was he one of Crow's informers? He then looked at the four goons standing close to the front door. *Could be one or two of them. Pinkie—now there's a thought!* He never paid that goon very well, but only tossed a few pounds his way when he did a job—not enough to pay the rent on the flat he lived in. Badger was his closest goon and knew everything that was going on. He would make a good informer.

The lock on the back door rattled, and Badger walked in carrying a large cardboard box. Declan approached, and the box got dumped at his feet. "The shops are all closed at this time; had to go to a friend's house and buy this lot from him," Badger said, nodding down at the box.

"Take it up to that room and get that tart to change the bed and tidy up the place. Get her to help that guy into bed, but not to get in beside him." Declan watched as Badger shouldered the box and hefted it up the stairs.

Maybe he had put too much trust in this big man, always having him there listening to his plans and all his dealings. He headed over to the bar and nodded for his usual drink, leaning heavily on his elbows. A sudden vision of Barton entered his head, and a cold shiver ran through his body. The only other person to send this feeling through him was his drunken psychopathic father, and that had been long ago. How could this man Barton bring it all back? Only the once had he come in contact with Barton, in the back office, and that lasted only a few minutes.

His decision to send this big ape to hell the way he had his father had failed too many times. His drink was pushed in front of him. He silently cursed the interruption, picked it up, and downed it in one swallow. He then banged the empty glass down and nodded for another.

Badger had that angry, sinking familiar feeling when he noticed that distant, out-of-focus gaze in Declan's eyes. Had he been drinking too much too quickly, or had he been sniffing a line? This was when he had to fight the urge to slam his fist into Declan's face. This was the reaction when things were getting tough and out of Declan's control, when he knew he was cornered. Always at times like this, when Declan was out of it, Badger was left to clean up the mess, and he often had to take the flak if things went wrong when his boss sobered up.

He lifted Declan's drooping head and comatose body up by the back of his collar and dragged him onto the nearest seat, pointed a big finger down at him, and said, "One of these days I'm going to make sure you never wake up again."

"Make sure we get our money first," came the familiar voice from behind him.

Badger swung round and came face to face with Pinkie. "The same goes for you if you open that big mouth," he snarled as he pushed Pinkie to the side with a big hand to his chest. "Now help me get him into the office."

He was surprised by the way the girl gently changed the dressing on his hand. Judd got the feeling that this young woman was experienced at this; perhaps she'd been a nurse in her earlier years. She had helped him onto the bed, but he refused to get under the covers and lay stretched out on top. "What's your name?" he asked. "I'm not trying to become familiar with you; I just want to know what I should call you. Any name will do."

She grinned at him, exposing a missing tooth at the front, in a smile that never travelled to her brown eyes. She turned her attention to his feet and began bathing them in warm water smelling of disinfectant. When finished, she wiped his feet with a towel and soon gathered up all her equipment and headed for the door. Before she stepped out, she turned, looked into his eyes, and said, "Trudie."

His smile stopped her for a while before she pulled the door and closed it behind her. Judd was puzzled by the expression on her face. The mistrust in her eyes had gone; she had seemed to relax during the time she was nursing him. *Maybe*, he thought, *if she was a nurse in her past, this brought on pleasant memories. Or*—he didn't want to dwell on it—*was it because she was with a man who didn't want her for herbody?*

Visions of the past few weeks floated through his mind: the old man he had been hired to kill, the journey he had made in an attempt to carry out the contract, the young girl who had almost died when she interfered with the case carrying the syringe containing the venom, the old guy at the bus stop wearing a similar blue cap as his target had the habit of wearing, the woman he accidently shot in the woods, the two old women and that creep of a man who lived in that old house with them. The shock when the final face appeared brought him back to the real world and made him jump out of his delirium; it was the man with the brown eyes, long black hair tied up in a tight ponytail, and stubble—a huge muscle-bound ape that Judd decided would have to be hit from a distance with a high-velocity round. The last thing he needed was for this big man Barton to be hunting him down when he had carried out the contract on his father. This meant he would have to break his golden rule of never killing for personal reasons. Self-preservation has to be considered in some cases, and this was one of them.

The struggle to stay awake was wearing him down; it had been many hours since his last sleep, and he drifted away with the thought that his first job, once he was fit, was to eliminate the son of Tom Barton.

The haunting echo of a female voice rang in his ear from a distance. *Another vision*, he decided. A hand rested on his shoulder, and he blinked his eyes open; her face was only a few inches from his. He made to jump up, but she restrained him. "I have to change your dressing," he heard her saying. Judd smiled, remembering who she was, and relaxed, letting her get on with working on his injured hand.

"Are you hungry?" she asked as she cleared away her implements and dirty dressings.

Remembering where he was, he asked, "Do you have food in a place like this?"

Packing the stained bandages into a plastic bag, she replied, shaking her head, "No, but I could send out for something to be delivered."

"I don't think I have any cash with me."

She grinned on her way out the door. "All been taken care of."

"I hope you're being paid for this," he replied, but she was gone behind the closed door. With his arm in a sling, he had trouble getting onto his feet; and when he finally did, he almost screamed with the pain when his weight went on them. Even with the massive padding she had wrapped around them, it still felt as if he were standing on broken glass. He flopped himself back down on the bed when the door flew open, and in she came carrying a tray with plates of food and a coffee pot on it.

Placing the tray on the bed beside him, she said, "Better take advantage of this while the boss is on a bender."

He guessed she meant he was out cold from drugs and booze but had to ask. "What do you mean, 'on a bender'?"

She grinned, shrugged, turned, and left. Was this idle advice or a warning? Whatever, it was, it set his warning bells off, and a rush of fear ran through him. He had to get out of this situation, and soon. He knew he needed help, but whom could he turn to?

The jacket he had taken from the creep in the old house lay over the chair at the opposite side of the bed where he sat. More pain came as he reached over for it only to find that the pockets had been emptied. He was now with no phone, no cash, and no means of transport. He had heard Crow's warning, but would the owner of this place take notice of it? The only person who came to mind was Trudie. Did he know her well enough to trust her? Perhaps given more time, he would. The trouble was, how much time did he have?

A heavy-handed knock came from the door. The handle turned, and a big face appeared with a grin. Judd, disturbed from drifting back into a deep sleep, was confused. He thought he was having a nightmare when he glanced at the deep-set eyes lodged under a protruding forehead. He was about to roll out of the other side of the bed when he remembered this was the goon who had accompanied the boss of this place.

"Just checking to see if everything is all right," Badger said as he entered. In truth he was checking that Trudie hadn't been giving this guy extra servicing that might end up causing more injury and therefore delaying his stay.

"I'm good," Judd replied, grinning.

Nodding to the tray and the empty plates on the floor beside the bed, Badger said, "I'll get someone to clear that away. Did you enjoy the food?"

Judd nodded and watched the big man turn and leave the room, closing the door gently. This visit gave birth to another concern. Was this big guy assigned to make sure he didn't escape?

CHAPTER 29

Twisting his shoulders from side to side in an attempt to free his hands from the cable ties was Barton's first reaction before opening his eyes. He soon realised he was free of them. Bright lights shone down on him. He closed his eyelids tightly to shade them, but it had little effect. Twisting his head gave him no relief from the stinging pain in his eyes. A hand touched his shoulder. He turned and came face to face with a young girl wearing tinted glasses. He tried to get up, but she held him firmly down. It was then that he realised he was no longer lying on the stone floor, but in a soft bed. "Where am I?" he asked her.

She stepped back and smiled. "You're in hospital. A couple found you lying at the side of the road and called the ambulance."

"What's wrong with me?"

Picking up a chart from the foot of his bed, she became more serious. "It seems you're suffering from a drug overdose and slight exposure."

"How long have I been here?"

"You were admitted last night."

"I need to get out," he said, trying to get up.

She replaced the chart and reached over and held him down again. "You can't go yet; the police are coming to interview you, and you don't have any clothes. You were brought in here naked. One of the local charities are bringing something in for you to go out in." She relaxed her grip and smiled; taking a step back, she went on. Reaching for the chart again, she stood poised ready with her pen. "I need your name and details."

Time to do some acting, Barton decided, panic rising in him. "I can't remember my name … can't remember anything."

She replaced the chart. "In that case, we need to do some tests; you won't be getting out today."

Watching her closing the door, he cursed himself for not coming up with a better lie. All he could do now was hope that this charity brought him clothes, giving him time to get into them and get out of this hospital before the coppers arrived.

Taking in the surrounds of the small cubicle, he discovered a small window looking outwards on a dark, starry night. On the opposite side was the door where the nurse had slipped out of; it was half panelled with a glass top. Light from above reflected off her tinted glasses as she sat at a desk opposite.

She appeared to be studying some charts but very often glanced his way. Barton was beginning to think she had been posted there to keep an eye on him. He swung his legs out of the bed and discovered he was wearing a white hospital gown. Instantly the girl was opening the door,staring at him. "I need the toilet," he explained.

She reached over, held him by the upper arm, and led him to a door in the corner of the cubicle. "Can you manage yourself from here?" she said. "I have to leave the door open for safety reasons."

She was nowhere in sight through the open toilet door, but he guessed she would be close by. Doubts entered his head, and he began to wonder whether this was an NHS hospital. He turned and could see the bed; it looked like standard hospital equipment, as did the cabinet and single chair.

He then remembered the small window. *Why does it have steel meshing on the outside of it? Could this be an asylum or a medical ward in a prison?* He flushed the toilet, and as if by magic she was at the door, reaching for him. "Where is this place?" he asked as she ushered him back down on the bed.

"A scan has been arranged first thing in the morning," she replied, stepping out through the door. "If the results are good, then the police can have a word with you, and when you get some clothes, you can go." She left him with a wide grin on her tanned face and closed the door. *Am I being paranoid*, he wondered, *or was that a grin with a hidden secret behind it? Is all this a part of Randel's plot? If so, why go to all this trouble?* As quickly as the thought entered his head, he dismissed it. He remembered the needle pricking the back of his neck and drifting out of consciousness. Had they dumped him naked at the side of a road to be discovered, as that nurse said, by a couple, and the ambulance crew had dropped him off thinking that this place was where he had escaped from?

With his adrenalin in overdrive, he couldn't lie there any longer and sprang out of bed to the window.

"What are you doing?" the girl cried from the open door.

"Just stretching my legs," he said without looking round at her.

"Well, when you're done, get back in that bed."

Her tone of voice stirred him. This wasn't the mannerism of a nurse. Still not looking in her direction, he asked, "Is that an order or a request?"

"Take it whatever way you want," she snapped, and she closed the door.

Reluctantly, he turned to see her seated at her desk. As if by instinct, she looked straight into his eyes through the glass panel on the door. He quickly returned his attention to the window and could see the headlights of a car driving into what looked like a small parking spot two storeys below him. *Not much hope of climbing out this way with no clothes or shoes.*

The car engine stopped, and the area fell into darkness. The vehicle doors opened, and in the cabin light he spotted the face of the man standing at the far side. Once again, that same countenance rang bells in his memory. Any doubt he had about this place was gone. *This must be part of Randel's game.* Without glancing in her direction, he got back onto the bed, feeling the girl's eyes on him with his every move. Now he knew he was no longer a patient in a hospital; he was a prisoner.

He lay staring up at the tubular light, thinking about the girl with the tinted glasses. A quick glance around and he saw she was still sitting behind the desk. He wondered whether the two men who had come in that car were her relief, or maybe the fake police she had talked about. No sooner had the thought entered his head than he heard male voices outside the door.

They stood in front of the desk, blocking his view of her. Although he couldn't make out what was being said, he detected that a heated argument was taking place.

The explosion, when it came, made him jump up, and he saw one of the men stagger back holding his upper arm; soon blood seeped through his fingers.

The other man disappeared from view, and he could she the girl standing, holding what Barton thought was a Ruger MAX-9 pistol, smoke still drifting from the barrel. What worried Barton was her expression; a wide grin lingered there, exposing the space where she was missing a tooth. He couldn't read what was in her eyes for the reflection from the light above her head on her glasses, but hewas certain she showed no regrets for what she had just done.

The wounded man staggered out of sight, and she pointed the weapon in the direction he was heading. Calmly she placed the weapon in one of the drawers of her desk and sat down, her eyes looking in the direction that the men had gone.

Barton took advantage of this, got up, and started banging on the door. She turned her attention to him, got out of her seat, and rushed towards him. Before she had a chance to put her hand to the handle, he jerked the door open.

She staggered forward into his arms, and he threw her at the bed and heard her skull crack on the metal frame. He didn't need to check that she was out cold. He slammed the door and retrieved the weapon from the desk drawer.

He discovered he was in a brightly lit short corridor with doors on either side. He ignored them and headed for the one that was ajar at the end. This led him to a steep set of stairs leading down to another corridor. Again one of the doors had been left open. He reached it in time to hear the car drive off.

Gone was his chance of getting something to wear. Had planned to catch those two men, hold them at gunpoint, and make them strip. All he could think of now was the nurse's uniform that the girl was wearing. It was a bit too small but was better than what he was standing in.

He bounded back up the stairs and rushed along to the door. Shock hit him when he looked through the glass panel; she was gone. Gently he turned the handle and pushed the door in,prepared for an attack. It never happened. Before entering, he recced around but could find no trace of her. The toilet door was closed; he remembered leaving it open on his last visit. *Pointless creeping up to it*, he decided. *She must know I'm here*. He charged at the door, kicking it with a bare foot. It flew open, banging against the wall. She wasn't there. Holding his breath, he listened for the slightest movement. At the point where he was about to give up, he couldn't hold his breath any longer. He heard the rustle of her uniform behind.

With the weapon in his hand, he swung round but was too late, she came at him with a baseball bat raised above her head. His instinct made him raise his arms in defence of his head, but the impact never came; she had misjudged her target, and the bat struck the top of the door jamb.

He dived at her, his shoulder striking her midriff. With arms clenched around her waist, he bulldozed her across the floor, landing on top of her on the bed. Barton was surprised at the amount of fight in her, but his weight exhausted her, and she had to give up with a mouthful of curses and swears that would have embarrassed a gang of building site workers.

As he held her fast by the wrists, he noticed that her glasses were gone and was shocked at how beautiful her brown eyes were. Through it all, he couldn't help himself from smiling down at her. He found her, despite the missing tooth, an attractive girl. They locked eyes for a while, and she smiled back at him. The anger in her eyes was gone. He relaxed his grip on her arms, and she folded hers around his shoulders. He felt her responding to his emotions as she thrust her pelvis up to meet his.

"I'm as good as dead if they find out about this," she sighed, fastening up her jacket. "I'm supposed to make sure you don't leave. They even gave me that gun and bat to threaten you with." She nodded at the weapons now lying on the floor at their feet.

Still clad only in the white hospital gown, sitting next to her on the bed, Barton asked, "What's all this about? Who are they that you are talking about?"

She stood up, shaking her head. "I'm in enough trouble; I dare not say any more. I've wounded one of their thugs, and now I've just fucked the guy I'm supposed to babysit."

"I won't tell anybody about that," Barton assured her.

Declan lay slouched across his desk, his head resting on his arms. He jerked himself up when the office door opened. He saw Badger approach. "What time is it? What fucking *day* is it?"

Leaning on his big hands on the desktop, Badger reached over and glared into Declan's bloodshot eyes. "If it's your intention to get your hands on Barton, you had better move."

Declan sat up, resting his head on the back of his padded chair. "I feel like shit." He focused his eyes on the desktop clock. "How long have I been out?"

"A few of hours," Badger replied, grinning. He got himself settled on his usual chair. Seeing his boss suffer like this delighted him.

The sudden memory of the injured guy upstairs in one of his rooms made Declan sit up, his small bloodshot eyes popping out at Badger. "Has Crow come back for that guy?"

"Not yet," Badger replied, shaking his enormous head.

Declan sighed and retreated to his relaxed position. "Have you been checking on him?" he said, staring at the light on the ceiling.

"He seems to be doing okay." The noise from Declan slapping his hand on his desk seemed to resonate through the building. He then jumped to his feet. "Fuck, I forgot that truck was due to arrive this morning."

Badger held up his hand. "The driver will give us a call when he's about an hour away. Pinkie's on his way out there just now."

"We'd better get out there and make sure things have been sorted out for their arrival." Declan said, staggering towards the door. "First we'll go upstairs and check on that guy."

The stranger lay face up on the bed. Badger silently opened the door and approached. He nudged the prone figure with a finger to his chest. "Still out cold from the drugs I put in hiscoffee."

Cautiously, Declan approached. "I hope you didn't overdo it. if Crow turns up and finds him like this, we're all dead."

"He'll be fine, should waken up in an hour or so. Anyway, I'm sure Crow must know it's going to take a few days before this guy will be able to get up and about."

Precariously descending the stairs ahead of the big man, Declan said, "Get that whore to keep a close eye on him, and phone me when he wakes up."

Pinkie was standing at the door, blowing smoke rings up in the air from a roll-up cigarette, when the four-by-four pulled up a few inches away from him. Declan jumped out and slapped the cigarette out of his hand. "You're supposed to be getting things sorted out for the truck arriving."

Pinkie staggered back. "I-It's all been done, Boss," he stammered.

"It had better be!" Declan shouted as he pushed the door open. The ex-army gymnasium had been in use by the locals before the council built a new one and had been abandoned only weeks before Declan leased it, so it was in good condition and didn't need a lot of renovations. The floor had been recently varnished and had a good, fresh sheen to it. He had invested in redundant service beds. He grinned at the sight of the layout, happy that it had been laid out without making the hall look overcrowded. His team had followed his instructions to the letter. Beside each bed he had ordered a small wooden locker, also ex-services, to be placed on the left top side of each bed. Pillows, sheets, mattresses, and duvets had been laid out on every one of them.

Like a sergeant on the CO's inspection day, he marched the length of the hall. Everything was as he had instructed. His most expensive investment was the modern kitchen and toilets. And once again, he was happy with the job that had been done. "All we need now is one of the whores to entertain the immigrants." He grinned up at Badger.

"We're short of women," the big man reminded him. "Take another one away from the club and you'll only have two to entertain the punters."

"Then those two will have to work harder until we find more. The one we left to look after that injured man of Crow's, she looked fit enough."

"Who's going to look after him?"

"Bring him here."

"If Crow turns up unexpected and the guy's not at the club, what then?"

Declan grimaced and headed back into the hall. Sensing the big man at his back, he said, "I'll phone Crow and explain I have found better accommodation for his guy. I'll ask him to phone when he's coming to collect, and we can ship him back." To the left of the main entrance was a door that led to what was once used as a cloakroom but that Declan had had his team convert into an office with a partition separating it from a small bedroom. This was to accommodate the person whose job it was to entertain the immigrants. Once again, he was impressed by the job that had been done. When his inspection was over, he sat at the desk in the office and was amused by watching Badger squeeze his bulk onto the chair opposite. The space between the edge of the desk and the wall wasn't wide enough for the seat to be pushed clear before bumping into the wall.

The suddenness of the text signal from his mobile made both of them jump. Declan snatched it from his pocket and began thumbing at the screen. He thought his blood had turned to ice water when he read the message. He had to read it over a few times to be certain he was reading it correctly. "Bloody fucking hell!" he shouted. He handed the phone over to Badger. "Read that."

After reading it into himself, Badger dictated it out loud. "'I'm in a queue at Dover, waiting for custom officers to check the container on my truck. The area is crawling with police officers.' That's not good."

"Return the text!" Declan cried. "Tell him to keep us posted."

"What's documented to be in the container?" Badger asked, trying to get up out of the chair when Declan jumped out of his.

"Rolls of denim cloth."

"If the immigrants stay silent and still, they might pass him though."

Declan shook his head. "When they pull him over the weighbridge, they'll know it's not denim rolls." He barged out and through the open main entrance door, and Badger followed him in time to see him push Pinkie down the step. Pinkie landed on all fours on the concrete paving but still managed to retain his cigarette between his fingers.

As Badger was about to start up the four-by-four, Declan's mobile sounded again. This time it was a call ringtone. He snatched it from his pocket and saw Trudie's name. "What is it, bitch?" he shouted. For a while he was silent, listening to her message. "What the fuck do you mean he's missing? The man could hardly walk. You'd better find him, bitch, before I get back—or you're dead."

"What now?" Badger asked as he got the vehicle started and on the move.

"That whore has let Crow's man disappear."

Badger, waiting for a gap in the traffic at the road end, said, "He can't have gotten far in his condition."

"Are you saying he could be hiding somewhere in the club?" The big vehicle jumped forward as Badger risked getting onto the road when a small gap between two cars approached at speed.

"Where else could he be?"

The vehicle hadn't quite stopped when Declan jumped out and started banging on the rear door of his club. He rushed in, pushing the goon to the side, and rushed up to the bedrooms. Trudie was sitting on the edge of the bed, her head bent over, her face in her hands. One of his bouncers was standing in front of her. They both looked up when the door flew open. "Have you found him?" Declan screamed, and he rushed at her, pushing her flat on the bed and holding her down by the neck.

The bouncer butted in before Trudie had a chance to reply. "We've looked everywhere."

Declan spared him a quick glance and returned his attention to the girl beneath him. "You were supposed to look after him and make sure he didn't hurt himself further." He yelled. He then balled his fist and landed a punch to her face. "Where were you when he managed to get out of this room?" Again he landed a blow, and he was about to deliver another when Badger grabbed him and pulled him offher.

"We're not going to find him battering fuck out of her!" Badger shouted.

As Declan struggled to get free from the big man's arms,his mobile sounded a text massage. He stepped out of Badger's reach and grabbed his phone from his pocket. All eyes were on him as a grin dawned across his features. "The truck's on its way; they waved him through." The grin faded when he noticed the blood coming from Trudie's mouth. "Get yourself cleaned up; I've a job for you. Think yourself lucky I didn't kill you, so if you fuck up on this other job, you know the consequences." He turned to Badger and the bouncer.

"We need to find this guy," he said, pointing a finger at the bed, and he strode out of the room.

After a search of the club, Declan was satisfied that the stranger wasn't on the premises. He gathered the goons and bouncers in the bar, gave them a description of who they were looking for, and sent them out on a search of the local area. "He can't have gone far," he said to Badger. "Not in his condition."

The big man nodded. "The trouble is there are so many places for a body to hide around here."

"We need to find him and get him and that whore out to that gymnasium before that truck arrives."

CHAPTER 30

Counting the crisp new fifty-pound note into the big, rough hands of Pinkie in the back of the four-by-four, Crow threatened, "Be sure and give that girl a share of that." As he handed over the last note, he added, "We don't want her upset and spilling her guts out under pressure."

"Don't worry about Trudie; she's a tough nut, that one," Pinkie replied, folding the notes and slipping them into his hip pocket. "She assured me that your injured man is in a safe place."

"Where might that be?" Crow asked as Pinkie stepped out of the vehicle.

"As she says, in a safe place; she wouldn't tell me," Pinkie said, and he walked towards his own car.

Nevil got the four-by-four moving. "Pull up somewhere out of sight along the road," Crow ordered.

"When he drives past, we follow him. I think he could be heading for that warehouse or whatever it is."

As the little man had predicted, Pinkie drove past in his red VW. Nevil let a few cars past before heading in the same direction. At the first set of traffic lights, they could see the little red vehicle a few cars in front. This was one of those dreaded multi-exit junctions with four lanes leading up to the line. At the last minute, the vehicles in front took to a different lane, leaving them directly behind Pinkie.

"Hope he doesn't look in his mirror and see us behind him," Nevil said.

A few seconds before they got a green light, the red VW shot out and swerved in front of the other traffic, causing a squeal of brakes and blasts from horns. Nevil realised he had no chance of doing the same without causing a collision and had to wait till his way ahead was clear. "I think he spotted us," Nevil said. "There's no chance of us following him now."

"He's not the brightest spark I've met; I think that swerve he made was a last-minute panic. If he thinks he has lost, us he'll about-turn," the little man said. "Park up on one of those streets, and I bet he'll drive past in a few minutes."

The few minutes became almost an hour before Pinkie drove past. "Where the hell's he been?" Nevil said as he pulled out onto the main road a few cars behind again.

"It's where he is going that is my concern. Wherever it is, I don't think it is very far."

Without giving any signal, they saw the VW make a last-minute right turn.

"Drive on past for a few yards," Crow suggested. "If my memory serves me, there's an old army barracks up that road, behind those shrubs. Park up and we can sneak in and recce the place."

They soon discovered that they would have to walk farther than they had intended to; finding a safe parking place was the problem. To their left and up a steep banking was a succession of blocks of flats that looked neglected and run down but still occupied by tenants.

"I don't like leaving the car here," Nevil said, pointing up at the houses.

Crow followed his pointing finger, nodded, and got out of the car. "You stay and guard it; I'll go in myself."

Although he cursed the destruction of his highly polished brown shoes on the marshy ground, he was in his element, exercising the tactics he had employed during training and in war zones back in his military days. Sooner than he had expected, he came across the red VW parked on what would have been the parade square. He ducked behind a tall bush. The evening sun was sinking behind a tall, long building. Unlike the rest of what appeared to have been the barracks, it was in good condition and looked as though it had been in use recently. A narrow blade of light shone through a partly open door. The figure standing next to it he instantly recognised as Pinkie, the small red glow from his cigarette lighting up his face. *Not military trained*, he mused. *A bloody idiot—a prime target for a sniper.*

Thinking he had seen and learned enough, he decided to get out and return to his car. The metallic click that came from behind him was no strange sound. A hand gripped the collar at the back of his shirt and dragged him to the ground on his rump.

Two figures stood over him, each with a handgun pointing at his face. "Who the fuck are you? What are you doing here?" one of the figures said. He reached down and grabbed Crow by the shoulder of his jacket and lifted him clean off the ground.

The little man took a swing at the figure holding him up, but his fists never reached the target. The other figure reached over and gripped his other shoulder and Crow felt himself being carried across the parade square, his toes barely scraping the ground. He was eventually pushed in through the door of the building. The layout of the interior brought him back to his days as a raw recruit in the officers' training camp.

He was dragged to the end of the room between rows of single beds to a set of doors. At the door to his left, they stopped and released their grip on him. Because of the angle his feet were at, he couldn't maintain his balance, and he felt himself stumble into the nearest wall. He risked a glance at the two men who were laughing at him lying there at their feet. He recognised one of them as being one of Declan's bouncers. "You … Tell your boss he's a dead man!" he shouted at them.

This brought on more laughter and earned him a kick on the thigh. He screamed with the pain and felt himself being lifted again by one of the goons while the other opened the door. Only the light from the main hall shone in through the small room he was pushed into. He felt himself being thrust onto a single bed, face down. The door closed with a thud, and he was enveloped in darkness. A few minutes passed as he listened for footsteps or voices from outside. All seemed deadly silent, and he turned over and threw his legs off of the bed. Dubiously, he stepped forward, frightened he would collide with something and make a noise that carried through the building.

With a deafening thump, the door flew open, bouncing off the wall. Crow was caught in the light from the hall. His soldier instinct made him drop to his knees and take cover. A tall silhouette delayed a long moment, casting a long shadow across the floor and onto the bed.

"Are you all right, sir?" the familiar voice asked.

"Nevil, what are you doing here?" Crow said with a nervous grin, getting up off the floor. "You're supposed to be guarding the vehicle."

"I thought you might need some help, sir, so I drove the four-by-four halfway up the drive, flashed the lights, blasted the horn. This got the attention of the mob guarding this place. They ran down to see what was going on. That's when I jumped out and sneaked up here. I think we'd better get out of here, sir, before they charge back, realising they've been duped."

As Crow was about to dart around the bed, an explosion erupted from behind Nevil. The tall black driver staggered forward and landed on the bed, face down. Once again, Crow's military instinct cut in and he dived to the floor. From his position below the bed, he saw several pairs of legs walk through the door and over to where Nevil lay.

Two more shots were fired, and he tightly closed his eyes and held his ears, expecting the same fate.

Instead of the expected impact from the gunshots there came a vice-like grip of a pair of hands on his ankles. He felt himself being dragged from beneath the bed all the way out the door into the hall. The grip on his ankles was released, and he felt himself being elevated onto his feet.

"I thought it would be you," Pinkie said, pushing his face close to the little man's. "Sorry about your driver; the boys got a bit overexcited when they found that abandoned four-by-four down the driveway. They thought a war had started and the mob had sent some muscle out."

After a few attempts to free himself from the hands gripping his arms, Crow gave up and said, "By killing my driver, war has now started."

"Only if we let you go to open your mouth about it." This voice came from behind the group, and all eyes turned to Declan and Badger, who were standing a short distance from them, both armed and pointing their weapons at the little man. Declan nodded to the goon holding Crow, and he was released.

"He was caught snooping about in the shrubs," Pinkie said, standing behind the little man.

Declan brought his pistol up and aimed it at Crow's head. When the shot came, the powder blast hit Crow's face, but the round missed. He heard a crash behind and turned to see Pinkie lying on top of a locker that had smashed under his weight.

"No need to get too concerned about that piece of shit," Declan said, and he returned his aim to Crow. "Think yourself lucky. I need you to get Barton. I've already got someone trying to get him for me, but I think you would be a sure bet at getting him. I know you are in contact, so if you want to live, you'd better get started."

"If I don't have contact, what then?"

"You know what."

"That will be three bodies you will have to dispose of."

"One more won't be too much trouble; I've already got the hole dug."

"Do that and you bring the whole cartel down on you."

"I'm ready for them," Declan declared with a grin, waving his gun round at the goons, who were now all standing with an assortment of weapons pointing at Crow.

Reading the expressions on the goons' faces, Crow could see they didn't show Declan's enthusiasm. "Is this all the troops you have?"

Declan laughed. "I bet you would like to know that answer." He turned to Badger. "Give him your mobile."

Before taking the phone from the big man's hand, Crow looked at the bunch of thugs and then at Declan.

"Why go to all this trouble to get Barton? The man I brought to you is a professional shooter; he is relentless—never gives up on a job— and not too expensive. Hire him to get Barton; then you can get on with your business.

"There's only one way to save yourself," Barton said. "We have to get out of here. You'll need to come with me if you're already in trouble. I need to get some clothes. This pea-shooter will come in handy." He reached down and picked up the weapon.

"I've stashed the clothes you came here in—not a very good fit." Trudie got up off the bed, went to the desk, and pulled open one of the drawers and dumped the bundle on the desk.

He was conscious of her staring at him as he took off the hospital gown. He took his time putting on the clothes Billy Bunter had unwillingly supplied. He grinned. "I enjoyed having sex with you," he said, trying to squeeze into trainers that were about a size too small. "We must do it again."

"Any time you want," she replied, retrieving the bat from the bedroom and joining him with it over her shoulder.

Barton nodded at the weapon. "Not very easy to conceal if we have to get about in a public area."

"We shouldn't need to if we're in a public area." She led the way down the corridor and down the steep stairs to the outer door. Slowly she opened it inch by inch. Quickly she closed it and ushered him hurriedly back up the stairs.

"What's happening?" he asked.

Gasping for air, she got behind her desk and pointed to the bedroom. "Get back in bed. The big man in the wheelchair—the guy who paid me to babysit you—is out there in his car. He'll be sending his thugs up to fetch us. I couldn't see how many there are, but we stand a better chance if they think you're still out cold from the drugs they gave you."

Barton checked the weapon, made it ready to fire, rushed into the bed, and covered himself with the duvet and lay still. He stole a glance at Trudie sitting behind her desk and noticed she had recovered her tinted glasses. Her head turned quickly down the corridor, and within a moment two men stood in front of her desk. After a brief conversation, the men turned and looked in his direction.

Barton lay still, controlling his breathing; this was an exercise he had done in the past and had often caught his antagonists off guard. The handle operated, and he heard the door open. *Two short paces … he estimated*, and he threw the cover off to reveal the gun pointing at them.

They stopped when he jumped out and pushed the nearest one back against the other. They both stumbled backwards through the door. The strike from behind created a cracking sound when she brought the bat down on the guy closest to her. The man in front of Barton turned—a natural reaction that lasted a only split second, but long enough for Barton to hit this man above the ear with the butt of the pistol. The guy let out a groan and fell to his knees but wasn't out cold; it took another two attempts before he was.

Trudie stood with the bat raised, ready to deliver another blow, but the two men didn't move. Jumping over the unconscious men, Barton grabbed her wrist. "Let's get out of here," he said, and he ran, dragging her behind. At the door, she withdrew her arm and gripped his jacket, holding him back. "That fat man in the wheelchair will be down there; I know he carries a gun. If he has heard the rumpus, he'll be ready for us, and he won't be on his own."

"So what do you suggest we do?"

She shook her head. "The only thing I can come up with is we stay here and hope he sends whoever is with him up to see what the delay is, then we jump him as well."

"The next guy he sends up is going to be careful and prepared, not like these two." He jabbed his thumb over his shoulders at the two unconscious bodies, "We'd better move them out of sight." Barton picked up the nearest one and dragged him in behind the bed. Trudie struggled with the lighter one. He rushed over and lifted her task by the heels, and they dumped him in the toilet. She returned to the desk while Barton got behind the room door.

Time dragged on, and no one appeared. Barton was about to change their plan when he heard Trudie's chair being pushed back, and he glanced through the crack at the back of the door and sawthe broad shoulders of a man in a grey suit who was obviously confronting her. Barton wondered where he had come from, for he hadn't detected any movement.

Jerking the room door open, he rushed at this guy, jamming the pistol into his spine. "Get down on your knees," Barton ordered. Without turning, the man obeyed. The next moment shocked Barton by the speed of Trudie's reaction. She brought the bat down on the man's head with such force that Barton was sure she must have killed him. *Thick skull!* was the only exclamation that came to his mind when the guy didn't fall; instead he got up onto his feet and staggered back against Barton, and they stumbled through the open door and onto the bed.

Rolling to the side and pushing at the same time, Barton managed to get out from under the man, who was fighting to keep him pinned down. He was about to hit the guy with the pistol when the bat swished past his head and hit the man on the back of the skull; this put him out. Although Barton was relieved that the fight with the man was over, he was concerned that he wouldn't have him as cover if, as the girl said, Randel had a gun.

Turning with the intent of cursing Trudie, Barton was in time to see her run around the far side of the bed, bat held high, ready to strike at the man Barton had hit with the pistol and was now attempting to get up. "Don't!" he shouted, and he dived over the guy she had just knocked out in time to knock the bat out of her hand.

She let out a yelp and made a dive to recover her weapon. Barton grabbed both her wrists and pinned her against the wall. "We need one to be walking!" he shouted at her.

With blazing eyes, she hissed at him, "Let me fucking go!" and she struggled like a wildcat, kicking, scratching, and spitting.

Barton held her firmly until she calmed down. "We need him for cover if Randel has a gun." He released her wrists but could feel that the fight in her wasn't over. He couldn't help but admire her feisty demeanour as she strode over and recovered her bat. In a single movement, she picked it up. She then strutted out of the room, slapped the bat on the desk, and dumped herself down on the chair behind it.

With one hand holding the pistol close to the groggy man's face, Barton helped him up onto wobbly legs with the other. "Walk as best you can," he ordered, "but try any heroics and you're finished."

They had to give the man a chance to gather some of his equilibrium before attempting to walk him down the steep stairs. Randel wasn't waiting in the lower corridor as they were expecting him to be. Trudie signalled that she would stand guard at the entrance. Barton, holding the man in front for cover, opened the two doors at the bottom of the corridor. Finding the rooms empty, the only move left was to attempt to go outside.

Holding the man by the back of his suit collar and pressing the pistol into his spine, Barton pushed him towards the exit door, expecting to find Trudie waiting there. The door was open, and she was nowhere in sight. The dark winter evening had fallen, and the car park was in darkness. Pushing the man ahead of him, Barton searched for the large black limousine that had transported Randel.

A sudden blinding beam of light dazzled them. Barton pushed the man to the ground and dived flat himself, but it was all in vain, as the large car drove up to them and stopped inches from the man's face. Barton scrambled to his feet, and his captive attempted the same but was pushed back down, and Barton held him there with his foot on the man's back. "Stay down," he said in a hoarse whisper, "or I'll put one in the back of your head." He jabbed the muzzle of the pistol into the back of the man's neck.

The car interior illuminated, and a man sitting next to the driver stepped out. The head lights got switched off. Barton took a step backwards, training the pistol on the approaching figure. "Don't come any closer or I'll put one of these bullets in your head!" he shouted.

The figure stopped at the same moment the man on the ground got up and charged. Barton felt himself being driven towards the figure. All three of the stumbling bodies smashed into the bonnet of the vehicle. From somewhere out of the darkness, more figures appeared, and Barton felt numerous hands gripping him and hauling him away from the car.

Lying on his back on the wet tarmac with a group of figures towering over him, Barton groped around with his hands, searching for the weapon.

"If you're searching for this, you can save your energy," the deep voice at his feet said, holding up the weapon he had got from the woman. He made to get up but was quickly pushed back down. "What's going on?" Barton cried.

"You'll soon find out," another voice from the group said. The strong beam of light, this time from above, again hit him in the eyes, blinding him.

The constant throb from the helicopter deafened him as it descended a short distance away. The blast from the rotor blades caused the gang around him to brace themselves. Without warning or signal, hands from all directions grasped him, and he felt himself being elevated and getting carried like a casualty. He twisted and kicked but was held firmly. They rushed him towards the waiting craft, struggling to carrying him and ducking below the moving rotor blades. He heard the sliding door opening and felt himself being hauled inside and dumped on the floor.

Two of the gang got in beside him, while the remainder retreated from the biting gusts from the blades. The door was closed, and soon after he felt the helicopter lift off. In the dim light from the interior, he glanced around and caught the sight of a burly-looking man with an unkempt frizzy salt-and-pepper beard and a head of hair that was similar. In spite of the risk of fire inside the craft, a precaution he'd had drummed into his head whilst in the forces, this character had a big cigar going. He hooked a big finger around it and pointed it at Barton. "If I have any trouble from you," he roared, "these guys will throw you out!"

Still lying on his back and feeling the vibrations of the craft, Barton looked at the two goons sitting facing each other on the plastic bench seats, glowing with pleasure at the thought of dumping him out the open door and letting him fall.

An attempt to get up resulted in a large boot thumping into his rib cage from one of the goons. "What's all this about?" he shouted at the bearded guy, hoping to be heard above the sound of the engines. All he got in response was a cloud of cigar smoke blown at him and a toothless grin from the small mouth.

Having lots of experience in travelling in helicopters, he could tell by the engine sound when the craft was making hight or descending, and he could tell by the sound of the tilt of the blades when the pilot changed directions or held the craft at a hover. Most of the drops he had been involved in during his time in special forces had taken place at night. This craft was on tilt and descending. The engine sound softened, and then came the familiar soft bump as it landed on uneven ground. He was pushed back down when he tried to get up. The sliding door made that metallic swishing sound he was familiar with.

The gaping blackness outside brought back memories that could have meant this might be his last mission. He thought those days were gone, in his past. The wind from the rotor blades blasted in on him, and he felt hands grip his ankles. He knew it was hopeless putting up a fight and let himself be carried out. He soon found himself looking up at the night sky through the turning blades.

The engines made a sudden blast, the props picked up speed, and he watched the craft lift off. For a moment it hovered; then the nose dipped slightly, and soon it disappeared into the night sky. The hands that held him down now lifted him onto his feet. He struggled and fought against their grip on his arms. The two goons took a step back. "What's going on?" he demanded. He got no response from them and noticed them looking past him. Barton turned and followed their gaze. A short distance away, a group of lights appeared heading towards them; by the way they bucked and bounced on the rough terrain, he guessed they must be quad bikes.

Soon the machines approached, the riders steering the bikes around them a few times before stopping and dismounting. Barton stood behind the two goons and watched them having a conversation with these riders. They all looked at him, the one nearest nodded, and the rest rushed at Barton, forcing him to the ground. He felt his hands being wrenched behind and secured. Next he was being lifted and pushed on past the parked bikes and onto a farmer's track.

The two goons followed close behind him, now and again pushing him forward. The quad bikes started and soon caught up, their lights shining on the track. The way ahead was rough with overgrown weed and rocks, Barton stumbled a few times, as did the goons walking behind. Without warning, the bikes raced past and stopped at what looked like a car park.

Once again they raced around it and came to a halt next to a building. Barton noticed the remnants of another building in the beams from the quads; the structures reminded him of an abandoned farmyard.

The riders dismounted and formed a line in front of the machines; the goons behind pushed him towards them. The riders then formed a circle around him. This, Barton decided, was a well-drilled performance.

The two goons entered the circle, and they all closed in on him. His eyes drifted around the deadpan faces that he could see in the glow caused from the beams of the quads. From between the ends of two of the buildings, another set of blinding lights appeared, approaching slowly.

The circle of bodies opened up, and the large limousine entered, stopping a few inches from Barton's legs. The cabin lights came on as the driver got out and pranced to the rear of the vehicle. A moment later, the driver was helping a big man into the wheelchair.

CHAPTER 31

"That guy's not fit to hunt anyone down, never mind that baboon Barton," Declan said.

"Judd's one of the best," Crow corrected him, "and as soon as he's fit, I can guarantee he'll find Barton and deal with him."

"Not what I want," Declan quickly interrupted. "I want to deal with that bastard myself."

"Barton's known personally by a lot of the top men in the syndicate; you had better let an outsider do the job."

"Fuck you and the syndicate," Declan swore, and he lifted his pistol to Crow's head and cocked it. He never got the chance to squeeze the trigger before Badger's big hand pushed the weapon down, pointing it at the ground.

"Best not kill him, Boss," the big man said. "You'll bring the whole mob down on us and start a war."

With a sudden twist of his hand, Declan freed Badger's grip from the weapon. He then stepped back and said, "I'm not going to kill him yet; I need a few answers from him." He waved his pistol at the dead driver. "I think the war has already started."

Crow stuck his head around the side of the goon he had taken cover behind and said, "That's not necessarily the case." He waved his hand at the dead driver. "He's a small fish—a disposable commodity. The mob chiefs don't need to know about him."

Declan waved the gun in the little man's direction. "And what about you? You know about this place; how do I know you're not going to open your mouth about my little side job?"

"I suspect they already know about it." Crow stepped out from his cover behind the goon. "They seem to be well informed about your operation. You must have an informer in your mob."

Again Badger put his hand on the pistol and pushed it down. "Don't listen to him, Boss; it's obvious how they got to know about the warehouse when Barton burned it down. He had to have been inside and seen what was going on. That girl you left in charge was friendly with him; she would have filled him in."

"I suspect you know who the big boss is?" Crow took a step closer. "Well, he's back in this country, and Barton was one of his key bodyguards before all the trouble began. He might know of Barton's whereabouts."

"How do I get to talk to him?"

"You don't. Only through me will you get the answers you want."

"Can you phone him?"

With a shake of his head, Crow said, "No chance of that. He doesn't trust mobile phones." The little man was fighting for his life; he knew that all it would take was a slip of the tongue and it wouldbe a bullet in the head. "You would be best advised to wait a few days for Judd to recover rather than involve the big boss. I'll have a word with Judd and get a good price from him."

"I've got someone holding Barton's parents; all I have to do is get in touch with Barton, and if he wants to save them, he'll come running," Declan replied with a grin as he lowered the weapon. He waved to the goons standing next to Crow. "Bind him up and lock him in that room. Make sure he can't make a sound." He supervised Badger and the three goons cable tying the little man's hands and tossing him on the bed. They used two rolls of duct tape on his head mouth and legs. Satisfied, Declan locked the door and led the goons outside just as the container truck pulled up in front of them. He caught Badger by the arm as he was about to head for the driver's cabin. "Get going back to the club and get that whore Trudie out here to cater for this lot."

Declan watched the driver climb down from his cabin. "You took your time. Where have you been?"

The young man shook his head and shrugged his shoulders. "I had to take a break; it's the law. We can only drive for so many hours; then we have to stop."

"Okay," Declan replied after a time of studying the driver. "Drop your trailer over there." He pointed to the side of the building. The driver looked in the direction he was pointing and walked over and studied the ground by walking and stamping his feet on it. "That doesn't feel like solid ground; I can't drop it here."

"Well drop it as near to there as you can!" Declan snapped at him, and he and stomped away to join the rest of his goons. "As soon as the truck pulls away, get those doors open. We don't want any deadbodies falling out."

The driver pulled the unit away from the trailer and drove off up the track. Declan and the goons rushed to open the doors at the rear of the shipping container. They all gasped in horror, and Declan staggered back with shock. The container was empty.

"What the fuck's going on here!" he shouted. In a few seconds, he was shouting the same question into his mobile.

He disconnected with a collection of swear words and rammed his phone back into his pocket. A wave to the goons signalled them to follow him back into the building. Crow was lying in the same position. "Get him up!" he shouted to them. A moment later they had the little man sitting up on the side of the bed. Declan took pleasure from ripping the duct tape from his mouth, knowing the pain it would cause.

"The cargo that was in a container that was just delivered here has gone amiss. I've reason to believe you might know something about it."

With his blue eyes still watering from the agony of the tape being torn off, Crow shook his head. "I don't know anything about a container," he managed to say through the stinging around his mouth and cheeks.

As Declan was about to step over and slap the little man, his mobile sounded. Badger's name came on the screen. "What is it? I don't need any more bad news!" he shouted before Badger could get a word in.

When he managed to get his message over, Badger informed Declan the girl Trudie had done a runner. "Nobody knows where she is!" the big man's voice bellowed in his ear.

"Get everybody out looking for her!" Declan shouted. After ramming his mobile back into his pocket, he turned his attention back to Crow, delivering the slap. "I got it from a reliable source that you hired guys from your old set-up in London to hijack that truck and sent another in its place."

The added pain from the slap made it difficult for Crow to reply quickly, and he had to shake his head to clear the fuzz from his vision. "I don't know what you are talking about. As I told you, I don't know anything about this container."

"You're a fucking liar!" Declan screamed, and he landed another slap. This time the little man fell back on the bed with the impact and heard the cocking mechanism operating on the pistol and braced himself for the shot. Instead it was the sound of Declan's mobile that disturbed the silence. "What the fuck is it now, Badger?" Declan shouted, jamming his mobile between his shoulder and his ear whilst holding the weapon with both hands aimed at the little man lying on the bed. "Say that again!" he screamed into it. Badger repeated his words about the police finding Trudie's body in a back street covered with trash. Like a statue, Declan stood there over the bed, gazing down at Crow but not focused on him.

Gradually Declan lowered the pistol. His shoulder dropped, as did his mobile, which crashed on the floor. One of the goons instantly picked it up but held onto it, knowing not to disturb Declan while he was in a shocked state. Declan craved for his escape in a line of cocaine and a bottle of vodka. But out here in the sticks, they weren't available. He could feel his craving developing into uncontrollable rage. This was when he needed Badger; he was the only one who could control him in this state. Lying on the bed, the little man had become a giant rat with a snake's head, ready to strike at him. Declan raised the gun and squeezed the trigger. The explosion was deafening in the confines of the small room. The beast kept coming. Again he squeezed, and he kept on doing so until there were no more rounds in the weapon.

Still the beast came at him. He struggled, realising now he had been pinned to the floor and was unable to move. He screamed at the heavy body lying on top of him. He gazed into the eyes of the beast, but now they had changed; no longer were they the cold yellow serpent's. Slowly he recognised the deep-sunken brown eyes of his minder. He burst into a ludicrous fit of laughter and threw his arms around Badger's neck.

Lifting Declan clean off the floor and ramming him against the nearest wall, Badger roared at him,

"You've done it now!" He forced Declan around, making him look at the bloodied corpse of the little man on the bed. "Now the war starts. I'm out of here; you're on your own." Badger pushed him onto the bed on top of Crow's body and followed the rest of the goons out of the room and out of the building.

"I've made your job easier for you," Randel said, grinning, "My guys got hold of the truck that was heading for that other property that Declan Craig leased. They changed the container and told the driver to continue—threatened him to keep his mouth shut. I had a tracker fitted to the container, and we have located where it is." He raised his arm above his head and snapped his fingers. The interior light of the big car came on, and a figure from the passenger's seat got out.

The figure walked between the big man and Barton and placed a leather bag down on the ground. Even in that obscure lighting, Barton could tell this was a female, and when her glasses reflected off the beams from the vehicles, he was in no doubt as to who she was. Nevertheless, he was shocked, wondering why she was here after the way she smashed the in heads of Randel's goons with that bat. He wasn't sure; was that a nod of her head or, maybe, a trick of the light as she stepped backward to the side of the big man's wheelchair? "What's going on?" Barton shouted at Randel.

Jabbing his fat thumb at her, Randel replied, "This lady will accompany you to that location, where she will video you taking this case into the building. You will open it up and set the timing device. After that, you can make your escape. I know that right now, the little maggot Declan is in that building and is somewhat incapacitated. So he won't be any trouble. I'm not sure if his minders are there also, but I'm sure that if they are, a man of your experience will be able topull the job off under their noses. You have no other choice but to succeed if you want me to cancel the contract on your father."

Barton made to step forward, but the group stepped in on him and restrained him. "So it was you who set up the contract on my father?"

Randel shook his snowman-shaped head. "What reason would I have to do that?"

"Hell only knows what you people's reasons are."

Plucking one of his cigars from his top pocket and slipping it into the side of his pencil-line mouth,

Randel said, "As an extra bonus, if you succeed, I'll tell you who is responsible for that."

"It looks as though I don't have a choice," Barton replied submissively. As he was about to ask where this warehouse was located and how would he get there, the sound of a chugging old petrol engine could be heard from a distance.

All eyes turned in the direction it was coming from, and soon the pink Land Rover appeared. *Bloody hell!* was Barton's first thought, *Not that cursed thing again.* It pulled up next to the limousine, and a long-legged youth jumped out and handed the keys to the nearest goon and sauntered back in the direction he had driven from.

Randel nodded to the goon with the keys, and the goon tossed them at Barton; they landed at his feet. "That is your transport," he said as the flame from a lighter lit up his face and he got his cigar going. The woman strode forward and picked up the keys and the bag. She made a distinct display of having a gun in her other hand, and the glance she gave him left him in no doubt she would use it. She handed the keys to him, and he felt the cable ties being cut.

Barton rubbed his wrists and took the keys from her.

"Shall we go?" Trudie said, and she got round behind him and, as a reminder, jabbed the gun into his back. As they approached the Land Rover, Barton observed two of the goons drop the tailboard and climb in the back. That cancelled out any idea that may have entered his head about jumping this woman. When she got into the passenger's seat beside him, she began to twist and turn, reaching her hands around the back of the seat.

Barton started up the engine and said, "This old thing doesn't have seat belts, if that's what you're looking for." He remembered from his previous experience with this old vehicle that the brakes were deadly—a feather-light touch, and you had to brace yourself from headbutting the windscreen. His advantage was that he could grip the steering wheel for support. The disadvantage was that the two guys in the back would be thrown in on top of him and the woman, providing she didn't fly out the front window first. But that idea wouldn't come into effect until after he planted the bomb inside that warehouse. He had already anticipated that the two goons and this woman had been instructed to kill him after they had made their escape. That way Randel would be able to deny involvement to the rest of the syndicate bosses using the video that the woman had made and claim his boys had caught the bomber and dealt with him.

Mathew Matlock, nicknamed Mad Matlock, had seated himself in the passenger's seat beside Badger. The other three were jammed in the rear of the four-by-four. Normally, to make things more comfortable he would be in the back because of his smaller size. The three big men in the back seat were quick to get out of the cramped space they had been in when Badger stopped the vehicle at the rear door of the club. Mad Matlock followed Badger into Declan's office.

"What are we doing here, Badger? he asked.

Badger had begun to open desk drawers, pulling out the contents, searching through them, and returning them with an unsatisfied grunt. Next, using a screwdriver, he opened the metal filing cabinet. Again he searched through papers, with the same results. He slumped himself down on Declan's seat and let out a deep sigh.

Mad Matlock sat himself on the chair in front of the desk and repeated his question and added, "What are you looking for?"

Badger, with his elbows on the desk and his head resting in his hands, looked at the smaller man. "We need to get back to the old barracks and kill that bastard."

"Can I ask why?" Mad Matlock said.

Badger got stiffly out of the seat and looked down at him. "It's the only way I can see to stop the syndicate from sending troops out to get revenge for the murder of Crow." Deciding to leave the other three goons to look after the club, Badger and Mad Matlock drove out to the old barracks and found Declan lying on the floor next to the bed where the corpse of Crow lay. The bed was now covered in the little man's blood. Declan lay curled up on his side, whimpering and thumping the floor with his hand. He was so far gone in his cold turkey that he didn't acknowledge their entrance.

Badger gripped his shirt and turned him over onto his back; and with his big hands round Declan's neck, he squeezed the life out of him.

Mad Matlock patted Badger's shoulder. "I think he's gone now."

Easing his grip, Badger slowly rose to his feet, studied his victim, and nodded. "Let's get to fuck out of here," he said, and he turned for the door. As Mad Matlock was closing the outer door, the sound of a vehicle approaching made them dart back inside.

Badger cursed the design of the building; it had no windows at the front or on the door, so there was no way of knowing what the vehicle was or who was in it. They quickly slunk their way back into the small bedroom beside the bodies of the big black driver, Pinkie, Crow, and now Declan. Soon they heard the sound of the vehicle doors opening and closing. This sound confused Badger; he had never heard that crude metallic sound from car doors before. He remembered that on the side wall of the room a sliding peephole had been built into it so that the person entertaining the immigrants could keep an eye on them. He located this, opened it, and could see all the way to the outer door.

"What's happening?" Mad Matlock asked. "Has anybody come through that door?"

Badger held up his hand to silence him. A dragging two minutes passed, but still the door didn't move. "I don't know what's going on out there. I heard the door of that vehicle open and close. So where did the occupants go?"

"I don't like this," Mad Matlock complained. "This is when I think I'm going to piss myself."

"You can start pissing yourself when the mob charges through that door," Badger whispered.

The charge never happened, and after ten minutes had dragged by, Badger decided they should go outside and investigate.

"Where are you going?" Mad Matlock asked in a panic.

"Out there to see what's going on," Badger replied, opening the room door.

"I can guess what's going on; they're out there waiting for us to show face and blow us to fuck."

"If that's the mob, they would have done that the minute that vehicle stopped. They would have charged in showering us with automatic fire, and they wouldn't have advertised their approach with that noisy machine."

Keeping a low profile, Badger made his way to the front door, Mad Matlock's heavy breathing at his back making it difficult to hear anything that moved outside. Inch by inch, he opened the door, every so often stopping and listening for movement. When it was wide enough for him to step out, his attention was drawn by the headlights of the vehicle that had been abandoned close to the four- by-four. What struck him as being odd was the closeness of the headlamps.

Mad Matlock's head appeared at his shoulder. "That's an old Land Rover, used in the army years ago," he whispered. They both shielded their eyes, trying to see what was beyond the vehicle, and gradual relief came when they noticed the lights were beginning to dim, and soon they went out. In the light from inside the building, they were able to make out the shape and colour of the Land Rover.

"It's been painted pink," Mad Matlock gasped. "This is too creepy; I think I'm going to piss myself."

"Don't piss yourself yet," Badger said. "You stay here; I'm going to get my gun out of the four-by-four. Warn me if you spot any movement."

"I think I'll come with you; we can jump in it and get the fuck out of here."

Badger pushed a big hand against the smaller man's chest. "That might be what they want us to do. Stay here to make sure they don't get inside; I'll only be a minute."

"Looking at the paint job on that Land Rover and the way it has been abandoned," Mad Matlock said, holding Badger back by the arm, "this could be kids from those flats pranking about."

"I've thought of that," Badger said, pulling his arm free. He darted head down towards the four-by-four and sighed with relief that nothing had happened when he got there. He soon got inside, grabbed his pistol from under the passenger's seat, and ran back pushing the smaller man in the door.

Mad Matlock staggered back as Badger closed the door. "What's happening?" he shouted at the big man.

"Nothing," Badger replied, standing to the side of the door and cocking his weapon. "That's what's now bothering me."

"Why?" Mad Matlock asked. "Isn't that a good thing?"

Badger shook his head, holding the pistol at shoulder height. "Do you remember that big guy with the ponytail? Barton …? This, is his field of play. The mob could have sent him instead of a squad of thugs; he could be anywhere."

"Now I am going to piss myself. At least with a squad of thugs we could run and hide; with that guy, it's like hiding from your own shadow.

Badger agreed with a nod. "If it is him they have sent, we'll just have to play him at his own game."

Mad Matlock moved to the other side of the door and pressed his back against the wall. "How are we going to do that if we don't know where he is?"

We stay put, stay silent, and hope he thinks we're sleeping."

"He could have spotted you going to the car when you picked up that gun, and with the noise that old engine made, who could sleep through that?"

Badger shrugged. "If it is Barton, then he has to get in here, and this is the only way in." He nodded at the door.

It had been a slow, painful struggle for Judd getting out of the club, even with the help of Trudie's younger brother. She moved him with the arm his injured hand was attached to over her shoulder, the youngster taking the weight of the other. The most time-consuming and trickiest part of his escape was distracting the bartender. She had to abandon them halfway down the stairs and report to the bald bespectacled little man that she had heard sounds coming from the cellar. This seemed to have taken a lot of time, and with the help of the youngster, Judd got himself seated on the steps.

When she returned, he noticed she was breathing heavily, and with her brother's help, they got him onto his feet. He asked her, "What was the hold-up?"

"Don't ask," she promptly replied. "I've managed to get the cellar door locked, so he'll not get out in a hurry." Trudie's brother—Drew, she had called him— had a small van waiting at the back door, and Trudie instructed him to reverse the vehicle close to the door. Soon Judd was lifted into the rear, and they got on the move. As he lay on his back, feeling every bump and turn, he started thinking how simple it had been to persuade her to help him. At first he had doubts, thinking, *Could this be a trick to get rid of me on the instructions of the owner of the club?* Even after miles of painful travel, the doubts were still there. In his lifestyle, paranoia was a constant companion that had helped him survive. Trudie was a lovely woman, and Judd sensed she had developed fondness for him, but he knew he had to fight against feeling the same.

The van pulled to a stop. A moment later, the back door swung open. In the background glow from nearby streetlamps, two silhouettes stood looking in at him for a moment. One climbed in; Judd recognised him as Drew. The other he guessed must be a friend. They slid him out on his rump and then carried him in through the open door of a cottage. Even in the dim light Judd could see the place was surrounded by high hedges, making it difficult for pedestrians to see what was going on. After a few awkward manoeuvres along a narrow passage and in through a narrow doorway, they finally got him settled onto an old, dusty sofa.

Trudie walked in with a trayful of mugs containing hot drinks. The two youths took one, and she handed one to him. With her drink in her hand, she sat next to him. She looked at the youths and smiled. "Thanks, you two," she said, holding up her mug. "That's a good job you've done; I owe you for that. But you mustn't mention this to anyone."

After the youths had downed their drinks and left, she said, "We need to get that dressing changed; I'll drive to the chemist's and get some bandages and disinfectant." She finished her drink, got up off the sofa, and collected the empty mugs. "I'll be back soon." She handed him the remote for the television and left.

Judd was getting bored watching television; he had lost track of the time but guessed she must have been away for over an hour. He needed the toilet, and he didn't know where it was in this old cottage. Slowly and painfully, he got onto his feet, and using the walls and furniture as support, he made his way out of the living room. Two doors faced him in the passageway. The first was the kitchen; the other was a bedroom. His feet were causing him so much pain that he lay on the single bed, thinking that maybe a short nap would help squash his need for the toilet.

He jumped out of his sleep thinking his bladder had given way. He could feel the wetness below him. He swung his legs out of the bed and was faced with a small window. The sun was shining in on the floor in front of him. He got up and almost fainted with the pain in both his feet and his hand. Slowly he made his way back into the passageway. He stopped at the open kitchen door, listening for Trudie moving about, but heard nothing. He struggled into the living room. Still no sign of her. Panic was something he had always managed to control, but this was different; he felt vulnerable, had no means of defending himself, had no idea where he was, had no mobile to call for help. Had there been a landline in this house, he would have surely spotted it. He resigned himself back to the sofa, and his memory drifted back to the debate between Crow and the owner of the club.

Could this be the way for the club owner to regain some leverage on the little man? With the remote in his good hand, he was about to turn the television on when the sound of the front door lock being opened made him drop it and struggle onto his feet. Before he managed to reach the living room door, it swung open, and the two young men stood grinning at each other. Judd recognised them instantly as Trudie's brother and his friend. "Hi!" he greeted them, feeling relief that help had arrived, his relief was short-lived when the expression on the youths' faces changed and they rushed at him, knocking him back onto the sofa.

"This is for the way you brutalised my sister!" Dew shouted at him as he and his mate drew long-bladed knives from behind their backs. Judd's attempts to defend himself were futile against the onslaught of knife stabs.

When finally the fight was drained from his body, he could do nothing but lie there until all the pains were gone. The light in his eye went out, as did his life.

CHAPTER 32

"The turning's not far from here, according to my satnav," Trudie advised. She leaned forward, peering out the small steamed-up windows. Barton pulled the Land Rover to the side of the road and stopped.

"What do you think you're doing!" she shouted.

Barton cut the lights and shut off the engine. "We don't know how many there are up there. We have to create some kind of distraction."

"Okay, bright arse, what do you propose?" she threw back at him.

"The only thing I can suggest," Barton said, "is that we let those two guys in the back drive up there, abandon this, and run like fuck. We can sneak up through that rough terrain while that gang are investigating what's going on. We get inside and hope we have time to set that timing device and do a runner ourselves." Her glasses reflected off the glow of the street lighting as she looked at him. He felt the pistol being jabbed into ribs. Barton moved away from the discomfort and said, "Unless you have a better idea, with the noise this old banger's making they're going know we're coming and be ready for us. We'll all get blown away before we even get out of this thing."

"I was told you were a tricky bastard, so try anything and I'll empty this magazine into the back of your head." She made an obvious play at releasing the safety catch. "Now get out and stand clear for me to get out." Barton complied with her orders and watcher her slide over to the driver's seat and step out, all the while the weapon being pointed at his face.

The two men in the back were reluctant to agree to carry out Barton's plan, protesting that they were the ones taking all the risk. "You'll be taking a bigger risk sitting in the back, not knowing what is happening up front," he pointed out. "The minute you pull up near that building, you both dive over the seats into the back and jump out the back tailgate. You won't be seen if the vehicle is facing the doors with the headlights on full beam."

The shorter of the two looked at his companion. "What do you think, Chuck? It seems to make sense."

"You forget we're here to help keep an eye on him." Chuck nodded towards Barton.

"What if we stop short of the building, get out the back, and push it nearer?" the shorter man said.

"Just get in the front and drive it in there!" the woman shouted, pointing the pistol at them. "I'll keep an eye on him."

This short distraction gave Barton time to glance at the weapon she had in her hand, and if his guess was right, it was a Glock 19 Blowback. All it would take to block it was a handful of mud on the recoil mechanism, and looking at the rough ground they will have to cover, he could see that mud was in no shortage. Seeing the weapon being pointed at them, the two men backed stepped towards the Land Rover. A short debate took place as to which of them would drive. The clicking sound of her pulling back the cocking slide of the gun soon sparked the decision.

Returning her attention to Barton, the weapon now aimed at him, Trudie stepped over and pulled the bag containing the explosive device out across the back tailboard just as the vehicle pulled away. She handed it to Barton. "Don't drop the fucking thing; it might go off. Now get moving." She waved the weapon in the intended direction.

The bag was about the size of what used to be called a weekend case; he estimated it to be about fifty pounds in weight. *Going to make quite a bang*, he decided. He was right about the mud. The ground beneath was marshy; in some places they were sinking up to their ankles. She was breathing hard behind him; he thought maybe she was a smoker and quickened the pace in the hopes she might trip over some of the undergrowth. It was too soon for that to happen, and he found himself at the edge of the wild terrain and standing on what looked like an abandoned parade square. Parked close to a large building was a large vehicle. Next to that stood the old Land Rover, the headlights still shining on the door of the building. He wondered whether the two goons had managed to escape.

Barton had to make a quick dive behind a nearby shrub when the door opened a crack, and he hoped she had the same reflexes. She had, and he was relieved when she stumbled on top of him. He was glad that the light wasn't good where they lay and the beam from the old vehicle would dazzle anyone one looking in their direction. He did manage to notice that when she stumbled over him, her gun hand sank into the mud. Would that be enough to jam the weapon?

Side by side they lay behind the shrub and watched as the door opened fully. Two figures stood for a time looking at the vehicles. The smaller of the two stepped back, and the other did a crouching dart towards the vehicles. In the dim light from the Land Rover, Barton recognised the big man; he could never forget the way he'd nearly broken his hand when he landed a punch to his jaw.

The door to the four-by-four opened and closed quickly, and the large man darted back into the building, closing the door behind him. "That's a bit of a bummer," he whispered in the woman's ear. "It looks like they're not going out to investigate what's going on."

"What do we do now?" she whispered, at the same time trying to clear the mud from her pistol with her hand.

"We need to get into that building without being spotted. We'll have to find another way in."

"How am I going to make a video of you with all those people in there?"

Barton's mind raced for a while, and he finally said, "If we find another way in and it's safe to do so, you can take your video outside that door or window of me setting the timing; then we can lob it inside and run."

Almost an hour later, soaked and mud caked, Trudie grabbed his arm. "What do we do now, smart arse? We can't find another way in."

"This is an old army gym; there must be a toilet with a window," Barton said. "I've been in enough to know they always have one." He continued scouting around the building with her at his back but could find no windows or fire exits. At the darkest corner, he stepped back, looked up, and noticed a faint light on the roof. "A skylight," he whispered, pointing up at the faint beam.

"How are we going to get up there?" she whispered back.

"That shipping container we just passed … I could get on top of that, hoist you up, then we can jump from there onto the roof."

"Then what?" Barton was already creeping his way along the wall and could hear her stretching her pace to keep up. "We open the skylight and I set the timer, giving us time to get back down and get away."

"I don't like heights," she complained, and she watched him climbing up the container doors. "You can stay down there," he said from the top of the container, "but how are you going to video me setting the timer and dropping the case through the window?"

He reached his hand down, and she had to jump a few times before getting a secure grip. Luckily she was a lightly built woman, and he whisked her up with little effort. They stood together looking at the distance they would have to jump. Barton could see no problems with it; it was well within his capability. But she took a quick step back.

"That looks a lot farther from up here than it did on the ground!" she gasped. "I'll never do it."

"If we fuck about here any longer, it'll be daylight and they will shoot us off the fucking container." He stepped to the edge, threaded his fingers together, and held his hands at crotch level, palms up. "Take a step back, jump towards me landing one foot in my hands, and I'll throw you over."

Trudie stood there for a long, doubtful moment puffing out her cheeks and shaking her head. Finally, when she decided she had no other choice, she took the plunge.

With the combination of her momentum and Barton using all his strength, she landed on the roof with a noisy yelp and a thump that Barton was sure must have been heard. Time ticked by as he stood listening for a reaction from below inside the building, but all he could hear was her whimpering and swearing, saying she was struggling to maintain her grip on the frame of the window and was bleeding from somewhere. He wrapped the handle of the bag around his shoulder and took a run and jumped, landing on top of her. He just managed to clasp his hand over her mouth before she started to yelp again. "We need to get this window open before I set the timer and you begin videoing with your mobile."

Opening the window proved to be impossible; it had been bolted to the rafters. Trudie whisked out a nail file from her pocket and handed it to him. Barton got to work gouging out one of the glass panes. When he finally succeeded, he nodded. "You can start videoing now." Barton had the bag open and was surprised to see that the device was simple and homemade. Within a few minutes, he had it all set, giving them fifteen minutes to get clear. He glanced up at her expecting to see her mobile in operation, but all she was doing was trying to piece it together. "What's the hold-up?" he asked.

"I had the fucking thing in my hip pocket. When I landed on my arse, it got smashed."

Getting the bag through the window was a squeeze, and Barton had no doubts that the noise it made when it landed on the floor must have been heard. "Never mind that thing." He pointed to her phone. "We need to get out of here." The container top was slightly lower than the roof of the building, and after a bit of persuasion, she jumped, screaming all the way until she landed heavily on her feet and teetered on the edge until Barton landed next to her, grabbed hold of her arm, and pushed her flat on the metal roof.

They lay for a while listening for a reaction from the noise she had made. Barton started to doubt whether there were people inside when no response came, but when he remembered the two men at the door and the vehicle parked at the front, he decided that whoever they were, they could be playing him at his own game. "Time to get off this," Barton whispered, getting onto his hands and knees. Trudie crawled behind him towards the rear, and taking both her hands, he lowered her down, but she was still a few feet short, and she let out a howl when she landed on the ground. He climbed down beside her, lying crouched where she had landed. "You're a noisy little cow," he whispered. "They must know we're here." He stood up and helped her, but she fell over. "What's wrong now?" he again whispered.

"I think I've broke my ankle," she whimpered.

"We need to get away from here," he said, lifting her up and folding her arm around his neck. "The thing in that bag is due to go off at any moment, and it's going to blow us to fuck with it if we don't." He ran, dragging her into the shrubs. When he thought they were at a safe distance, he pushed her down flat on the marshy ground and dived down beside her. "Close your eyes and hold your ears," he advised her.

The minutes passed, and nothing happened. He lowered his hands and got onto his knees, looking in the direction of the building. "It's well past the time I set it for," he said. He glanced down at her still holding her ears and snatched her hands away from her head and repeated himself.

"Maybe all this mud and water got into the electric timing device," she suggested.

He wondered how it happened without him being aware of it. Maybe his attention had been so full of the present predicament. In any case, he suddenly realised that the dawn chorus had begun and grey light had filled his surroundings. "We need to get away from here," he said, and he rose stiffly. Again he had to support her over the rough ground. When they reached the roadside, her two companions appeared from behind a bush. The tallest of the two took her other arm, and at that moment the explosion shattered the morning stillness.

CHAPTER 33

Tom Barton and his wife, Jean, were in their small kitchen. She was preparing cups of tea when they heard Paddy Barns shout from the living room, "Come on, boys and girls! Never mind the tea; come and have some more of this vodka! It's the best money can buy."

"I don't like that man," Jean whispered. "He strikes me as being a bit of a con man," Tom replied, "but what could he be after?"

"He's your friend; you brought him here."

"Well, he did take us out, and we had a lovely meal and some good wine, so it can't be money he's after."

Jean grimaced. "If it's money he's trying to get from us, he's in for a big shock, as we don't have any."

"Why is Richard not answering his phone?" Tom said. "I've tried a few times, only to get the same response. Hope he's all right."

"So do I," Jean replied, handing him a mug of tea and heading into the living room with a mug in each hand. Before she opened the door, she turned and whispered to her husband, "I can smell him from here, the dirty little poo bag."

Paddy was stretched out on the sofa, the empty vodka bottle lying on the floor next to him. He grunted and snored, constantly braking wind, the odour of which made Jean stop in her tracks and recoil against her husband. "How are we going to get rid of him?" She complained.

Shaking his head, Tom stood over Paddy, bent down, and picked up the empty bottle. "That's why we need to get hold of Richard; he'd soon send him on his way."

From somewhere a mobile phone sounded. Paddy jumped up, knocking the bottle out of Tom's hand. Paddy rummaged through his pockets and pulled out his mobile. "Yes, it's me," was all he said, and they watched as he listened to the caller, every now and then shaking or nodding his head.

Jean almost jumped out of her skin when the little Belfast man disconnected his mobile and did a silly dance, punching the air and cheering. "Looks like you've had good news," she said.

Paddy gave her a broad toothless grin. "Very good news," he replied. "Now let's try to contact your son."

"I've tried," Tom said. "He not answering."

"Why do you want to contact our son?" Jean asked, placing the mugs on the coffee table at the side of the sofa.

"A mutual friend of ours wants to have a few words with him."

"What mutual friend?" Tom uttered sharply. "I can't remember him mentioning your name as a friend or any associates of yours."

Still maintaining his broad grin, Paddy said, "You know what it's like, sure. You have a few drinks in the pub and get into a conversation, and before you know it, you tongue runs away with your reasoning. Towards the end of the evening, you've found yourself a new friend, and the next morning you can't remember half the things you told this person. To cut a long story short, your son said he wanted to buy an item from this mutual friend, and the friend wants to know whether he's still interested."

Tom and Jean looked at each other, and that look sent the message to Paddy informing him he had just been rumbled. He jumped up off the sofa saying he had to run and meet someone and was opening the front door before Tom and his wife got out of their chairs.

"What was that all about?" Jean asked as they watched Paddy trot down the street.

"I think he realised we have just caught him out in a lie. We know Richard's not in the habit of overdrinking and letting his tongue get out of control to a stranger—or, for that matter, to anyone." Tom got settled back on his chair as Jean cleared away the empty bottle, glasses, and mugs.

She almost dropped the items she had in her hands when the screech of a braking vehicle intruded on the silence they had shared whilst thinking about the experience they had gone through with the dirty Irishman. They both rushed to the door in time to see that a vehicle had mounted the pavement at the end of the street, and the driver was out shouting at something under his car. It was obvious there had been an accident, and like the rest of the neighbours, they rushed to the scene.

Jean instantly recognised the person trapped under the car and gazed at her husband. "It's Paddy."

Tom pulled her by the arm. "Come on, Jean; there's nothing we can do here." Slowly they walked back to the house. "The emergency services will get here soon, and so will the police. We don't want to get involved. I hope the neighbours didn't see him leave our house; there could be a lot of tricky questions to answer. Judging by his manner and the way he talked, it's obvious he's some kind of crook."

It was a natural reaction for Barton, he had seen much too often in his past that even at this distance an explosion of this magnitude could cause injury. He dived headlong into a shallow ditch at the edge of the road, dragging Trudie with him. Chuck and his mate were stunned and confused by the power of the blast, and they got thrown backwards onto the road. Luckily there were no traffic this early; otherwise they could have been added to the potential casualties.

It seemed as though the entire world was in a state of shock as the seconds passed in sheer silence. But just as unexpectedly as the first blast there came a second one; this one was less powerful but seemed to have more effect on the ground, and Barton felt it shudder beneath him.

"What the fuck's happening?" Trudie shouted from beneath him. "Were there two bombs in that bag or what?"

Barton remained in the same position, holding her down, "I don't think that second blast was a bomb;

it could have been gas tanks or something. Stay where you are in case there are more."

"We need to get out of here before someone reports this and the coppers come racing here," she said, struggling to get up.

Barton held her down. "Give it a few more minutes; we can't take the chance of there being something else that could blow up."

He had soon carried her for a good half mile along the road, with Chuck and his mate staggering behind, and still there was no sign of the emergency services. *Okay, we're out in the countryside, and maybe a few miles from the nearest police and fire station, but surely the sound of them being on their way should be heard from here?* The first vehicles that came racing up behind them weren't what Barton was expecting. The two black four-by-fours pulled to the side of the road ahead of them. The doors flew open, and the driver waved for them to get in. Barton pushed Trudie into the rear seat of the nearest, while chuck helped his mate into the front vehicle. They had barely moved a hundred yards when the emergency services came charging towards them and flew on past, sirens blaring and lights flashing.

The four-by-four drivers soon put their feet down, and a few minutes later they were on the motorway. After the shock of the two explosions, Barton was hit by another; from somewhere hidden in her mud-caked clothing, Trudie fished out her pistol and jabbed it into his ribs. He flinched away from it and said, "Is this how you treat a guy who just saved your life?"

"I think we're on our way to see the big man in the wheelchair, and he knows you have a vendetta against him."

"As he has against me," Barton replied. "It's all down to who pulls the trigger first."

"He's got bodyguards all around him, and they're all well trained for the job; I don't see how you can hope to win."

"So why are you holding the gun on me?"

She indicated to the men in the front four-by-four. "It's our job to make sure you don't disappear. As long as he knows where you are, the big man can relax." Barton grinned at her. "I wouldn't like to be in your shoes when you tell him you couldn't get that video shot. That was the whole point of the job; now he can't prove to the syndicate he wasn't responsible for setting it up."

The vehicles pulled onto the slipway signed for Stafford. "We'll just have to wait and see what he has to say." She gave the weapon an extra jab at his ribs.

"Do you think that had you succeeded in getting that video, he would let you live and take a chance at you not mouthing off to the syndicate, what you did, and who you did it for?"

"Mr. Randel is one of the top members of the syndicate; he'll think of a way round it, and they'll listen to him," she replied with a confident grin.

As the two four-by-fours pulled into a side street and stopped outside an office block, she ordered him out. Barton asked, "Why should he go to all that trouble when he can just as easily get us all killed and that would be the end of it?" He was staring into her eyes, trying to read her reaction, when his door opened. There, standing holding the door with a grin, was the shortest of the two goons from the other vehicle. Chuck was at his side, and he grabbed Barton's jacket and attempted to pull him out. Barton swiped his hand away and stepped out. "Touch me again and you're a dead man."

This time Trudie stabbed the pistol into his back with such force that it took his breath away. His natural reaction was to swipe around using his elbow as a weapon. He felt it hit the target and heard her jaw crack. She yelped and fell back against the vehicle; the weapon fell out of her hand and landed at Chuck's feet. Barton dived for it but was too late, and Chuck swiped it away with his foot. The two men jumped at the same moment and soon had him on his knees. This time the weapon was jabbed into the back of his neck, and he felt himself being wrenched onto his feet and pushed through a set of double glass doors.

Facing him was a long, wide brightly lit corridor with numerous doors on either side. The two men walked close behind him; he felt their hands on his shoulders as they edged him towards an open lift. Had Barton the choice, he would have found the stairs and climbed them; he hated using lifts, being somewhat claustrophobic, and having no other choice in the matter made him feel worse.

There was no need to push him out of the lift; he had stepped out before the door had fully opened. Trudie stepped out behind them, still holding her jaw and cursing him. Another long corridor faced them, and Chuck's mate walked ahead, knocked on one of the doors, and pushed it open.

Randel was in his wheelchair behind a large desk and, as usual, belching smoke from a big cigar. His pencil-line mouth widened in what could have been a grin or a frown, but his grey eyes remained cold. "I heard you managed to blow up that building," he said, wrapping his fat fingers around his cigar and placing it on a glass ashtray.

He turned his attention to the woman. His eyes widened, and he nodded at her, pointing at her face. "What happened to you?"

She stabbed a finger at Barton. "That's what happened. He thumped me."

This time it was a definite grin. "You're lucky that's all that happened to you. Did you get that video?"

A deathly silence filled the office as the big man glanced from face to face.

"We didn't get a chance to," Barton said. Now it was his turn to grin, guessing what the results of Trudie's failure would be. Chuck and his mate gave him their account of what they had done, denying any knowledge of what happened prior to the explosion. Randel lifted his cigar out of the ashtray, took a long pull at it, and blew the smoke at the faces in front of him. He nodded to the two men. "Take her away and shut her up in a room or a cupboard; I'll get someone to deal with her later."

Taking a step closer to the desk, Barton jabbed his thumb at the woman by his side. "She's not to blame. She did all she could; she was behind me all the time with that pistol at my back. It's not her fault the building had no other entrants. We knew the goons were inside, and the only way in was through that door. If we had charged in, we would have been blown away and the bomb wouldn't have been planted."

Randel waved his fat hand at the two men, and Barton was powerless to protest further as they dragged Trudie out the door. "As you no doubt know, she seriously injured some of my boys," Randel said when the door closed and he and Barton were left on their own. "I gave her a second chance, and she blew it." Barton took a step closer, and the big man whipped a gun from an open drawer in his desk and aimed it at Barton's head.

Barton stepped back and held his hands up. "You wouldn't use that in here; the noise would bring everyone in this building hereto investigate.

"Don't bet on that," Randel said, stubbing his cigar in the ashtray on his desk. "My boys will have me out of here before these desk jockeys can get up off their arses, and an alibi has already been set up."

"The last time we met, you said you could have had me killed long ago. Why didn't you?"

"I could have, but I decided that you could be useful to me." "How's that?"

"That contract out on your father. I can get it cancelled, but I'm the only one who can do that. And that, Barton, is my lever on you. Once you have carried out a few other jobs with success, I will cancel."

"You said you would do that when I blew up that building; do you expect me to take your word for it if I do other jobs for you?"

"Do you have a choice?" Randel grinned and placed his pistol on the desk within reach of his fat fingers.

"There's always a choice if you can find the time to discover it," Barton replied, taking a sharp glance at the weapon, his mind racing to work out a distraction good enough to give him the opportunity to dive for it. "When you say you're the only one who could cancel that contract, that means it must have been you who took it out."

Randel caught Barton's glance and placed his hand over the weapon, shaking his snowman-shaped head, the layers of flesh rubbing against the collar of his white shirt. "I didn't hire the shooter, but I know who did, and I have the power to call it off."

"You do that now and I'll consider doing those jobs." Barton knew what the answer would be, but talk seemed to be the only distraction he could think of.

The big man chortled, and his entire body seemed to wobble down to the wheel on his chair. "I'll give you credit, Barton, for being a comedian. You say you'll consider? Ha! If you want to see your father alive again, you'll do these Jobs."

Barton was about to reply by asking what the nature of the jobs were when a mobile phone sounded. The big man cursed and dragged it out of his breast pocket.

Without giving himself time to think, Barton dived over the desk. He was a split second too late to grasp hold of the weapon, but his momentum carried him over on top of the big man, and they crashed backwards. The blast sent a burning shock through Barton's chest; the gun in the big man's hand had gone off, and he was sure he had been hit.

The expected struggle from the big man below him never happened. Randel lay motionless, his small, deep-set eyes staring into Barton's. At first those eyes blazed in shock, and gradually the fire left them. It was when Barton eased himself off the big man and his wheelchair that he noticed the blood at the top of the Randel's bald head, and black powder burns peppered under his fleshy chin. He didn't need to check to know that he was dead.

Just as Barton stepped backward around the desk, the door burst open. He swung round to see the two goons charging in. Chuck stopped suddenly, but his mate continued over and gazed down at Randel's body. A long moment passed as they all stared in shocked silence at the big man lying with his head in a pool of blood. Hismate turned to Chuck, panic written all over his face. "Let's get the fuck out of here!" he cried.

Without hesitation, Chuck charged out with his mate behind him. Barton followed, but at a steady pace. He needed to find that woman, and he knew she had to be somewhere in the building. In the corridor, all the doors were open, and the occupants from the offices were all standing in groups, waiting in a panic to dive into the lift to get out and away from the gunshot.

Barton took to the stairs, where he had to squeeze past others who were rushing to get out. He managed to get out of the glass exit doors in time to see the four-by-fours speed away. A woman came rushing out the door and stopped, gazed at Barton, and screamed, pointing at his bloodstained clothes. "Are you the one who got injured?" she cried. Barton followed her pointing finger to see that the clothes he had taken from Billy Bunter were soaked in the big man's blood. There was nothing for him to do but run, knowing that within a few minutes the police cars would come screaming in.

Trudie was standing at the junction, her hands sunk deep into her pockets. Barton ran up to her, and she looked at him and yelled, "What's going on?"

"There's been an accident," he said, grabbing her arm. "Now let's get out of here before the coppers arrive."

Trudie held back. "You can't walk down the street in that state." She pointed to his clothing. "We'll have to hide you somewhere till I can find you something to wear."

Barton nodded towards her mud-stained clothes. "You don't look too well dressed yourself."

At the other side of the street, a narrow lane passed between two tall buildings. Trudie steered him across and pushed him into a corner. "Stay there," she said, looking around for signs of anyone passing nearby.

Barton hunched down, making himself as invisible as possible in the darkest part of the corner. He decided to give her five minutes. If she didn't return, then he was off to find clean clothing. Five minutes is a long time when crouched in an uncomfortable position and when having no timepiece, He was playing a guessing game. *That's it*, he decided. He could neither see nor hear any sign of her, so he got up and searched around. The only signs of life came from the traffic on the main road.

Barton edged his way along the lane, stopped at the end, and glanced around the corner of the building. He quickly darted back when the sound of sirens from a short way off blasted his hearing. When he reached his hiding place, she was standing in the shadow.

"I thought you had buggered off," she said, unfolding a set of blue work overalls from her arms. Handing them over, she added, "I think they'll fit you." She grinned.

Barton stripped off Billy Bunter's clothes while she stood there admiring his physique. "Where did you get these?" he asked, stepping into the overalls and zipping up the front.

"From a washing line just down the street."

"I need to get a phone," Barton said as they reached the end of the side street.

"Well, you know what happened to mine," she replied, limping along beside him and struggling to keep up, still nursing her cheek with her hand.

"I also need to get wheels."

"And I need to get to a hospital," she complained. "My ankle is killing me, and I think you've broken my jaw, plus my arse bone feels as though it has been hit by a sledgehammer."

They walked a few paces in silence, dodging through people heading for the shops, Barton all the while eyeing the cars parked at the side of the street. Most of the properties had been converted into flats, and the few that hadn't were boarded up.

Farther along the street Barton noticed a run-down hotel that looked to be still in use. By the side of it was a small car park, and a few cars were parked close to a wall. Barton turned to talk to Trudie and discovered she was quite a way behind, limping as fast as she could.

When she caught up with him, he was standing against the wall and was studying the vehicles lined up a few yards away. "A right load of old bangers," she said. "We'll be lucky to get any of them started."

He selected a blue Vauxhall Corsa because, in his opinion, it would be quicker and easier to get into and get started.

She grinned at him as she got into the passenger's seat. "Did you pick this one to match your overalls?"

Having got the car started and driving, he asked, "Where do you live?"

"Not far from here, why?"

"We need a place to rest up for a while and sharpen my thinking."

I'm not sure my flat would be safe in light of what has happened. The syndicate will be on the hunt."

"My place was bombed, so we can't go anywhere near there."

"Maybe for a short time we could be safe at my place," she said thoughtfully, "but don't get any ideas;

I'm in no condition for that, and I really think I need to go to hospital."

Following her directions, they ditched the car a short walk from her flat. It was an attic with low ceilings, and Barton had to lower his head to move about. They sat on an uncomfortable two-seater sofa drinking coffee without milk or sugar and watching television. He turned to her with a grin and asked, "By the way, what is your name?"

She returned his grin. "Marlin."

At the sound of that name, Barton suffered a memory flashback from almost a year before. It felt like a sudden blast of ice water had invaded his bloodstream. He could see her lying on that sheepskin rug, visualise her mutilated body and her baby lying drowned in that bath of cold water. He put his coffee mug on the floor at his feet and jumped up.

She sprang up beside him and whined in pain at the sudden movement. "What's wrong? Did I say something?"

Barton shook his head. "I've got something to do, and I need to get started now." Leaving her standing holding her mug with her tinted glasses perched at the end of her nose, her eyes wide and her mouth open, he headed out the door and bounded down the stairs.

Sitting in the small blue Corsa, he couldn't shake off the feeling that he was responsible for the deaths of Marlin Bank and her baby. If he hadn't been so besotted with the woman Nancy, he would have been with her. Or if he had stayed away, this would never have happened. He had vowed over her dead body to get the person responsible; maybe then his conscience would easeoff.

Armed with his golf club, Tom Barton stood ready to strike; his wife, Jean, was at his back, wielding a candlestick. At the sight of his son clad in the blue overalls, Tom laughed and relaxed his weapon and opened the door as Jean replaced her weapon on the shelf. "I like the suit," his father said, walking behind him into the living room. "Have you decided to take on an honest job?" he asked, pointing at his boilersuit. He and Jean stood together by the living room door,looking at Barton as he got seated on the sofa.

"I thought I'd come and see if you both were all right," Barton said. "Have you seen anything of that guy with the white hair recently?"

With confused looks on their faces, they both shook their heads. "We've had so much happening here we never gave it thought," Tom replied, sitting on his chair as he began rolling a cigarette. "Make the tea, Jean," he said, "and I'll run through with Richard all that has happened."

Barton was listening to his father's experiences, but his mind was on Randel's accidental death. If, as the big man said, he was the only one who could call off the contract on his father, that could only mean that the white-haired shooter was out there waiting for a chance, and with no one left to call it off. The only alternative was to call Crow and see whether he could help. "Can I borrow your mobile?" he asked, interrupting his father midway thought telling his story.

After numerous failed attempts, he handed the phone back to his father. He was sure something must be wrong; this was unlike the little man not to respond to a call. There was only one thing left to do, and that was drive to Crow's house first thing in the morning.